Praise for
CONVINCE ME

"*Convince Me* will keep readers guessing until the very end."
—*New York Times* bestselling author KARIN SLAUGHTER

"When a seemingly perfect husband, son, and friend is tragically killed, his house-of-cards life comes crashing down, exposing the twisted secrets and lies he's been hiding for years. Nina Sadowsky is a master storyteller. From the very first page, the story flies, giving life to the characters and plot until all has been revealed. *Convince Me* is one hell of a read!"
—WENDY WALKER, *New York Times* bestselling author of *All Is Not Forgotten*

"One of the cleverest psychological suspense novels I've read in years . . . tense, gripping, and fast-paced . . . lies piled upon lies and an entire cast of unreliable narrators that will have you wondering if anyone is telling the truth . . . I raced through this wickedly deceptive thriller in one sitting—highly recommended!"
—KAREN DIONNE, #1 internationally bestselling author of *The Marsh King's Daughter* and *The Wicked Sister*

"A propulsive thriller that starts with a bang and never lets up until its final shocking reveal . . . In *Convince Me*, Nina Sadowsky's brisk, energetic prose spills across the page, tightening the noose around the central terrifying question: How far would you go to learn the truth about the people you love?"　　—CARLA BUCKLEY, author of *The Liar's Child*

"This thriller tells a story that couldn't be more timely for this 'post-truth' age. It concerns liars and the damage they cause, with the stakes of manipulation, gaslighting, and all-around deception drawn out on the small stage of domestic suspense. It's my favorite kind of book, because it all felt personal. I was constantly asking myself, What would you do in that situation? even while I was trying to solve the mystery. But when the solution finally arrived, I never saw it coming. This book felt like a Roman candle. You watch it take off, then it just keeps climbing with one twist after another until it finally goes *boom*."

—LEE MCINTYRE, author of *Post-Truth*

Praise for

THE EMPTY BED

"A reverse-engineered action movie . . . The quick cuts make the book the perfect solution to a widespread problem this time of year: seasonal short-attention-span syndrome."

—*The New York Times Book Review*

"There's a definite cinematic vibe to Sadowsky's novel, especially as the characters rush around Hong Kong in Jason Bourne–type chase scenes. Catherine and her mysterious network are impressively connected and intriguingly motivated, and the woman herself is a fascinating study of power, empathy, and efficiency. . . . Surrender to the action and intrigue . . . and enjoy this whirlwind adventure in Hong Kong."

—*Kirkus Reviews*

"Entertaining."

—*Publishers Weekly*

"A sly, wry look at privilege and the price it can exact . . . a globe-trotting, jetsetting quest to avenge some of society's most pressing ills . . . Nina Sadowsky thrills again with her filmic vision of a troupe of unlikely superheroes."

—JENNY MILCHMAN, *USA Today* bestselling author of *Cover of Snow* and *Wicked River*

"Who better to find a missing woman than an expert in making people disappear? This unputdownable novel has flawless prose, a compelling premise, and textured settings that become characters in their own right. There is no more sleep once you crawl into *The Empty Bed*."

—K. J. HOWE, internationally bestselling author of *Skyjack*

"Nina Sadowsky weaves another thrilling chapter of the Burial Society series, mixing classic Hitchcock conspiracy with the sexual tension of a modern noir. Sadowsky's characters exude a razor-sharp wit that yanks you along on an adventure that keeps you guessing until the glorious conclusion."

—TED SULLIVAN, producer and writer of *Riverdale*

Praise for

THE BURIAL SOCIETY

"A complex but strangely exciting thriller."   —*Booklist*

"A deeply unsettling, compulsively entertaining Rubik's Cube of a novel . . . Every time you think you've unlocked the puzzle, Nina Sadowsky introduces a new twist that makes you start guessing all over again."

—MICHELLE RICHMOND, *New York Times* bestselling author of *The Year of Fog* and *The Marriage Pact*

"*The Burial Society* is a twisty, can't-let-go read! The heroine can trust no one as she struggles to help abused and endangered women in a world of secrets and shadows. . . . A dynamite psychological thriller by a new master of the genre."

—KAREN HARPER, *New York Times* bestselling author of *Falling Darkness*

"Addicting and chilling . . . a smart, sophisticated, terrifying trip to the City of Light."

—SUSAN ELIA MACNEAL, *New York Times* bestselling author of the Maggie Hope series

Praise for

JUST FALL

"[A] tense, wild fever dream of a debut."

—*Entertainment Weekly*

"What a terrific novel! *Just Fall* arrived in the mail this morning and I read the book in one sitting, which I haven't done for years. Nina Sadowsky's premise is original, her voice is clear, her storytelling skills are remarkable, and her pacing is perfect."

—SUE GRAFTON

"Character-rich and compulsively readable, *Just Fall* is a marvelous surprise. Exploring the universal need for family and human connection, and the costs incurred when those bonds are severed, *Just Fall* takes the reader on a wild ride through the psyches of two damaged people who hope to find redemption in each other. The writing is lush, the insights sharp. This novel is a winner."

—DIANE KEATON

BY NINA SADOWSKY

Just Fall

The Burial Society

The Empty Bed

Convince Me

Privacy

PRIVACY

BANTAM BOOKS

NEW YORK

PRIVACY

A Novel

NINA SADOWSKY

A Bantam Books Trade Paperback Original

Copyright © 2022 by Nina Sadowsky

Published in the United States by Bantam Books, an imprint of Random House, a division of Penguin Random House LLC, New York.

BANTAM BOOKS is a registered trademark and the B colophon is a trademark of Penguin Random House LLC.

LIBRARY OF CONGRESS CATALOGING-IN-PUBLICATION DATA
Names: Sadowsky, Nina, author.
Title: Privacy : a novel / Nina Sadowsky.
Description: New York : Bantam Books, [2022] |
"A Bantam Books Trade Paperback Original"—Title page verso.
Identifiers: LCCN 2021052763 (print) | LCCN 2021052764 (ebook) |
ISBN 9780593356401 (paperback) | ISBN 9780593356395 (ebook)
Classification: LCC PS3619.A353 P75 2022 (print) |
LCC PS3619.A353 (ebook) | DDC 813/.6—dc23
LC record available at https://lccn.loc.gov/2021052763
LC ebook record available at https://lccn.loc.gov/2021052764

Printed in the United States of America on acid-free paper

randomhousebooks.com

2 4 6 8 9 7 5 3 1

Title-page photo: © iStockphoto.com

Book design by Dana Leigh Blanchette

This book is dedicated to the memories of my parents,
Jean Sadowsky, who always saw the best in everyone,
and Edward Sadowsky, who always inspired me
to do the right thing.

PRIVACY

Watching

She's so relaxed, so easy in her own skin, with her long blond hair bound up in a ponytail and her T-shirt, damp with sweat from her morning run, knotted below her breasts to expose a taut abdomen. She radiates youth and health.

She's also seemingly unaware of the dark temptation her very light ignites.

Would that change if she knew I was watching?

She's oblivious to the telephoto lens I wield from an anonymous sedan parked down the street, which is precisely what makes my surveillance so exquisite. People reveal so much when they don't know they're being observed.

Jacarandas arch overhead, velvety purple blossoms exploding off their branches and falling to carpet the pavement below. The day is new and the air heady, sweet with the scent of blooming flowers and salty with tangy breezes from the Pacific Ocean.

My target is every bit as fresh and lovely as this postcard perfect Southern California day.

She pulls the tie from her blond hair, which cascades down around her shoulders. A drop of sweat rolls into her cleavage. I pull the camera away from my eye. Squirm against the leather of my car seat.

It's 6:47 A.M. *Her pattern is the same every day, Monday through Friday. Out for a run by 6. Back to her house no later than 7. Out the door to her job as a biology teacher at a Catholic high school between 8 and 8:15.*

Sometimes I wait for her. Cool my heels for the hour she takes to shower and change and then trail her the six blocks she walks to reach the school and the church next to which it squats. She grew up in this neighborhood; she attended this same school.

I admire that, the commitment to tradition and religion, her desire to give back to the community that raised her. A good girl with values. She's popular with the students and the parents too, or so I hear.

Despite my rigorous observations, she remains an enigmatic puzzle. My thirst for information about her is punishing. She is a mystery I am determined to crack.

She disappears inside her bungalow. I don't have the time to wait for her today; I will have to miss the swish of her long, stick-straight blond hair as she walks confidently to a job she loves, the greetings of colleagues and students as she enters the gates.

Today I have other things to do, and will have to miss those few extra moments of delectable observation. But tomorrow? That's another story.

CHAPTER ONE

Daisy Sullivan had come into Dr. Laina Landers's office already crying messy tears and they haven't abated yet, forty-three minutes into the fifty-minute session.

Daisy, a freelance graphic designer, had received a call from her bank that very morning. A woman with the unlikely name of Jupiter Sterling had apparently gotten ahold of Daisy's tax return and had tried to cash the check for quarterly estimated taxes that Daisy had written to the government. Daisy had seen a scan of the check, with *U.S. Treasury* miraculously erased and replaced by *Jupiter Sterling*. The amount had been large enough for a savvy teller to twig, and Jupiter Sterling herself stupid enough to try to cash the check at Daisy's bank using her real name and her own ID.

The check was stopped. The credit agencies were notified. Jupiter Sterling is in custody. But none of these measures eases the sense of violation that consumes Daisy. Her Social Security number *"is in the wind,"* she's sobbed repeatedly since entering Laina's sanctuary. *"I'm going to be looking over my shoulder for the rest of my life."*

Laina's calm face doesn't give it away, but with seven minutes to go in the session, and despite her genuine sympathy for Daisy's distress, she's feeling the pressure to get her client pulled together.

"Daisy?" Laina interrupts. "Can you listen to me for a moment, please?"

Daisy blows her nose into the wad of damp tissues already clutched in her hands and nods.

"What happened with your taxes is upsetting. I get that. But the culprit was arrested, you've issued a new check to the government, notified the credit bureaus, spoken with your bank. I wonder if this sense of violation that you're talking about has another contributing factor?"

"Like what?"

"Why don't you think about it for a moment and tell me what comes to mind. Take a couple of deep, mindful breaths."

To Laina's relief, Daisy does as she's been instructed, closing her eyes and taking a deep inhale through her nostrils, filling her belly with air. She holds her breath a long moment before releasing it through her mouth with a hearty sigh.

"That's good, Daisy. Do another."

Laina takes advantage of Daisy's closed eyes to sharply observe her client. Always attractive in a pale, blond, washed-out kind of way, Daisy's become almost blurry around the edges since her husband announced five months ago that he was leaving her and their two young children. Within three days of this pronouncement, he disappeared without a trace to "find a new path," considerately emptying only half of their joint bank account.

A "pandemic-life crisis," Laina dubbed it, and poor Daisy's husband isn't the only one. The ricochet effects of a world turned upside down are still being felt.

Scores of people she knows, and virtually everyone she treats, were bludgeoned one way or another. Parents or children lost, or siblings or friends. Jobs and savings accounts evaporated into thin air as if by an evil fairy's malicious spell. Schooling interrupted, dreams delayed, marriages broken beyond repair. Laina herself can't claim to be untouched.

Daisy's eyes snap open. "You think it's about Mark Victor, don't you?"

"Is that what you think it's about?" Laina parries, hiding her surprise. Mark is a friend of Daisy's who'd delivered some "benefits" when Daisy found herself newly single after eight years. As far as Laina knows, there had been a few stress-releasing tumbles and then a mutual agreement to stay friends. Daisy hasn't talked about him much since.

Daisy lifts her pale blue eyes to hold Laina's dark brown ones in a firm, resolute gaze. "He took pictures of me. You know, *naked*. When I was asleep. I think he might have even drugged me! God! How did you know? I've been so scared and humiliated, I haven't said a thing to *anyone*."

With a barely perceptible twitch, Laina reacts to both the bomb Daisy's just dropped and the realization that they have about four minutes left in their session. She has Ken and Connie Ito, a pair of hard-driving surgeons struggling with fertility issues, in for a joint counseling session immediately after this, and Ken Ito does not react well to being kept waiting.

"I mean, talk about a violation!" Daisy splutters on now that the floodgates are open. "I thought we were friends. I couldn't believe it. I still can't."

"Did you ask him to delete them?"

"Of course I did! I have *children*. But he laughed, said

they were 'too sweet' to give up, and when I pushed him, he got crazy angry. After that I just backed off."

"I am so sorry that happened to you. You must feel so betrayed," Laina says empathetically while concealing her surprise that Daisy had kept this incident to herself. Daisy has legitimate life issues to contend with, as well as a diagnosis of moderate to severe anxiety and depression, but Laina's used to Daisy laying every detail of her life and then some bare in their sessions. She'll have to delve back into the Mark Victor of it all with Daisy next week, probe deeper into why Daisy had kept this secret.

"I live in constant fear," Daisy whispers. "That the photos might, you know, show up somewhere."

"Do you have reason to believe he's planning to post them?" Laina asks, a concerned furrow forming across the bridge of her nose.

"No! I mean, I don't know. But I don't think so." Daisy stares at Laina with wet blue eyes. "I feel better now that I've told you. I don't know why I didn't."

"I'm glad telling me gave you some relief. But can I ask you to do something? Think about what role shame might have played in your decision to keep Mark's behavior a secret."

Daisy nods eagerly. The two of them have had many conversations about shame and the role it has played in Daisy's life thus far.

"And let me remind you," Laina continues, "Mark is the one who did something shameful here. Not you. He took advantage of you and taunted you about it, proving he wasn't the friend you thought him to be. That's his shame. Not yours. The same way Jupiter Sterling should feel shame for her attempted fraud. The same way Brad's behavior is his shame," Laina adds, looping Daisy's errant husband into the equation.

"I don't want to start mistrusting everyone," Daisy whispers, her eyes filling with tears once again. "But it's hard."

"Did you have any sense about Mark?"

Daisy's eyes shift. "I guess I did wonder a bit. He was really Brad's friend, before the asshole took off. I was too stupid to see what was what."

"You were in shock, hurt, and vulnerable. He exploited that. You weren't 'stupid.' Stop judging yourself."

"Thank you," Daisy says as she tosses her wad of tissues in the trash.

"You're very welcome. I'll see you next week, okay? Remember to be compassionate toward yourself. You've been through a lot. And don't drive until you're calm and ready," Laina suggests. "Take a few minutes to pull yourself together."

"Will do." Daisy smiles at Laina and for a brief instant Laina sees the appealing, bright-eyed girl Daisy had been before the hard edges of life caused her to fade.

Laina escorts Daisy out and takes a moment to jot down a few notes.

She ponders Mark's motives in letting Daisy know he had taken the pictures. She marvels at the passivity that led Daisy to retreat from him instead of fighting back when he revealed what he had done. Daisy had never been a particularly assertive person, but she had really folded in on herself since her husband took off, Laina reflects. She's become so withdrawn she's listless, almost paralyzed. It makes Laina's heart ache for her. Laina wonders if that bastard Mark Victor is using the pictures he took of Daisy in some nefarious way, posting them on the Web for profit or holding on to them for blackmail purposes. She also wonders if Daisy is his only victim and suspects she is not.

It's appalling how easy it seems to come to some men, the power trips and exploitation, the manipulations and the slickly easy betrayals of trust.

Laina blinks, batting away the sudden stab of deep sadness that hits her as she contemplates the perfidy of men and the damage it can inflict. Sliding her pad with the jotted notes into a desk drawer, Laina locks it and then presses the button under her desk. The entry door to her office swings open and she adjusts her face and her attitude for the Itos, but it's her partner, Dr. Harley Weida, who appears in her doorway.

"Got a minute?" he asks, tugging at his hair in a characteristic gesture. Harley's a big man, with square, capable-looking hands, thick black hair, and a salt-and-pepper beard. He wears pricey, understated clothes and favors expensive watches, of which he has a collection. Today's choice is a Hublot Big Bang chronograph. He emanates easy charm and a kind of SoCal casual luxury, moving through the world with the confidence of a man accustomed to success.

"I have the Itos coming in. Can it wait?"

"It won't take long. I just want to know if you've found a new therapist." Harley pushes both hands through his hair, which then stands in spiky clumps. Somehow it only serves to make him more attractive. "It's been a few months and I'm concerned about you."

"I haven't yet. But I will," Laina replies. "Don't worry about me. I'm good. Really."

"I only ever want what's best for you," Harley assures her with the warm smile known to pierce even the most armored. "You know that, right?"

"Of course I do." Laina smiles back at him, swallowing her irritation at what feels like condescension from her partner. "But stop worrying, I'm fine."

"All right. Listen, Megan and I want to invite you for dinner next Saturday."

Laina laughs, hoping to cover her exasperation. "Not another fix-up?"

With a wry grin, Harley confirms that it is.

"I'll need some details before I say yes," Laina says. "The last attempt was a disaster."

"A well-meaning disaster," Harley replies.

"Even so, a disaster," says Laina. With relief, she turns her attention to her clients as the Itos come into view. "Come on in. Dr. Weida is just leaving."

An hour later, after showing the Itos out, Laina sits back at her desk to collect her thoughts and record her notes. Couples counseling is a relatively new arena for Laina. Her focus has always run more to teens and young adults, but one patient asked if she could come with her husband, which led to one referral and then another. But Laina has to admit she's not as comfortable treating couples. The Itos, for example, seem to have a coded communication she can't quite crack, one that shuts down Connie, causing her eyes to run skittish and her mouth to press into a thin line when things get tense. The Palmers and the Hutchinsons are two couples Laina considers more successful outcomes, but she still feels she gets her best results one-on-one. When their new teen clinic opens, she plans to scale back on the joint sessions.

Laina logs out of her computer with a decisive click of her mouse and pushes back her desk chair. Every choice in Laina's office reflects her preference for soothing colors and soft textures, order, calm. Her desk sits across from the one large, west-facing window, outside of which the fireball of a setting sun shoots orange and crimson streaks into the shadowy mysteries of encroaching nightfall.

Laina sighs, running a hand through her shoulder-length brown hair. She loves the peaceful refuge that is her office, every object lovingly chosen to celebrate the triumph that was opening her own practice, but that doesn't mean she wants to live here. More than ready to head home for the day, grateful that it's Friday night and she has a quiet weekend ahead with the highlight a long-planned dinner with her friend Bex, she slings her bag over her shoulder and walks out of her office, shutting off the lights as she goes.

The halls of the clinic are dim; everyone else has already gone home for the night. The office doors lining the corridors are all closed tight; the cheerful reception area is empty. Laina sweeps up a few scattered magazines and stacks them neatly on a table before stepping out into the corridor and turning back around to lock up.

The name of the clinic, BETTER LIFE, is emblazoned on the front door. Even though it's been almost five years since the clinic launched, Laina still feels a thrill of pride every time she sees the distinctive font. BETTER LIFE's very existence as well as its growth are a result of Laina's discipline and determination, proof that difficulty, even tragedy, can be overcome and people *made better* with the right kinds of support.

Laina bristles remembering Harley's expressed concerns

about her own mental state. The driving desire to help others bound the two of them together when they first met and then decided to partner in the clinic, but Laina has to admit that she's bothered by Harley's recent efforts to help *her*. Despite their history together, or maybe because of it, his worry about her psychological health seems patronizing, as do the repeated attempts he and his wife have made to fix her up with "eligible" men. Would he be that overbearing and intrusive with a male colleague? Laina guesses not. Besides, Laina likes her life the way it is. She has her work and her friends (admittedly a small group but solid, which is all she needs). If a man were to come into the picture organically that would be fine, but she resents this pressure on her to couple up just for the sake of it.

With the door to the clinic locked behind her, Laina glances quickly left and then right. She's annoyed with herself for her unease, but she's felt apprehensive and on edge for days now. She may have reassured Harley that she is completely fine, but in her heart and gut, she knows that *something* is *wrong* in her world, even if she can't name what or why. It's just a feeling, an uneasy, creepy sense that some danger is edging ever closer.

She tries to shake off her fears, but nonetheless slides her keys between the fingers of her right hand and forms a fist around them, creating an impromptu set of brass knuckles before striding down the hallway to the elevator and punching the CALL button.

The elevator glides open as if it had been waiting for her. Laina confirms the car is empty and hurries inside, using the keys threaded through her fingers to press the CLOSE DOOR button and then jab at the button for level A of the underground garage. She looks down at her tight white knuckles, keys bristling between them.

What woman hasn't done this? Laina thinks ruefully. If only she could sort out why exactly it is that she's had this weird sense of dread. She never used to feel unsafe in this office building, quite the contrary.

But everything's changed, hasn't it? The whole world is different now.

The elevator door slides open. Scanning the largely empty parking garage, Laina spies her car, a late model Jeep, sitting in its parking spot under a pool of light way at the far end. She moves to the car quickly, eyes darting, heart pounding, slipping in and out of the circles of light cast by sporadically placed overheads, her heels clicking hollowly on concrete.

Laina reaches her Jeep, pressing her key fob to beep it open. Flings her bag on the passenger seat and slams her door closed. Relocks the car with a jab at the button. Hits the ignition. As the car purrs to life, Laina grips the steering wheel with both hands, trying to steady her breath. *You're being ridiculous,* she thinks. *Calm the fuck down.*

She puts the car into gear, but the lilt of her cellphone makes her startle. She digs in her satchel for it, forcing a chuckle at her own jumpiness. But the laughter turns to a frown as she reads the caller ID: PETER HUTCHINSON. After hesitating for a moment, Laina answers the call. "Peter? Is everything all right?"

"Nothing's all right!" Hutchinson's ragged voice booms through the car's Bluetooth speakers. "I'm going to kill her! I swear I'm going to pull the trigger!"

"Please talk to him!" It's Clare, Peter's wife, her voice

faint in the background and torn by tears. "Dr. Landers! Please! He has a gun!"

Laina gulps in air, desperately trying to maintain her cool. She pushes that ugly word *gun* away from her thoughts and focuses on her patients. Peter and Clare Hutchinson have been seeing Laina for eight months, working through the cracks and fissures in their marriage. While Clare had shown emotion in their sessions, Peter maintained a consistent façade of reserved respectability. Laina's never even seen him lose his temper.

"Where are you, Peter?" she asks, struggling to keep her voice steady as she reconciles the man she knows with the ravaged voice on the phone.

"My house! My own goddamned house," he answers with a laugh that sounds like a sob. "The place is crawling with cops, but just let them try to stop me! There's no other way! It's all gone too far!"

"You're wrong, Peter!" Laina exclaims. "There's always another way! You know I'm on your side, right? How about I come to you and we talk this through? Please, Peter. You called me because you want to talk, right?"

Laina's breath catches in her throat. Terror strikes with the realization that Clare's life hangs on the success or failure of her words. There's what feels like an infinite pause, an eerie suspension of time and place, as Laina feels the weight of that responsibility settle heavily on her shoulders. Peter is quiet and Laina can hear Clare sobbing faintly in the background.

Laina turns up the volume in her car but all she can hear are Clare's wretched weeping and Peter's heaving breaths.

"Peter," Laina says softly, "I'm already in my car. Just let me get over there, okay? So we can talk in person."

"All right," he finally grunts.

"I'll be there as quickly as I can. And, Peter, please, I know you don't really want to hurt Clare. You don't, right? You know that and I know that! So, stay on the line with me while I drive, okay?"

Hutchinson hangs up and Laina swears out loud.

All of her personal anxieties swept aside, she guns the Jeep and hightails it out of the garage, her mind racing. She jabs at her phone screen to call him back, but it goes directly to voicemail and she hangs up. What could have happened to set Peter off like this? She'd seen the couple just days ago and they'd seemed solidly on track in a way about which Laina had felt a good degree of pride, and the Hutchinsons had seemed to share her happy enthusiasm. They'd overcome so much grief and loss, and seemed on the way to repairing the many fractures in their relationship that had manifested as a result.

And for Peter, repressed, uptight Peter, to threaten Clare's life? *Unthinkable.*

Oh my god. Is this why I've been feeling so uneasy? Did I miss something? Did I suspect something?

Laina jams on the brakes just in time to avoid skidding through a red light. She reminds herself to breathe. *You're not going to be able to help anyone if you crash the car!*

Flashing red cherries and a phalanx of police greet Laina as she turns onto the Hutchinsons' street. In this neighborhood of grand houses oozing moneyed respectability, this chaos seems out of time and place. Nosing her car into a parking spot, Laina tries to mentally prepare herself to confront Peter. A pulse flutters in the hollow of her throat as if it will choke it closed.

What will I say to him? What are the words that will make Peter put that gun down?

She spots a reporter with a trailing videographer. Of course there would be press; what did she expect? Peter Hutchinson is the well-heeled scion of a wealthy and deeply embedded local family.

Laina sucks in air, acutely aware that if she fails in her mission to have Peter surrender his weapon, it may not be only Clare's life that is at risk. She clutches at the steering wheel to steady her shaking hands, batting away the terrifying snapshots of blood and bodily carnage that insist on invading her mind.

Peter called her. There must be a reason why. Some part of him doesn't *want* to kill Clare—or anyone else. He *must* want to be stopped.

Laina pulls down the mirror on her sun visor to take quick stock of herself. Her skin is pale, her brown eyes so dark they are almost black. She stares at herself, willing a bravery she doesn't feel. Snapping the visor closed, Laina steps out of her car and finds her legs loose beneath her. She steadies herself with a hand on the roof of the Jeep. Gulps in another deep breath.

You can do this. You were trained to do this. Made to do this. Go get him.

Smoothing her skirt with her hands and cursing the high heels that seem to barely support her wobbly legs, Laina approaches the first uniform she sees and explains who she is and why she's come. In rapid succession she's asked to repeat her story to first a pair of detectives and then a police hostage negotiator. Her words tumble forth with intensity and fervor. *"If you just give me a chance, I think I can defuse the situation,"* Laina entreats each man in turn until they finally agree. *"Peter Hutchinson called me."*

It couldn't have taken more than five minutes to convince them, but it felt like hours. At last, Laina sets forth across the Hutchinsons' lawn toward Peter, who holds a gun in his right hand and restrains his wife by her neck in the crook of his left elbow. Tears streak down Clare's face. Her eyes are unfocused in terror as her husband rubs the barrel of his pistol in soft circles over the planes of her face.

Laina's heels sink into the moist earth, causing her to struggle toward Peter and Clare. Despite her awkward gait, despite the absurdity of the almost comic *squelch* of her heels as they pull out of the sod, she keeps her eyes locked on Peter, and as she gets closer, she speaks to him in a soft, reassuring tone.

"Hey, Peter, hi. It's me. I've come just like you asked."

"Too late!" he yelps. "It's too late." He jerks Clare's body back against his own and pushes her down to her knees. Points the gun at the top of her head.

"Talk to me, Peter. Please." Feeling like she's moving through liquid resin on the brink of solidifying to amber, Laina inches closer to the couple. She tries to tune out everything and everyone around her except for the desperate Peter Hutchinson and the petrified Clare. She tries to mentally catalogue everything she's ever learned about hostage situations.

As soon as she's in reach, Clare clutches at Laina's leg.

Laina sinks down to her knees and grasps Clare's hands, keeping her head tilted up and her eyes locked into Peter's. "Talk to me, Peter," Laina entreats. "I want to listen. I want to help."

"Everything is broken," Peter chokes out. "Our family is broken."

"I hear you saying you believe your family is broken," Laina replies. "That must feel awful."

Peter nods at her savagely. "It is awful."

"I'm so sorry you feel that way. It must be really painful. But I don't really believe that's the case," Laina continues. "You and Clare have weathered so much together. You can get through whatever it is that's upset you. Why don't you tell me about it?" She can sense, rather than see, uniformed police stealing closer to them, hunched low to the ground and ready to spring.

"I never will," Peter says with deadly calm. "I'll never tell anyone." He presses the barrel of the gun into Clare's hair.

"Okay, Peter," Laina quickly reassures him. "You don't have to. I respect that. But how about letting go of Clare? I know you don't want to hurt her, Peter."

Clare whimpers.

"You know you don't want to hurt her, Peter," Laina repeats. "Think about your sons. Think about your family. You've gone through so much with both your boys."

Hutchinson grinds his jaw. Laina can hear the grainy sound of his teeth grating against one another, can practically feel the tension radiating from his muscles and tendons. That pulse in her throat comes to life; Laina can hear her own heartbeat loud in her ears.

"I'm going to blow her fucking head off!" Hutchinson

yells. He jerks his wife away from Laina's grasp and cocks the trigger. "And you're next!"

Time, which had slowed, shudders to a stop. Laina stares down the barrel of Peter Hutchinson's pistol and wonders if this is how she is going to die.

CHAPTER TWO

"You gotta love this weather," Calvin Murray declares, rolling down the windows of his rented midsize to allow the salty breeze passage through the nondescript car. His companion, Mike Amis, merely grunts in response. It's probably the third time tonight Cal has made this pronouncement, so he isn't surprised by Mike's tepid response to his trite observation.

But here's the thing: Cal doesn't really know Mike Amis yet. And if Cal's learned one solid thing in his years on this earth, it's to trust slowly.

They're chasing a story involving Medicare fraud, the Russian mob, and human trafficking originating out of Belarus, which is why they're parked outside a Russian social club here in what's been dubbed San Diego's Little Odessa, hoping for a sighting of the alleged ringleader, a Russian national named Sergey Petravich. There's news here, Cal feels it in his bones, but their quarry hasn't arrived after almost five hours of lying in wait and Cal's stomach is growling. He's about to suggest they pack it in when his phone rings.

"Murray," he answers.

"It's your brother from another mother, Cal."

Cal smiles. Takes the phone off speaker and presses it to his ear. "What have you got for me, my man?"

The caller replies succinctly, then rattles off an address. Cal repeats the address back as he pulls on his seatbelt. "On our way." Hunger pangs forgotten, Cal shoots a grin at Amis.

"Finally. Something with some juice!" Cal exults. "Peter Hutchinson is holding his wife at gunpoint."

Mike lets loose a long, low whistle. "That'll for sure top the eleven o'clock."

Adrenaline rockets through Cal's body. This could be his first chance to make a splash here in San Diego. Only a few weeks into this job after a stint in Savannah, and with his eyes pointed firmly north to that magical land of opportunity, Los Angeles, Cal is all too ready to make his mark.

Of course, Cal doesn't actively wish for others' ill fortune, but if Peter Hutchinson is going to behave like a murderous lunatic, he's fine with capitalizing on the man's bad judgment for his own advantage.

Cal hits a saved number on his phone and connects through to their station's assignment desk. He greets the assignment editor on duty enthusiastically; Cal may be new in town, and he may have felt the cloud of his color descend the first time he entered the newsroom, but he knows all too well the vital importance of keeping himself in the assignment desk editors' good graces and he's worked hard to win them over. He relays the pertinent details of the developing story, asking for a chopper to meet them at the Hutchinsons' house. Then he silences the phone, plugs the address into his GPS, and pulls away from the curb.

"How'd you get a connect in the PD so damn quick, any-way?" Mike inquires after Cal rings off.

Cal smiles. "I've been lucky enough to find a Murray on the force in both of the cities where I've worked so far—first Salisbury, Maryland, then Savannah. A legacy of Irish cops, creating a brotherhood of information. I happened to be particularly fortunate here in S.D., Officer Callum Murray, known to his friends as Cal Murray just like yours truly, wel-comed me with open arms."

Cal can feel Mike staring at him and chuckles. "You don't think I pass for Irish?"

"You're Black," Mike replies flatly.

"Too true," Cal replies cheerfully. "Still, the Murray Magic seems to work every time." He slips a quick glance at Amis, trying to read the sentiment lurking behind the sur-face of Mike's irrefutably true statement, but his videogra-pher's face is carefully neutral.

Cal had been warned by his brand-new agent, Ryan Greenspan: *"San Diego, this market, is a stepping-stone to L.A. but also a bastion of white conservatives. Watch your ass."* Cal's no fool; he knows he was plucked for this job be-cause the station needed to hire a Black face as part of their PR campaign to combat a recent lawsuit alleging racial bias. Nonetheless, Cal's nothing if not a pragmatist. The offer got Cal out of Savannah just before what he dubbed "the sum-mer swelters," and Ryan has already lined up some freelance work in L.A. in order to get him on the radar there.

Taking a turn a little too sharply, Cal throws out an in-stinctive arm to protect Mike, then slaps his hand back on the wheel with a muttered "sorry."

"I wouldn't have even known who this clown was if he hadn't launched his campaign just last week. What kind of fool does that? Announces he's running for Congress and then puts a gun to his wife's head?"

"A fool who doesn't want to win?" Mike hazards.

"Surely, there's an easier way—" Cal breaks off as he pulls the Chevy up behind a police car. He and Mike flip into action, grabbing Cal's microphone and Mike's camera, testing sound levels.

Cal turns to survey the scene. Police throng the Hutchinson house. A competitor has set up shop a little ways down the street and is talking earnestly into the camera. Mike jerks his head at the carefully coifed and curvaceous reporter. "She's obviously got a whole other kind of magic working that's getting her tips. I thought we might have an exclusive."

"It's not about being first or only. Just about being best," Cal replies, unfazed. "Let's find our spot." He gestures, assessing the scene.

A florid-faced Peter Hutchinson stands on his immaculate front lawn, holding a gun to the head of his keening wife. They're illuminated by what Cal guesses are "gotcha lights," motion-activated floodlights throwing deep shadows back behind the pair. The neighbors to the right of the Hutchinsons, a silver-haired man and his younger bottle-blond wife, stare in transfixed horror from their expansive front porch, clutching at each other for support.

But it's the preternaturally calm woman advancing on the crazed would-be congressman and his trembling wife who catches Cal's eye and tickles his reporter's instincts. *This* is the story to follow.

"Any idea who that is?" Cal asks Mike, jerking his head toward the lithe brunette.

"Not a clue," his cameraman replies.

Cal scans the lineup of squad cars and the cops milling between them. He catches sight of his namesake and strolls over, offering a discreet fist bump. "Thanks for the heads-up," reporter Cal thanks cop Cal. "Who's the woman?"

"Shrink," says Officer Cal Murray. "Couples counselor. Can't say this situation indicates she's done a hell of a job, but Hutchinson called her himself and the chief is letting her take a shot."

Cal feels the familiar flip in his gut. He's right. That woman is the story. "Know her name?" he probes.

"Dr. Laina Landers."

An involuntary guffaw escapes Cal's lips. "You're kidding, right? Sounds like the name of an evil villain in a DC comic."

Officer Murray laughs in reply, but Cal is already on the move, directing Mike to a spot and situating himself camera right so the drama playing out on the lawn behind him is center of frame. He speaks into his headset, confirming the chopper is on the way and that they're going live. His news director gives him the green light to start rolling with the simple phrase, "Candice is on the blur button." Back in the control room, Candice is now more or less the equivalent of God. Her decision about when to blur whatever tragedy might unfold is writ in iron.

Cal rolls his shoulders and sets his face for the camera: approachable, not intimidating, respectfully grave given the tragic scene unfolding.

"I'm Cal Murray, live for Channel Five, reporting from

the exclusive neighborhood of Rancho Santa Fe, where newly announced Republican congressional candidate Peter Hutchinson is holding his wife, Clare Baker Hutchinson, at gunpoint. So far, we don't have any information about what might have sparked Hutchinson to threaten his wife in this way. The couple have been married for twenty-one years and share two teenage children. About to speak to Hutchinson is a woman said to be—"

Cal's rudely interrupted by a beefy cop with huge fore-arms who stands between him and his cameraman. "We don't want anyone in his eyeline. You've got to move." Cal hesitates and the cop bristles. "I *said,* get a move on."

Cal nods at Mike and they jog down the sidewalk looking for another good angle. Cal keeps talking into the camera. "We've been asked by law enforcement to change our loca-tion. Let's see if we can't find a better spot while you take a look at the helicopter shot."

The Channel Five Newscopter roars overhead.

Mike cuts his camera. From the cover of a large hedge, Cal peers over at the scene playing out on the crisply mani-cured lawn. Peter Hutchinson's face is mottled red with anger, his shirttails are pulled loose from his khaki trousers. The shrink is speaking softly, one hand reaching out implor-ingly. But it's the look on Clare Hutchinson's face that draws Cal's eye. She looks like she knew this was coming and is resigned to her fate. It makes him wonder: Spousal abuse? Drug addiction?

What's the story behind this story?

Cal beckons Mike to follow him and skirts around the edge of the neighbor's porch, crouching down to keep to the shadows.

"Here," Cal whispers. "Set up here."

Mike nods and frames the shot. Cal speaks softly into his headset. "We have a position."

The brunette shrink sinks down to her knees. She clutches Clare Hutchinson's hands in her own. Tears run down both women's faces, but the shrink's eyes are locked into Peter Hutchinson's; she talks softly while he grinds his jaw.

"I'm going to blow her fucking head off!" Hutchinson yells. He jerks his wife away from Laina's grasp. "And you're next!" He waggles the weapon back and forth between the two women.

The doc stays focused and calm; Cal has to give her props for that. She continues to speak, her words indistinct, her low tones making her message to Peter Hutchinson a secret.

With a sudden harsh cry, Hutchinson releases his wife. The shrink pulls Clare into her arms and the two women scramble away from Peter as he raises the gun to his own head, his hand trembling, his eyes darting wildly. Four cops descend, shoving him to the ground on his stomach, kicking the gun away from his grasping hands.

Clare Hutchinson's legs give way and she collapses in a heap several yards from her now restrained husband. Peter Hutchinson is hauled to his feet and hustled from the scene. The expression on the handcuffed man's face is one of utter defeat, the look of a man who knows he's just thrown his entire life away.

Two detectives approach the shrink and the sobbing Clare Hutchinson. The shrink bids them to *stay away* with a single raised hand. They obey. Clare practically climbs into the therapist's lap. *What was her funny name again? Laina Landers?*

Cal looks directly into the camera. "We've all just witnessed a remarkable turn of events—the couple's reported marriage therapist convinced Peter Hutchinson to release his wife. He's now in police custody." He listens to his earpiece. "More on this story at eleven."

Mike cuts the camera and Cal turns to see Landers stroking the crying woman's hair and murmuring softly into her ear. Gradually Clare's sobbing subsides.

"Wish we could hear her," Cal observes to Mike. "She must have some silver tongue."

"You're on our lawn! Get off our property!"

Cal spins to see the Hutchinsons' neighbors approaching, indignation simmering on both their well-maintained faces. He advances toward them, extending a friendly hand and affecting his well-honed newscaster speech cadence.

"Good evening. Cal Murray with Channel Five. What a thing to witness! Are you two all right? You must be shocked. Absolutely shocked."

The bottle blonde leaks tears, smearing her mascara. "You're so right," she wails.

Cal presses his advantage, signaling to Mike, who lifts his camera into position and begins to shoot. "Your names, sir? Yours and your wife's? How long have you and the Hutchinsons been neighbors?"

The silver-haired gent eyes the red light on Amis's camera anxiously, and Cal continues smoothly. "I bet you've never seen anything like this in your neighborhood before."

"Damn straight" is the proud response. "Lived in this house thirty-six years. This is a *good* neighborhood. Not like some." He pauses. Looks uncertainly at Cal. "No offense meant."

Cal doesn't blink an eye. "And how long have the Hutchinsons lived next door?"

"Wait one minute! We don't want to be on the news! Turn off that damn camera."

Cal signals to Amis to cut but also surreptitiously fishes his iPhone from his pocket and opens the camera app. He swipes to video and subtly angles the phone the best he can to capture the couple. "Absolutely, sir. But just for background, how long have you and the Hutchinsons been neighbors?"

"Nineteen years," the blonde replies, fluttering a hand into the crook of her husband's arm. "Do you think I should go talk to poor Clare?" Cal follows her eyeline: Dr. Landers has Clare on her feet. A female cop lays a blanket over the shaking woman's shoulders.

Turning a broad smile to the neighbors, Cal thanks them for their time. He oozes sympathy for their shock and suggests stiff glasses of scotch.

"Maybe a vodka tonic," the bottle blonde quavers, looking at her husband hopefully.

"Follow me," Cal barks at Mike. With that, Cal is sprinting toward Dr. Landers, Mike at his heels.

"Dr. Landers, Dr. Landers," Cal calls as he comes within reach. "How does it feel to have saved Clare's life?"

The doctor nods at the female cop, who escorts Clare Hutchinson away, then turns on Cal with a look of pure fury on her face. "How dare you shove a camera at us? That poor woman is traumatized!"

"You're the one I want to talk to, Doctor," Cal deflects smoothly. "What did you say to Peter Hutchinson to get him to free his wife?"

"I'm not speaking to you," she hisses before turning her back on him and striding away.

Both empathetic and tough, she swung from pure compassion with her patients to fierce protective reserve with Cal. She may have turned him down, but in doing so, she became all the more interesting to him. He also can't help but notice her ass swishing beneath a close-fitting pencil skirt as she retreats. *Damn. That's trouble.*

"Where to now, boss?"

Not for the first time, Cal wonders about the inflection in his shooter's voice when he calls him *boss*. Then he reminds himself: *I am silk, I am butter, making smooth moves all the way to L.A.*

"Back to the neighbors for a hit, then over to the station. We've got to tee this baby up for prime time."

He'll research the good doctor back at the station. She may have refused to talk to him, but he's damned if she's going to stop him from reporting on her.

CHAPTER THREE

Dear god, what a horrible, awful night.

After making sure Clare Hutchinson is admitted to the hospital overnight for observation, Laina goes straight home. In an exhausted daze, oblivious to the jacarandas arching overhead and the fragrant scent of night-blooming jasmine mingling with the tang of the sea, she unlocks the front door to her condo, grateful for the calming colors and meticulous order of her refuge. The acrid odor of fear has permeated her blouse and skirt, soaked into her hair and skin: sweat, oil, something metallic. She kicks off her shoes. Shimmies out of her pencil skirt and yanks her silk blouse away from her body. Peels off her bra and panties. She leaves her clothes in a heap and heads for the large square shower that is the pride of her en-suite bathroom.

Twisting on the taps, she shudders as she thinks about what might have happened if she hadn't convinced Peter Hutchinson to release Clare. Her eyes drift closed; she envisions the sharp report of a gun firing, an explosion of brain matter and bone.

She sways. Snaps her eyes open and clutches at a towel rack for balance.

Laina steps into the shower, desperate to wash away the

day. As steaming hot water courses over her pale skin, her fragile shell of composure breaks. Arms wrapped across her breasts as if she's shielding herself from a blow, face lifted to welcome the hot stream pounding from the showerhead, she sobs, mascara-streaked tears running down her face, the sound of her cries barely muffled by the rushing water.

When there are no tears left, she shuts off the faucet and squeezes the excess water from her slick, wet hair. She dries off with a towel made of thick, thirsty Egyptian cotton. Naked, damp hair hanging, she crosses into her bedroom and enters her custom walk-in closet. It's more of a dressing room than a mere closet, color-coordinated, meticulously organized, with point of pride a full-length mirror surrounded by a heavy wooden frame hanging on the back wall. Laina steps up to the mirror and examines the reflection of her bare body critically. She believes in the body's somatic response to trauma. Where has the stress of this day lodged itself? Her belly? Her back? She feels a telltale flutter in the base of her throat and draws even closer to the mirror in order to stare into her own dark eyes, wiping away a remaining smudge of teary mascara with a pinkie.

Laina climbs into her coziest pair of pajamas. She's exhausted but also wired. So wired, she knows sleep will elude her no matter how spent she may be. Her bare feet pad into the open-plan heart of her condo.

Laina customized the design of her unit to her exact specifications when she bought the place, thrilled to be in a position to do so. She's a self-made woman and proud of it. The modern kitchen is situated at one end, with clear sight lines across the length of the cooking/dining/living area to a large plate-glass window that dominates the unit's western wall.

The building is only a block away from the La Jolla Shores beach and sits on a slight rise. During daylight hours this perch provides a tantalizing view of a sandy beach and lapping waves and it delivers pretty spectacular sunsets as well. Even now, in the dead of night, moonlight glimmers off the roiling ocean, reminding Laina of nature's power and humankind's insignificance in comparison. She chose this location by the beach precisely for that constant, humbling reminder.

Laina picks up her discarded shoes and soiled clothes and puts them neatly away before pouring herself a glass of her favorite golden Sancerre from the leftover half bottle chilling in the fridge. She then settles into the ivory-colored sectional that dominates the living space, pulling a sage-green velour throw onto her lap. It's a favorite of Laina's, thick, textured, and luxurious, the blanket version of a hug.

But her body can't relax and she can't stop her mind from spinning about Peter and Clare Hutchinson. Had she missed a sign that he was becoming unstable? As Laina parses her memories of their last few sessions, she comes up blank. Nothing she observed would have led her to believe Peter capable of violence.

The couple had suffered significant losses on both sides when the pandemic blazed through Orange County (Peter's father and stepmother, one of Clare's two sisters). On top of all that, their eldest son had been in a car accident last year, sustaining injuries that required multiple surgeries and extensive rehabilitation.

It was too much grief to bear, all lumped together as it was, and it wrenched through what had been a marriage of at least routine contentment, if not great passion.

But some good also seemed to ultimately come from all the loss.

As the son, grandson, and younger brother of high-achieving, powerful men, Peter had always felt he was a bit of a disappointment, particularly to his father. After his father died, and after his son James survived the car accident that nearly ended his young life, Peter stood straighter, spoke more plainly, seemed purpose driven for the first time in his life. He'd inherited a fortune way younger than he ever imagined and decided to devote the rest of his life to public service.

If you could call the shark-infested muck of Washington politics "public service."

Clare seemed ready for this step into public life. Their kids were mostly grown and Clare was relieved and proud her husband seemed to be finding this new meaning and purpose. They'd had a rough, long haul and Clare expressed her hope the couple might become more of a team along the way, whether Peter won or lost the election.

Then Peter revealed his "indiscretion." "*Over for years,*" he'd assured both Clare and Laina. "*Short-term. Over the course of three conferences in eleven months.*"

As his words had sunk in, Clare's body grew taut and tight. Through everything they'd weathered, this couple had bent, mostly because Clare had stayed flexible in the service of making her marriage work. But the admission of Peter's infidelity made her rigid as steel.

But after months of working with them, it seemed the couple had finally moved on. They appeared a united front, waving and smiling along with their two boys at Peter's candidacy launch event just last week.

So, what made Peter Hutchinson, the buttoned-down and buttoned-up embodiment of white male privilege, suddenly snap?

What makes any of us snap?

Laina gulps more wine. In the end, he *wasn't* capable of violence, though, was he? He released Clare (although his own life is now pretty much as destroyed as if he had pulled the trigger). *Or maybe not. Maybe his money and connections will buy him an easier ride. Is that any better?*

Horrific images of Peter's and Clare's anguished faces threaten at the edges of her consciousness. Seeking to bat them away, Laina gropes for the TV remote and flicks on the power. Maybe an hour of something distracting. *Archer,* which never fails to make her laugh. Or *Sex and the City* reruns, as comfortable and easy as a well-worn shoe. The screen flickers to life.

Laina gasps. She's looking at *herself* on her TV. Her face has an unflattering sheen; her hair is damp, a few loose strands pasted over one eyebrow. She's snarling directly into the camera, *"How dare you shove a camera at us?"*

Her face disappears and is replaced by the face of the reporter she'd confronted.

"She may not be known for her reporter-side manner," he says with a cheeky grin, "but Dr. Laina Landers is credited with talking congressional candidate Peter Hutchinson out of shooting his wife in a tense standoff earlier today."

Laina stares as his lips move but his words fade because of the rush of blood pounding through her head. She'd barely remembered encountering the man. And there she is, on television, a headline! That pulse flutters in the hollow of her throat, and she swallows hard against the surge of emotions suddenly coursing through her. The image cuts away from the reporter to a shot of the building that houses BETTER LIFE.

"Bastard," Laina mutters. The exposure of both herself and the clinic is dredging up ancient, sickening feelings from a place she thought long buried. Her body flushes with horror and shame. She feels exposed, vulnerable, angry, afraid. She wants to turn off the TV, but her finger is somehow frozen, poised over the button that will mercifully end this torture. The reporter comes back on the screen.

"A life saved, but a campaign over. And that's me, Cal Murray, reporting to you live from Action Five." The reporter lets loose another cheeky grin and Laina finally jabs the power button on her remote. She forces herself to breathe evenly, fighting the faint tickles that signal her throat might be closing, her airways blocked. . . .

Laina determinedly churns her thoughts away from fear to self-reassurance. *You're fine. You're completely fine. Just breathe. You're fine.* Then fury and fire descend. *He has some nerve. Poor Clare. I hate being on TV. Hate it! Will this hurt the clinic? How dare he?*

Her cellphone trills. Laina reaches for it and frowns, not recognizing the number. "Hello?"

"Dr. Landers? I'm Caroline Newsome with the *Union-Tribune*. I'd like to ask you a few questions about Peter Hutchinson. . . ."

"How did you get my cell number?"

"Good reporting," Caroline replies cheerfully. "Now about those questions—"

Laina hangs up on her. The phone trills again almost immediately. NO CALLER ID. Laina silences the ringer and shoves the phone under a sofa cushion, just as the hardwired phone in the kitchen begins to ring. Laina hurries over to it and lifts the receiver, offering a tentative "Hello?"

"Dr. Landers, my name is Eddie Abdy, and I'm a reporter with—"

Laina hangs up on him and unplugs the phone from the wall. That horrible tickle in the base of her throat fights again for her attention.

She'd done the only thing she could under the circumstances, and possibly saved both Clare's and Peter's lives. But the unintended consequences of her actions are just now starting to hit home.

CHAPTER FOUR

After a day spent dodging reporters' phone calls, Laina's looking forward to the evening she's got planned, dinner with her friend Bex, who's in the process of gender-affirming surgery. Bex's transformation is making him happy in a way that both Laina and he celebrate, and today is the first time Laina will see him since his most recent operation.

A smile grows on Laina's face as she watches him cross the restaurant's outdoor deck to their table. Bex's appearance is a glorious thing indeed. He seems to fill his body differently. His shoulders are square instead of slumped; he's got a swagger in his walk. His very center of gravity seems to have dropped.

"Bex!" she exclaims, rising to her feet. "You look wonderful."

"Don't I, though?" he replies with a wink.

They settle into the routine of ordering drinks and food. When that's taken care of, Laina clasps her hands on the table and leans in. Aims a smile at her friend. "Okay. Tell me everything. How are you feeling?"

"Oh no. That's not happening," Bex replies tartly.

"What? Why?"

"Let's talk about you, the star of the evening news."

Laina releases an uncomfortable laugh. "I didn't ask for that. And frankly I don't want it. I have the funding for the new center on the line and I don't want to ruffle any feathers."

"Ruffle feathers? Are you nuts? People think you're a hero."

"I'd rather talk about you. How did your call with your mother go?"

"Moira insists on calling me by my dead name, but she is among those who think *you're* a hero."

"I'm not a hero," Laina blurts, uncomfortable with the characterization. "And I don't want to be one. Getting Peter Hutchinson to release Clare without her or anyone else getting hurt was the best possible outcome in a horrible situation. I keep thinking I must have missed something! I should have seen how close to the edge that poor man was."

Bex snorts. "Poor man? That living, breathing embodiment of white male privilege? You know if it had been a person of color waving that pistol around, it would have been a whole other, and not pretty, story."

"That's not the point. He's still my client. I have to have empathy for him. I do have empathy for him. And it's public record—he's suffered a lot."

"Who hasn't? But you don't see me trying to shoot anyone in the head."

"How could I have not seen this coming?"

"You're not God, honey," Bex admonishes her. "You can't predict everything. And you're not responsible for Hutchinson's actions, if that's what you're thinking."

"It's not just that. Reporters are hounding me."

"You know what they say. All press is good press."

"Not for therapists," Laina retorts. "And particularly not for this one."

"I think you've got it totally wrong," Bex replies. "Seize your fifteen minutes and use your newfound powers for good! We've spoken enough about the mental health crisis in this country that I *know* you have opinions. Get them out there."

Laina shifts in her seat and shifts the topic away from herself. "How did Moira take your invitation to come visit?" she asks. "Or my offer to meet with her?"

"Ah. Thank the heavens. Cocktails have arrived," Bex replies. "To get into that hornet's nest we definitely need alcohol."

The waiter sets down their drinks and Laina immediately lifts her glass. "To the new you," she says in a toast.

"This is the always me, that's the beauty of it," Bex replies with a happy grin. "The outside just finally matches the inside."

Across the deck, at a table set for one, Cal Murray polishes off a steak. He can't believe his luck; Dr. Laina Landers is at the very La Jolla steak house he randomly selected for dinner after a day of house hunting in the area. He can't quite hear her conversation over the sound of the ocean lapping only a few feet away, although clearly a toast of some kind was made.

Cal has only ever been a reporter in the internet age, but still he's constantly amazed by how much of his job can be done with a few easy clicks. He's discerning, of course. He checks and rechecks his sources before he runs with a story, knowing all too well how going off half-cocked can wreck a career. But still, there's a wealth of information about everyone out there, and Dr. Laina Landers had proved no exception.

Schooling, publications, the launch of the BETTER LIFE clinic, appearances at charity events. Cal knows she's a story first and foremost, but he liked what he saw of the woman (and it's more than just that ass). Her educational credentials are impressive, Berkeley undergrad, her PhD obtained from UCLA. She has a restrained social media presence (something Cal respects) and most of her postings are focused around her volunteer work with a local girls' empowerment organization. And he's pretty sure she's single.

He's genuinely attracted, but it also wouldn't be the first time he used his charm on an attractive member of the opposite sex in order to chase down a juicy quote or a promising lead. And he knows from experience he's appealing in a way that has crossed color lines.

What did Laina Landers say to get Peter Hutchinson to release his wife? What if you could bottle that?

They'd had footage no one else had, and his agent has been blowing up his phone since the segment aired. But Hutchinson's spectacular fall from grace will topple from the news cycle quickly. To keep his momentum going, Cal has sold his news director on a follow-up piece about Dr. Landers, and he's not going to let something petty (like her apparent complete unwillingness to talk to him) put him off.

Cal studies the man she's with. Tallish, stocky, a faint hint of beard. Jeans, boots, and a crisp button-down shirt, sleeves rolled up to the elbows, a hint of a tattoo peeking out. A date? Somehow Cal doesn't think so; he's getting a different sort of vibe from the pair, even if he can't quite put his finger on its pulse. Colleagues? Friends, he decides. They're easy with each other like they have history but there's no hint of flirtation.

He turns his attention to Laina. She looks comfortable and quietly sexy in a wrap dress and chunky, surprisingly funky sandals. Cal would have pegged her for slingbacks with a kitten heel, or a traditional pump, he realizes; these cork-wedged lace-ups she's wearing are a much more aggressive choice.

Cal believes he can predict what kind of lover a woman will be based on the shoes she wears. It's an idle theory, but also one that's often proven correct in Cal's experience. And shoes like the ones Dr. Landers are wearing? He feels a stirring in his groin.

A waiter whisks into view and sweeps away Cal's plate. "Anything else?" the waiter inquires.

"A dessert menu," Cal replies. "And a coffee." He doesn't want either, but he does relish the idea of being able to observe Dr. Landers from this discreet vantage point for just a while longer.

A slice of New York cheesecake and two slow-nursed cups of coffee later, Cal observes as Laina and her companion request their bill, and he rapidly does the same. He'd managed to find a parking space on the street, but with any luck, the doctor will have valet-parked and he'll have an opportunity to approach her at the valet stand.

In Cal's experience almost everyone has a key, one usually related to their own agenda. Find out what they want and you can get what you want. It's a simple philosophy, but one that has served Cal well in both his professional and personal life. He's been accused of being manipulative more than once, but Cal truly believes he's never unlocked a secret that its keeper didn't want to reveal. Besides, what kind of good investigative reporter isn't at least a little manipulative? It's competitive out there and a man has to use every tool in his box. The doctor's key, in Cal's estimation, is her ambition, as manifested by her plans for her new clinic.

Dr. Landers and her friend are locked in an embrace when Cal follows them out. He hears assurances of *"another dinner soon,"* and admonishments to *"drive safe,"* as the two part ways. The man takes the keys proffered by a valet, climbs into the red Mini Cooper idling at the curb, and pulls away.

"Dr. Landers?" Cal inquires softly.

Laina turns around, her features composed into a pleasantly bland expression. "Yes?" she says politely.

"I'm Cal Murray with Channel Five—"

She cuts him off, her politesse evaporating, her eyes narrowing. "I recognize you. You're that guy who ambushed me and poor Clare Hutchinson! Are you following me now? What is wrong with you people?"

He keeps a steady smile on his face as he responds. "Sorry about that. I was just doing my job. The same way you were doing yours. Pretty brilliantly, I might add. And I'm not following you, I promise! I happened to be having dinner here and recognized you."

"Well, I'm still not talking to you." She turns her back on him and looks pointedly at her watch before peering down the street to see where the valet is with her car.

"Ouch. And you didn't even hear my pitch."

Dr. Landers turns back to face him. Cal looks into her deep brown eyes. They're charged with skepticism, faintly mocking, a little amused.

"Okay," she says. "You want to pitch me something? Go ahead."

He swallows before responding. "Look, you were amazing out there. I don't know what you said to Hutchinson, but you saved his wife's life! And his. I get why you shut me down on the scene, but how you handled that crisis situation is newsworthy. Also, I've done my homework. I know you're expanding, have plans to open a trauma center for teens; this could be a great opportunity to get more support for your work. I think sitting down for an interview with me is a win-win situation. I'm not one for therapy myself—"

"Never tried it?" Laina interrupts.

"Nah. I'll admit it, I'm a skeptic. But you might be the one to turn me. You sure worked some magic the other night." He shoots her a killer smile.

"What I do isn't magic. It's based on research and training."

"So is cutting a woman in half, but that's exactly why I want to do this piece. To take away the mystery and mysticism of what you do. Magicians need to keep their secrets, but if more people understand what you do, it can only help them. You might even help me."

Laina runs a hand through her dark hair and he feels that stirring of attraction again.

"That's funny," she replies. "That's exactly what Bex was saying."

Cal inclines his head in the direction in which her dinner companion had driven. "Your date?"

"My friend," she clarifies, "but yes, he thinks I'm missing an opportunity."

"I think Bex is right," Cal offers, with the grin he knows delivers results 99 percent of the time. "I promise to work with you in a way that will let you influence the narrative. You're a story, you have to accept that. Better to get ahead of it, rather than behind it."

She holds his gaze for a long moment. Cal feels his grin crack just a little under the intensity of her scrutiny. "Let me think it over," she finally replies coolly. "I'll let you know."

He hands her a business card. "The number's my cell. I look forward to hearing from you."

The slightest hint of a smile pulls at Laina's lips. "I admire your optimism," she replies as the valet pulls up in a Jeep and hands Laina the keys. "But we'll see."

Watching

A new day, a different target. I don't limit myself. Tunnel vision is a fool's game, not likely to achieve the goals I've set. I have ambitions and I'm proud of them, despite the fact that "society" may deem my methods suspect. It's through observation that I learn. Once my findings are complete, I can act, but I'm cautious, careful, precise. I'm a planner and secrecy is essential for my success.

It's dusk and the light has that magical rosy quality uniquely conjured by the dissolution of day into night. She pulls into her driveway and parks, sitting in her car for a long few moments, her head of dark curly hair ominously still. I wonder if she's gathering her thoughts or her courage, as I suspect her home life is not a happy one. A curtain flicks and the face of her husband appears in the bay window. She raises her hand in a wave and gathers her belongings.

Am I imagining it, or does she seem to drag out these simple actions for as long as she can? Is there a reason she's afraid to enter her own house?

She appears strong in both body and mind, but people often don't understand their options, or they underestimate their own resilience, leaving them stranded in damaging relationships. I don't want her to suffer through that. I want to liberate her from her own misguided barriers to happiness. Women so often make bad choices; I'm providing a service, even if my subjects may not necessarily see it that way at first.

I wait for about half an hour after she enters the house, keeping my ears attuned for the sounds of the violence that I suspect may be occurring inside, but the curtains are closed and it's as if she's been swallowed whole.

In our culture of overexposure, the most potent secrets are held fast behind closed doors. I need those secrets to be mine in order to achieve my aims, so I've learned how to get behind those doors. This subject's door will be no exception.

CHAPTER FIVE

"Are you a hundred percent sure you want to do this?" Vanessa Calabres, Esquire, presses her client. "You can still pull out. I've got to say, it's a fucked-up world where a patient losing his shit on live TV creates a promotional opportunity."

"I don't disagree, but it's the world we're in." Laina twists her hands in her lap. "And I'm nervous, sure. But I think it's the right thing to do. There's a lot of stigma about mental illness. My work toward eradicating that is going to be the focus of the piece."

Vanessa releases a skeptical snort. "And you trust a reporter?"

"That's why we're doing it here, right?" Laina smiles. "So you keep me out of trouble?"

Laina crosses her legs and settles deeper into one of the two wing chairs that flank Vanessa's substantial, old-fashioned desk. The law offices of Calabres, Hitton, and Phipps are designed to evoke a sense of old-money security and Vanessa's private office is no exception.

Vanessa's phone buzzes and she answers. "Yes? Okay. Give us five. And then bring them to my office." She replaces the receiver and addresses Laina. "They're here. Why don't you go to the restroom for a few? I'll get them set up and see what I think of this Cal Murray, cub reporter, for myself."

Laina feels that pulse in the base of her throat. Her jaw tightens. She feels anxious, but hopes it's actually excitement. *Then again, maybe it is just anxiety.* "Okay," she says. She leaves Vanessa's office and heads into the ladies' room down the hall. Once inside, she leans her palms on a sink and stares at her reflection in the mirror affixed above it.

The face that looks back at her is familiar, of course, but today she looks alien to herself, her skin paler than usual and her makeup heavier (to prepare for her appearance on camera). The dark patches beneath her eyes are still evident despite the careful application of concealer. Not for the first time she wonders if this interview is a mistake.

Laina hadn't slept well last night, bolting wide-awake and bathed in sweat at 1:47 A.M. The dream that woke her is one she's had before, although its familiarity did nothing to make it easier to bear. In the dream, she's sleeping and wakes up to find herself bound, her mouth sealed with duct tape. Her arms are locked behind her back, her ankles and knees also secured by tape. She longs to break free; pins and needles prickle her heavy, immobile limbs, but all she can manage is an ineffectual writhing. Images swim past her eyes, blurry and indistinct. She strains to see. Is that her brother being dragged by his hair? Her mother with a gun at her temple? There's the sound of a gunshot. A splatter of blood on gray tile. She shrieks in horror but the tape over her mouth muffles her cries.

She woke screaming, like she has every time before.

It's been a long time since she's had the dream. And for a brief yet endless moment in the hazy interlude between sleeping and waking, the nightmare's horrifying images morphed into an imagined alternate to the standoff with Peter: Laina watching in horror as Clare's skull exploded and bled into the neat green grass.

Laina shook it off. Did what she always does after the dream. A quick shower and a change into clean pajamas. A cup of chamomile tea with honey. A breathing exercise to calm down. Soft music to help lull her back to sleep. Unfortunately, last night her usual routine failed her and she was awake for hours. Nerves about the interview, no doubt.

It's not too late to back out!

Laina admonishes herself to get a grip. This exposure will be good for the work she does. It might even do her good on a personal level to face her anxiety about being on TV. She touches up her lipstick and applies some pressed powder to quell the sheen on her face. Her final touch is a spritz of perfume; it won't show on camera, but she finds it good for her morale.

The law firm's receptionist, a thin young man with a nervous manner, comes around from behind the waiting room's built-in desk and beckons Cal and Mike to follow him down the corridor. Cal's on his feet instantly. He's got *all the feelings,* the tingle of excitement that lights him up when he's chasing a story for its own sake, but also the extra thrill of knowing that this interview could be a building block in the tower of his ambition.

Cal's first real mentor, Kingsley Stone, the news director in Savannah, frequently reminded Cal not to get ahead of himself. "Build your career one story at a time," Stone always advised. "Let the small pictures build to the big picture." Cal took this advice to heart, but now with L.A. so close he can taste it, and his agent's palpable excitement about Cal landing this interview, he can't ignore his burning hunger.

He tips a mental hat to Kingsley, as other nuggets of his ever-ready advice float through his mind: *"Always decide the objective of the interview in advance and control it. But don't be afraid to deviate if you see an opening. That's where you find gold. And always start with the third question on your list; the first two are probably warm-up bullshit and you never know how long you'll have."*

Cal pats his breast pocket, where he has a copy of the interview questions he's reviewed with his producer and Laina, through her lawyer. The lawyer had been a tough cookie over the phone; Cal thought he might lose the interview even after Laina had given him her verbal *yes.* Entering Vanessa Calabres's office with the smile on his face turned up full wattage, Cal finds his grin faltering when he sees Vanessa is alone. He stops short and Mike Amis, trailing behind, stumbles into him and almost drops his gear.

Cal assesses the stern face of the tall woman sitting behind a massive desk. He guesses she's in her fifties, with springy black hair woven through with silver, heavy-framed no-nonsense glasses perched on her nose, and a pugnacious jut to her chin that lets him know he's in for a testing. She rhythmically taps a mother-of-pearl pen on her desk as she looks him over.

"Hi," Cal musters, recovering his smile. "I'm Cal Murray; we spoke on the phone. This is Mike Amis, who'll be operating the cameras."

The lawyer removes her glasses and inspects Cal like he's a bug pinned to cardboard. "Vanessa Calabres, as you've no doubt deduced. Let's recap, shall we? I remain in the room for the entirety of the interview. We've previewed the list of questions you sent over and they're acceptable. I'd like to reiterate that my client won't answer any questions that violate patient confidentiality. And that I have the right to call 'Cut,' at any time, for any reason, at which point filming will cease."

Nodding agreement, Cal keeps his smile fixed. "Of course," he reassures. "And Dr. Landers?"

"She'll be right in. I'm surprised she agreed to this, if you must know."

Cal considers his answer. Anything flip, flirtatious, or self-flattering is likely to land the wrong way with this one. He goes for sincerity mixed with boyish charm. "My aim isn't exploitive; I think Dr. Landers understands that. Peter Hutchinson may have been the story when he had his wife at gunpoint, but there's a larger mental health story here. Domestic violence is soaring. People need to know what resources are out there for help."

"Aren't you the Good Samaritan," Vanessa remarks drily. "Not my experience with most journalists."

To Cal's irritation, Mike snorts a laugh, which he covers with a cough. Cal assesses the room and directs setup of the two cameras. "Mike will operate and cover Dr. Landers," he explains. "The second camera will operate remotely, angled on me. I can always reshoot my questions later, but I like to do it this way for a smoother edit. I wanted two operators, but"—he shrugs—"budget cuts."

Cal looks toward the door of Vanessa's office and sees
Laina standing just outside of its frame. She looks nervous,
a bit startled even, so Cal moves over to her immediately,
smile working, and grasps both her cool hands in his warmer
ones. "Dr. Landers," he says, "good to see you again. We're
just about ready for you."

He sits her in one of the wing chairs and settles opposite
her. Mike adjusts a bounce card to give Laina's face a little
glow. A sound check and they're off.

"I'm here today with Dr. Laina Landers, the woman who
successfully talked congressional candidate Peter Hutchinson into dropping the gun he had held to his wife's head for
over an hour while horrified neighbors and the police
watched. Dr. Landers, I have to begin by asking, what *did*
you say to Peter Hutchinson to get him to release Clare?"

A kind of mask settles over Laina's face. Her interlocked
hands clench in her lap. Cal wonders if she's going to freeze.
Or pull the plug on the interview completely. He pauses,
knowing that sometimes the best thing to do with a silence is
to simply wait until the interviewee fills it. Finally, she unclasps her hands and places them flat, palms down on her
thighs. She takes a breath.

"I can't say there was any one thing. And frankly, I can't
reveal exactly what I said without violating patient confidentiality. But in general terms, one of the aims of my work is to
help people process their past trauma. In doing that work, I
remind patients that their present is not their past, and part
of separating the two is focusing on what is positive in the
here and now. I relied on that technique."

Cal's impressed. She answered, but without directly answering. It's smart on Laina's part, but it doesn't give Cal the juicy sound bite he needs. "Can you tell me what was positive in 'the here and now' of holding his wife at gunpoint?"

Dr. Landers shoots a slightly panicked glance at her lawyer, who answers for her. "She's already made it clear she can't share any specifics that might violate patient confidentiality. Move on."

"All right." Cocking his head to one side, Cal asks, "Why do you think Hutchinson snapped?"

"'Snapped' is hardly a clinical term," Laina parries deftly. "And as I've not had the opportunity to speak to the patient since the incident, I'd hesitate to render a diagnosis. But I would like to emphasize that there are many stress management techniques available to anyone who is feeling overwhelmed. And that there's a stigma attached to mental health issues that we as a society must work to overcome."

Cal follows up with more questions, specifics about the techniques mentioned: an explanation of psychodynamic holistic therapy, which the doctor considers foundational to her work, and a dive into EMDR, a trauma treatment Dr. Landers feels is giving especially good results. It's a solid interview; his subject eventually relaxes, and even the sharp-eyed Vanessa settles back into her desk chair, but the whole thing lacks juice and Cal knows it. He debates playing the one card he's been keeping hidden. It's a rumor, nothing more, but one floated over to him by his namesake Cal Murray, proud man in blue in the SDPD.

Cal decides to throw it out there just to see if anything sticks. "I've heard that there might have been some kind of video that sparked the Hutchinson incident. Do you know anything about that?"

To his disappointment, Laina looks genuinely surprised by the question. "A video? What kind of a video?"

The attorney leaps to her feet.

Before she can speak, Cal sneaks in one more question, "Why don't you tell me what kind of video might be involved?"

"Okay, that's a cut," Vanessa says sternly. "I didn't expect much but I expected better than shock tactics. The approved questions included nothing about a video."

Mike looks to Cal for guidance, but Cal nods in agreement. "Okay. That's a cut. Hey, I'm sorry, I didn't mean to spring it on you—"

"The hell you didn't," Vanessa bristles.

"I just heard about it earlier today. A rumor, nothing more. I thought I'd float it, but this wasn't a deliberate ambush."

"What kind of video?" Laina demands.

"I'd advise you to discontinue this conversation," Vanessa says to her client. "This man has proven he's not trustworthy."

Cal ignores Vanessa and responds to Laina. "I wish I knew. But why are you so interested?"

"I'm concerned for my patients' welfare." Laina's back is stiff, her hands once again clamped together in her lap.

"Laina." Vanessa says just the one word, but it's laden with meaning. Cal catches the glance that passes between lawyer and client. This interview is over.

CHAPTER SIX

Coming up the driveway to the Hutchinson house, Laina wills away the pinch of anxiety rising in her throat. She flashes to her arrival here the last time. The soft spring darkness cut by the harsh red lights of police cars. Willing herself out of her car despite her almost paralyzing fear. Pleading with the cops on the scene. Her awkward progress across the lawn. Clare's abject terror. The shock of looking into Peter's eyes and seeing the depths of his agonized despair.

Laina parks and exits her Jeep, noting that there are a couple of cars already parked in the circular driveway. Laina's glad Clare isn't alone, although she hopes to speak to her privately.

Laina rings the doorbell. After a few moments, the door swings open, revealing a puffy, younger-looking version of Peter Hutchinson. Not the older son who was in the accident, Laina deduces; that young man, James, would still have visible scars. This must be Drew, aged sixteen, home from boarding school.

"Hi, Drew? I'm Dr. Landers? Your mother's expecting me?" Laina hadn't intended to end every sentence with the rise of intonation that indicates a question, but she's unsettled by the baleful glare the stocky young man is bristling in her direction.

"The shrink, huh?" he snarls. "Fucking lot of good you did."

"I understand you're angry," Laina says, keeping her tone carefully neutral. "It's only natural, and I'm sorry you're having to cope with that. I'll keep my appointment with your mother now." Laina steps forward and Drew reluctantly steps aside, allowing her to pass into the house.

Laina's been inside this house only once before, after James's accident. Clare had asked her to come and Laina had, although doing so bordered on a blurring of professional lines in a way that left her mildly uncomfortable.

She's no less uneasy now, despite the quiet opulence of the entry hall with its cavernous skylighted archway. A furious Drew Hutchinson lurks next to her, his sparks of rage almost visible in the streaks of sunlight beaming down into the hushed space. "And where will I find her?" Laina asks him, her face a polite mask, but her voice a command.

Drew grunts and gestures to Laina's left. He then departs up the wide staircase that seems to float up the center of the house, but not before giving Laina the middle-fingered salute. Irritation bubbles within her, *rude little brat*. But she reminds herself that he is young, and grieving, and probably without many targets on which he can unload his bitter anger. She can shoulder the burden of the piece of it directed at her. After all, she's seen far worse. She shakes the encounter off before squaring herself to talk to Clare Hutchinson.

Upon entering the room that Drew had indicated, Laina's eyes roam from one beautiful sight to another. Several fine oil paintings, all with a nautical theme, are hung prominently and lit expertly. Two long, low navy sofas flank a polished driftwood table that is itself a work of art. One wall boasts an enormous stone fireplace, with a basket of firewood on one side and substantial wrought iron andirons on the other. Sliding doors lead out to a richly flowered patio, creating a sense of being both inside and outdoors at once.

Clare Hutchinson's curled up in the corner of one of the navy sofas, a delicate-looking china cup cradled in her hands, a lightweight cashmere throw wrapped around her legs.

"Excuse me if I don't get up," Clare says by way of greeting. "I can't seem to get out of this corner much at all since I've come . . . home." Laina suspects from the dilation of Clare's pupils that she's been prescribed a sedative, which is no doubt contributing to her inertia.

"Of course. Don't worry about it," Laina replies, taking a seat opposite her.

"Do you want some tea? I'm having tea. Drew made it for me. He's been lovely."

"No, thank you. I'm fine. It must be a great comfort to you that he's here, though, Drew. And James?"

"Also home. He's at the supermarket just now." Clare's voice drops to a whispery growl. "The boys don't want me to go out. At all. Because of the journos. Vultures. All of them."

"Have press been hassling you, Clare? You can report that, you know."

Clare shrugs. "They've finally stopped hanging around the house at least. But ironic, isn't it? All those months staying home and now I can't go anywhere for a whole different reason. Not that I feel like going out, anyway."

"How's Peter?"

Clare trembles, an involuntary spasm that travels from top to toe. "His bail hearing's tomorrow."

"How do you feel about that?"

"Well, he's not welcome back in this house. The boys don't want him here and I don't either. I've hired a divorce lawyer and filed a restraining order." Clare looks at Laina defiantly, as if expecting her to challenge these pronouncements.

"Those choices are of course yours to make," Laina responds. "You need to do what will make you feel safe."

Clare appears mollified by this answer. "I am. I'm taking care of myself. And my sons. And we don't want him near us. I'm planning a whole new life," Clare adds.

"Oh?" Laina asks.

"Yes," Clare affirms. "I get the house, but I'm going to sell it and everything in it. Move us away from here and Peter's family. Maybe go up north, near my sister. Get something smaller. Live a little simpler. I'm thinking about getting a dog. Peter never wanted one."

A dreamy anticipatory light shines in Clare's eyes as she pictures this new version of her life, but she fights to keep her eyelids open as the sedative takes hold. "I'm sorry," she says. "I'm so tired. You said you had a question? Something you didn't want to ask on the phone?"

Laina hesitates. Clare seems so fragile. But if there's word around about a tape that somehow contributed to Peter's violent outburst, surely it's better for Clare to be aware of it. Particularly if reporters are sniffing after it for a story. Laina decides to wade in cautiously.

"Was there something that happened to set Peter off? That night?"

Clare gives her head a vehement shake without responding verbally. Laina presses the point. "Are you sure? Nothing?"

"No. He just went off."

"What about some kind of a tape? A video?"

Suddenly Clare's eyes are wide and focused on Laina's like laser beams. "What?" she gasps. "How do you know about that? No one knows. No one can ever know."

Watching

I slump into my swivel chair. I can't seem to fall asleep, so have come to check on things as a way of soothing myself. I bring my bank of computer monitors to life, their bluish screens bathing me in their reassuring glow.

My timing is excellent. It seems my Catholic girl has just taken a bath or a shower. She's wrapped in a plush terry towel and has another twisted around her hair.

She drops down to sit on the edge of her bed. Shaking loose her turban, she finger-combs her long blond hair, twisting through the tangled locks with infinite patience.

I have installed two cameras in her bungalow. One is fixed in the ceiling of her bedroom inside a carbon monoxide detector. That angle provides a constant view of most of her queen-size bed and a partial view into the bathroom that's adjacent to her bedroom. The second camera is installed in her laptop, so provides a surprise angle every time. Tonight, it's sitting open on her bed behind her, providing me with a view of her exposed shoulders and back.

She stands and drops the towel from her body. As viewed from the angle above, her bare breasts jut out, perspective foreshortening the rest of her frame. From the laptop angle I can see her ass, pretty much as round and perfect as an ass can be.

She quickly slithers into a silky nightdress with only the thinnest of straps. The night is warm, and her little bungalow doesn't have air-conditioning. She'll no doubt sleep with her window open. Again. I want to scold her, "Silly girl, don't you know how vulnerable you are? Be smarter than that. Protect yourself."

But of course, I do nothing of the sort. Silent observation is my mission until I've gathered the information I need.

True to my prediction, she opens the bedroom window as wide as it will go. Moonlight floods into the room, bathing her in its milky glow. She positions two fans, a large one on the walnut dresser opposite the foot of her bed and a smaller one on the adjacent night table. She tugs the thick cotton comforter off the neatly made bed and folds it, leaving it at the foot, and then crawls in between the top and bottom sheets.

I wonder about the sense of trust that allows her to be so careless. I can barely remember a time when I trusted the world to have safe harbors.

She usually reads before she falls asleep. At least, this is the routine I've observed since I was able to get the cameras into her house. When she turns off the bedside lamp immediately, I'm surprised. I decide I'll watch just a moment or two longer, conscious of feeling a little bit cheated that she changed up her pattern.

She sighs and turns over on her side. Sighs again and flips to her back. Her right hand creeps down between her legs and she begins to slowly and gently rock against it. My breath catches in my throat. Her left hand moves to cup her *right breast. She rocks and rubs for just a few moments, her left fingers pinching her right nipple, before coming with a small shudder.*

I'm aroused, who wouldn't be? And particularly gratified that my insomnia led to my witnessing this unexpected piece of her. In the weeks I've been watching her, I've never seen her touch herself like this, have never seen her with a man, or a woman, for that matter.

I was beginning to think that my little blond Catholic girl was all saint and no sinner and I'm relieved to see she may be more layered, after all.

CHAPTER SEVEN

"Just do it," Laina coaches. "Yell. Tell him how he hurt you. Tell him you're mad as hell! Go ahead. Scream as loud as you want. No one can hear you. Our offices are all soundproof."

It's a gorgeous day. Sunlight pours into Laina's office, radiating gold onto the cool blues and grays of the décor and finding fiery streaks of red in the dark hair of Laina's client.

Carmen Hidalgo is a newish patient; this is only their fifth session. She's a systems analyst, precise and methodical in her demeanor and speech. She came to see Laina because her father was sexually and physically abusive and she's fearful that legacy will impact her brand-new marriage. She'd explained that she'd had therapy in the past to help her process the abuse, but she thought it was important to keep up the work given her new situation and some struggles she was having within it.

Laina had liked Carmen at once. She was forthright and concise when describing what had happened to her. Self-aware about her pitfalls and triggers. Eager to put her past behind her and full of faith that Laina could help her do just that. But Laina has concerns, particularly about Carmen's concealment of her past from her husband. Without context, some of the behaviors Carmen has described—the flinch in response to a caress, difficulty relaxing during sex—have been construed as rejection by Rick, creating a widening rift between the newlyweds.

Today's role-playing exercise is designed to help Carmen release some of the rage she harbors toward her father. Laina has given Carmen permission to scream, to yell, to mime attacking her abuser with a sharp knife, has coaxed and assured her. Still, Carmen hesitates.

"Come on," Laina commands. "Tell him. Tell him that what he did was unforgivable. Tell him you're angry. Tell him you're sick of being angry!"

"You fucker," Carmen finally explodes. "You miserable prick! What you did to me is unforgivable! No little girl should have a father like you! You never should have touched me!" Carmen leaps to her feet and mimes stabbing an imaginary body in front of her. "Take that, you fucker! Take that, and that! Right in the heart you don't have!"

Carmen stops her vicious air assault and sinks back down into her chair, chest heaving. Tears well in her eyes and spill down her cheeks.

"Nice work, Carmen," Laina assures softly. "How does it feel to say it out loud? Good, right?"

Carmen replies with a tremulous nod. As her eyes dip down to her entwined hands, both she and Laina notice the bruise just peeking out from underneath the cuff on Carmen's right wrist, an angrily mottled purple mark. The two women lock eyes for a split second. Carmen tugs the sleeve down. Averts her eyes.

Laina lets the silence linger, hoping it will invite Carmen

to fill in the gaps. But while she fidgets and squirms in her chair, she stays resolutely silent.

Despite the fact that Carmen sings the praises of "my Ricky," today is not the first time that Carmen's exhibited a disturbing injury. There was the lump on her forehead (which she claimed was caused by an iron falling from a shelf in her linen closet) and the stab wound to her hand (she cited a self-inflicted cooking accident).

Laina speculatively connects the dots. Maybe Carmen can't talk to Ricky about the abuse because she's locked in a repetitive cycle. Telling him about her father would be tantamount to confronting her husband about his own mistreatment.

"Do you want to tell me what happened to your wrist?" Laina queries softly.

"I . . . It's nothing. It was stupid. I fell."

"You sure? You can tell me, you know. You're safe here."

Carmen visibly bristles. "Not if you keep pushing in that direction. I know what you're trying to get me to say. That my Ricky hurt me. But he hasn't. So stop it."

"I'm not trying to get you to say anything. I'm just observing that this is our fifth session and you've had a fresh injury in three of them. I'd be remiss if I didn't ask."

"I'm just clumsy, okay?" Carmen retorts with hostility. "I've had enough trouble in my life, please don't start making it up in the one place there isn't any."

"I'm just concerned about you."

"Well, don't be."

"It's my job to be concerned about you. That's why you're here." Laina steadily holds Carmen's gaze. Carmen finally looks away and Laina shifts tactics.

"Do you want to talk about how 'stabbing' your father made you feel?"

The question causes Carmen to look back at Laina. A slow smile spreads across her face. "Fucking awesome, actually." She rolls her shoulders. "It's like a weight off."

After Carmen leaves, while jotting down her notes, Laina fights a wave of anxious nausea. She's virtually certain Carmen is a victim of domestic abuse, albeit one who is in deep denial.

Will I have blood on my hands if I accept Carmen's denials at face value? She was seriously in the dark about the Hutchinsons, and that ended in catastrophe. These twin dilemmas feel like an anchor pulling on her neck, dragging her down to murky, viscous depths.

Laina raises her head to find her partner, Harley, framed in the doorway to her office.

"You all right there?" he asks. "You look a little green around the gills."

"I'm fine."

"Listen, Laina, if you want to take a few days . . ."

"Absolutely not. I have patients. We have meetings about the clinic."

"Is it too late to kill that interview you did?" Harley asks, abruptly shifting topic.

"Why?" Laina's surprised. She'd consulted with Harley before agreeing to do it in the first place and he'd been on board. "What's brought this on?"

"The Hutchinsons have come up in session with more than one client. I think we all might be better served by a low profile for the time being."

Abigail, their receptionist, strides past Harley and into

Laina's office, her face ashen and her shoulders riding high with tension. Abigail is plump and cute and friendly. She's great with patients, even if she struggles a bit with organization. Laina's fond of her and knows the single mother is grateful for the flexibility this job has afforded her schedule. But Abi's usual grin is missing today. She's agitated, bouncing nervously from one foot to the other.

"What is it, Abi?" Laina asks.

"We got a weird message on the voicemail," Abi tentatively offers, ducking her eyes to the floor.

"What? Speak up," Harley demands.

Abi raises her eyes to meet Laina's, seemingly afraid to look at Harley. "Somebody called and . . . they said . . . they said . . ." The receptionist trails off, her eyes nervously darting back and forth between Harley and Laina.

"Abi, what is it? Just say it," Laina commands kindly. "Whatever it is, it can't be that bad."

Abi looks at Laina with a face of helpless, distressed confusion. Her reply comes in a breathless rush. "Somebody left this crazy message. They didn't leave a name. But they said that Dr. Weida . . ." She looks at Harley and then back at Laina as if for courage. "That Dr. Weida . . . had told a patient he was treating in couples therapy that he loved her. That they should run away together."

"That's ridiculous!" Harley exclaims.

"You saved the message, right?" Laina lifts the receiver of her desk phone and punches in the code for the voicemail. Puts the phone on speaker.

The voice they hear is scratchy and low, deliberately distorted. The message is rambling and sinister, accusing Harley of being a fraud and a predator, before ending on the accusation that he asked a married female patient to leave her husband for him.

"I can't even tell if it's a man or a woman calling," Laina observes as the recording comes to an end, carefully keeping her voice neutral. "Can you?"

"This is absurd! It never happened. I can't even think of a patient who would make that kind of an accusation." Harley tugs his floppy forelock, a gesture of anxiety that Laina knows well after years of working together.

"I believe you, Harley. You know I do," she reassures him. Laina glances at Abi, who looks miserable. "Abi, I'm sure it's nothing, but I'm also sure I don't have to remind you to keep this quiet. It's a patient acting out. Or someone playing a prank. But don't say a word to anyone. False accusations can do a lot of damage. You can go back to your desk now. But really, don't worry."

"Of course." Abi departs, overtly relieved to have laid this burden on someone else's shoulders.

Laina turns to face her partner. "I'm so sorry, Harley. I know better than anyone you would never do something like this. We're partners and I have your back. But you also know as well as I do that this kind of an accusation, even if false, can derail a career. We're going to have to figure out how to get ahead of it."

"What the hell, Laina. Who does something like this?" Harley demands.

"Someone who's hurting."

"Don't patronize me. It's not your career on the line."

"Bullshit. We've been co-directors of this clinic since it launched. I have every bit as much to lose as you do."

"Do you think it could be Kelsey?"

Kelsey McKendrick had served as BETTER LIFE's receptionist prior to Abi, and while it was true her employment had ended on a sour note, Laina frowns. "I can't see her stirring up trouble now. Why would she? She got what she wanted."

"I just can't think of anyone else who has any kind of grudge."

"I think that Kelsey saw and milked a financial opportunity after she cracked her head open in our reception area. I don't think she holds a grudge of any kind. And anyway, maybe it'll turn out to be nothing, Harley. Maybe it was just a stupid prank. But don't worry, we'll handle it together whatever it turns out to be."

"Thank you. You know, for dismissing—"

"You don't have to thank me, Harley," Laina interrupts. "I *know* you. We should inform Vanessa and see what she thinks, but let's try to shake it off for now."

Harley looks doubtful. "I'll do my best. And while you're talking to Vanessa, see if she can kill that interview. Press can only draw more disturbed people our way."

Laina feels that sudden prickle of irritation that seems to color her every encounter with Harley lately. "We talked about it before I sat for the interview. You agreed," she says serenely (while making a note to herself to explore just what that prickle might be signaling).

Harley smiles at her, as if sensing her irritation and working overtime to ameliorate it. "I recognize that," he says, "but things have changed. The Hutchinsons have been a topic in my office all day. And now a threatening message? Come on, canceling the interview is for both our good. For the good of the practice."

A still, empty space hangs between the two partners until the soft chime signaling the hour peals out into the silence.

"I'll see what she says," Laina finally replies. "But I signed a release." She's a little surprised by her own reluctance to let the interview go. Harley makes some sense, as much as she might not want to admit it.

Harley sends a wry grin her way. "Thank you. Think about it is all I'm asking. We've built so much together. We both need to be careful. Particularly with the teen center in the offing. And ask Vanessa what she thinks about Kelsey too. Remember that she left a number of threatening messages on the machine before we settled with her."

"But not one since," Laina replies.

"Yeah. Until now, maybe," Harley says grimly.

Laina's cellphone vibrates and she checks the screen. It's Cal Murray. Her stomach gives a little flip. "I've got to take this," she asserts to Harley. "We'll talk more later."

Harley departs and Laina presses the button that swings her office door firmly shut. "Hello?" she says into her cell.

"Hi. It's Cal Murray. How are you?"

"I'm fine, thank you. What can I do for you, Mr. Murray?" Laina thinks about Harley's request to spike the interview and rolls her neck to relieve the tension suddenly gathering in her shoulders.

"Actually, I was wondering if you'd like to have dinner with me."

Laina falls silent as she ponders this request. *Is he asking me on a date? Like a real date?* Whatever his motives, a dinner would give her a chance to see what he knows about the Hutchinson video. Maybe even manage the situation a little in service of protecting Clare and her children. And give her a better feel about how he might edit their interview; Vanessa had advised her that how something is cut can radically alter perception of a person. Over the course of a meal there would be ample time to assess whether he's as empathetic as he appears. There seem to be a lot of reasons to say yes and no reasons to decline.

"You still there?" Cal asks.

"Yes. Sorry," Laina replies. "When were you thinking? I know the perfect place."

Watching

I think she might be on a date. This is the first time she's been on one in the course of my observations.

I wasn't entirely sure at first; she left her house in her car and drove to the Gaslamp Quarter, where she parked and walked. My first clue was her appearance. Her hair was long and loose; she wore a dress and a necklace glistened against her breastbone.

She met a man outside an Italian restaurant, tall and slender with the ropy build of a cyclist and a slightly receding hairline. He greeted her formally, almost awkwardly, seemingly unsure as to whether a kiss on the cheek or an embrace was warranted. He settled for a one-armed hug and an air-kiss that landed somewhere near her cheekbone.

She didn't seem to mind his awkwardness. She smiled at him in that shy, little girl way she has, a darting look from underneath her lashes, her crooked front tooth snagging her bottom lip. Now they're seated inside, enjoying plates of pasta and glasses of what looks like a hearty red. From where I'm positioned outside, I can see her date, but my quarry is partially obscured, her face split in half by a frescoed column.

I'm critical of the choice of restaurant. Frescoes and faux

Roman busts on pillars; the joint seems like it's trying too damn hard. I wonder if her date is too. Certainly, his choice of venue indicates as much.

He throws back his head and laughs appreciatively at something she says. I get a glimpse of her pleased smile in response. He pours them both more wine from the bottle on the table. I keep a sharp eye on that. Women need to be careful; some assholes will lace their drinks with anything that will let them have their way. I've never fully understood that. Where is the pleasure in taking someone unwillingly? Power, of course, I know that's the answer, but on a personal level, I don't get it. Convincing people to do what I want them to of their own volition is much more rewarding.

Positive manipulation, *I call it. Getting others to do what I want in a way that makes them feel good about it, even like it was their idea in the first place. Now, there's a skill. Dropping a roofie in some girl's drink is a rookie move.*

They're on to dessert. I think I spot tiramisu and my contempt for the date's stereotypes rises, even as I acknowledge I'm being petty.

When they emerge from the restaurant, the couple pauses. There's a magnetic pull between the two of them, I can see it, and I can see they both feel it. After a short conversation, they set off together in the direction of her car. I follow from a discreet distance, keeping to the shadows, my steps soft, my eyes sharp.

Once at her parked car, there's another moment of awkwardness, another kiss that doesn't land on skin but just grazes air. They both giggle, nervous, excited, clearly pleased with how the evening has gone.

A formal handshake and beaming smiles; then he turns

sharply on his heel and walks away, his head already bent over his cellphone. Her phone pings and she pulls it from a jacket pocket.

"I had a great time too," she calls after him, smiling.

He turns then. "Text me when you get home," he calls back.

I snap a shot of her date with my cellphone, his stupid, smirking, expectant face.

I need to know more about him. And it's amazing what you can find out about people if only you know where to look.

CHAPTER EIGHT

They wordlessly huff and puff up a last rocky stretch and finally reach a crest in the trail. The view from this spot is glorious, green scrub against sandy earth and iron-gray mountain, the Pacific Ocean a glistening expanse stretching out to a horizon line so similarly hued in shades of blue that it appears an almost infinite merge.

Laina places her hands on her knees and hauls in a lungful of air. Beside her, Vanessa pauses to take in the view. "That never gets old," Vanessa remarks. "You ready for the last stretch?"

"You promised me we'd take it easy today," Laina protests.

"Well, I lied. I need to let off some steam and something tells me you do too," Vanessa replies.

Laina takes a long pull from her water bottle. Breath recovered, the two women attack the last stretch of their hike, falling into an easy rhythm. The hot sun beats down on them. Sweat glistens in tiny beads along Laina's upper lip. "I wanted to ask your advice about a couple of things," Laina says as she swipes it away.

"Surprise, surprise. When else do you get up this early if

not to get me alone on a trail? What's up?" Vanessa's tone is teasing but without rancor.

"We had an anonymous call accusing Harley of impropriety. With a female patient."

Vanessa's sharp intake of breath whistles in Laina's ears. "Who took the call?"

"It was a message left on the reception voicemail. Abigail, Harley, and I all listened to it but didn't recognize the voice."

Vanessa stops hiking and pulls Laina to face her. The sun tilts directly in Laina's eyes and she has to squint; even so, she can barely make out Vanessa's backlit features. "Harley denies it, of course?"

"Yes," Laina confirms. "It seems absurd, really. Unsettling, of course, but more ludicrous than anything. Harley's devoted to his wife. Their kids."

"You know better than anyone how good some people are at concealing things."

"I should put that on a business card," Laina retorts wryly. "Harley thinks it might have been Kelsey McKendrick."

"And what do you think?" Vanessa replies sharply.

Laina shrugs. "I always thought she was more harmless than he did. And she's been long and quietly gone. But either way, is there anything we can do to get ahead of something like this?"

"You might want to get ahead of it alone," Vanessa suggests. "And let's pick up the pace."

"What do you mean?" Laina asks, falling into step beside her.

"Hear me out. You're expanding; do you want some

messy allegation against Harley to taint your every move? Deflect from the good you're trying to do? I know you guys have been in disagreement about the scope of the new clinic. Maybe it's time to fly solo."

"We've had some disagreements, sure, but that seems disloyal to even think about. Harley was so integral when I was just getting my footing here."

The bend in the trail's taken them to yet another sweeping vista. Dun-colored hills dusted with emerald brush and greeted down below by blue water etched with white foam. In the far distance, a handful of surfers atop their boards dot the azure surface with sleek black wetsuits and splashes of color.

Vanessa pauses to take in the view. "Being loyal to yourself sometimes means you have to do what's best for you, even if you have a history with someone. You're the star of that practice and everybody knows it."

Laina laughs. "You going to bill me for therapy as well as legal services? Anyway, I thought you liked Harley."

"Sure, I like him well enough. But I'm your friend in addition to being your lawyer. You said you had a couple of questions?"

"Yeah. Do you think we can kill that TV interview? Harley thinks more press will just draw more trouble."

"Another example of Harley looking out for Harley. You thought long and hard about that interview before you decided to do it, and suddenly you want to shut it down? What's good for Laina here? I think you have to answer that question before you make a decision about the interview, Harley, or anything else."

Laina takes another long pull on her water bottle as she

considers Vanessa's words. A hint of a smile crosses her lips as she realizes she's probably given similar advice to countless patients.

What *is* good for Laina? She'll have to give this real thought. Because surely it's her time. She's worked hard enough and well enough to be entitled to the good.

"The reporter asked me out," Laina confides.

"Did he now? Did you say yes?" Vanessa quirks an eyebrow.

"I did."

Vanessa puts a hand on Laina's arm to slow her stride. She tilts up her sunglasses and scans her client's face.

"I have to say I'm glad to hear it. First date since Mr. M, right?" Vanessa asks.

"Right," Laina confirms.

"It's about fucking time," Vanessa huffs. "Now I'll race you to the top."

CHAPTER NINE

"Journalism is dying," his father had said when Cal revealed his career path. *"I thought I raised a smarter son than that."* But Cal loves the feeling he gets when he's in pursuit of a story, the adrenaline-pumping thrill that comes along with the search for a larger justice. He's charged with energy, on the hunt, ready for wherever the next adventure will take him, determined to probe and expose and reveal.

The story that launched him into San Diego, an insurance fraud scandal that had led to the unmasking and prosecution of the beloved executive director of one of Savannah's largest medical centers, had begun as a result of a similar sort of tingle to the one now pulsing through his veins.

He'd been at the hospital covering something else entirely, a multi-car accident involving teenagers on their way to prom, when he happened to witness a whispered conversation between the hospital director, a towering and substantial woman, and a shorter, smaller man, who Cal later determined was her husband, a doctor employed by the medical center in the oncology department. Cal did a little research. The realization of the nature of the pair's marital relationship had put some of what Cal had observed into frame: The couple's tight-lipped tension could have been attributed to spouses reluctant to bring a personal argument into their workplace. But Cal's Spidey-sense tingled.

Always one to trust his instincts, he poked and probed, first discovering the "unconventional nature" of their marriage (both had multiple lovers, about which Cal couldn't have cared less) but shortly thereafter revealing the insurance fraud scam and all its illegally gotten gains: a renovated first home in Savannah's ritzy Ardsley Park, and a second home on Hilton Head with a soundproof sex dungeon.

The story had everything: money, sex, and scandal. Cal pieced the lurid puzzle together meticulously and broke the story live in front of the medical center just as Executive Director Audrey Hartwell was led away in handcuffs. Ryan had been on the phone to him in a nanosecond, excited and poised to sign him and then sell, sell, sell him. And he'd delivered; the offer for San Diego came in a mere ten days later.

Cal stretches and hoists his sturdy frame up from his lumpy bed in the rather sad and run-down corporate apartment in which the station has temporarily lodged him. It almost makes him laugh; on the one hand, he's congratulating himself on how far he's come (an agent at CAA, for example; he didn't even know journalists had agents when he got started), on the other, this place is a dump. It's as if the apartment had been designed to hurry its transient residents out as quickly as possible.

Cal takes a last look at himself in the closet door mirror that runs the length of one wall of the bedroom; the bottom corner of one of the sliders is shattered and leaves a trail of tiny splinters of glass every time Cal moves it. His reflection reveals a lemon-colored button-down shirt, black blazer, dark wash jeans, and a pair of Italian-made soft leather boots. He's the very image of subdued propriety, a conscious reflection of the image Laina Landers projects, at least in his research. Even if those sandals she wore the other night hinted at something a little wilder.

He's delighted she accepted his invitation to dinner. He would like to sit down with her formally a second time for the piece, sure, but he's also attracted to her in a way that has taken him by surprise.

He checks his phone. Time to go. He gathers up his keys and wallet and heads out. He's going to have to get rid of his rental and get a decent car. What's the point of his new job and higher salary if he's not living the life a little bit? He enters the elevator thinking maybe a Mercedes or a Beemer, something sleek with a powerful engine. He's dreaming of speed when the doors slide open revealing a freckled, auburn-haired woman in her mid-forties. The woman hesitates upon seeing him.

Time slows. The redhead's sidelong glances and nervous, fluttering hands reveal her fear of entering an elevator with an unknown Black man. She takes a step back and away. Her eyes slide back to Cal, who keeps his face neutral and pleasant, despite the fact that his perfectly fitted shirt collar suddenly seems a bit too snug. With a jerky nod and tight shoulders, the woman enters, careful to keep both her distance and a carefully flexed smile.

The elevator's descent seems interminable to Cal, and it must seem the same to the woman as she hurries out of the elevator with an audible exhale as soon as they reach the lobby. She crosses to exit the glass front door and Cal follows. Once outside, the redhead turns left. So does Cal; it's the direction his rental car is parked.

The redhead turns and sees him. Her steps quicken. Cal slows his in weary resignation, not wanting any trouble. Still, he feels a knot in the pit of his stomach. That woman may have felt unsafe upon encountering him in the elevator, but Cal knows he could just as easily have been the one victimized. Three quickly punched numbers, "911," along with his description, could be enough to end his life.

Unsettled, Cal climbs into his rental. He depresses the pedal on the Chevy and feels it lurch forward jerkily.

The dulcet tones of his GPS inform him he should take the next left. He abruptly changes lanes without signaling and makes the turn. Suddenly red lights flash behind him. A siren screams. Cal reflexively checks his speed (under the limit!) as his heart hammers in his chest.

Are they stopping me? Shit. They are.

He pulls over. Unrolls the driver's side window. Places both hands carefully on the steering wheel so they remain visible. He swallows hard, feeling the knot in his stomach tighten, fighting the waves of anger, frustration, and fear coursing through him.

The many harsh lessons with which his mother had battered him over the years run rapidly through his mind: *"Always present yourself respectably, in how you dress and how you act. Don't pop off; temper is not your friend. Try to never give them reason to stop you. Or shoot you. Learn to de-escalate."* Cal had resented the constant barrage when he was younger but has since come to understand she was just trying to keep Cal and his brother, Jacky, alive.

Cal gulps air, trying to control his hammering heart. He feels as if his chest might explode. He tries to compose his face and realizes his upper lip is beaded in sweat.

The flashing red lights zip right past him, the howl of sirens tearing away from him and into the darkening night.

Cal suddenly feels straitjacketed. He unclasps his seatbelt buckle and stumbles out of his car and into the street in a simultaneous rush of relief and furious anger, oblivious to the plumber's van barreling toward him. The van driver swerves to avoid hitting Cal, letting loose an angry blast of his horn.

Pull yourself together, man, Cal admonishes himself. *Nothing happened.*

Shit. He's late to meet Dr. Landers now. That won't get them off to a good start.

Laina gazes out at the spectacular, multicolored sunset, pleased with her choice of restaurant for her dinner with Cal Murray. Not just for the shades of violet, lavender, crimson, and ginger painting the horizon but also for Bex's reassuring presence behind the bar. Sea Now is where Bex and Laina first met, back when Laina was new to the area and Bex a bartender, not yet the restaurant's manager. He's behind the bar tonight to keep an eye on Laina and she's grateful for his reassuring presence.

From a prime table on the outdoor deck, Laina sips at her vodka and soda. Murray is late; only a few minutes, but she feels a prickle of anxiety.

Bex shoots her a reassuring smile and comes around from behind the bar carrying a fresh drink. "Late, huh?" he drawls as he places the cocktail on the table and lifts away Laina's depleted glass. "The man's losing points already."

"Stop it. You were the one who thought I ought to at least

check him out and get a vibe." Laina ducks her eyes away from Bex's. She'd of course only told Bex she was meeting Cal for dinner, nothing about her secret intent to try to protect Clare Hutchinson. "Stop stirring up trouble where there is none. Go back to the bar to relive your glory days."

"Ingrate," Bex retorts as he retreats to the bar. "And after you enlisted me as your bodyguard."

Despite her relaxed banter with Bex, Laina's anxious. She has a simple agenda tonight: finding out what Cal knows about the Hutchinson tape and, to the extent she can, shutting down any further speculation about it. She's not quite sure about Cal's agenda. Is it professional? Personal? Knowing would give her a better sense of how to handle the conversation, but she can't quite read his intentions.

Laina sips at her fresh cocktail. Glances at her watch. He's almost fifteen minutes late. Laina's anxiety rises. Clare had confessed to a retaliatory affair, with the additional devastating revelation that her lover had filmed the encounter without her knowing it. Peter had received the video via text and things had escalated from there. Laina's brain ticks over to poor Daisy Sullivan, similarly ill-used. *What is wrong with men? Why am I even on this date?*

When Cal Murray comes hurrying toward her, Laina is surprised to feel her anxiety dissolve in response to the openly apologetic look on his face and the urgency in his step.

"I'm so sorry, Dr. Landers," he says, extending his hand for a shake.

"It's quite all right. And call me Laina," she says, startled by the electricity the touch of his hand ignited inside of her. "Let's get you a drink; I'm afraid I've lapped you."

"It isn't really all right. I don't like being late and I don't like keeping people waiting. I won't offer an excuse, just an apology."

Points for owning his mistakes, thinks Laina. "Apology accepted."

Bex strides over in response to Laina's signal and takes Murray's order. "Hey, you're Laina's friend, right? Beck, was it?" Cal asks. "I hear you were a major reason Dr. Landers agreed to sit for an interview with me. So thanks."

"Bex, actually," he replies, "but good memory. Yes, I'm Laina's friend and I run this joint, so behave yourself."

"Always do until I don't," Cal retorts with a smile.

Laina studies Cal, the easy charm and megawatt smile. *What's underneath that smooth façade?* He's damn sexy, that's for sure, but he seems to know it, which makes her wary.

"I'll be right back with your drink," Bex replies, mouthing "he's cute" at Laina as he retreats to the bar.

They order food and in response to Cal's questions, Laina sketches out the highlights of her career. She learns Cal is new to San Diego. That they each have one brother. That they've both always been closer to their mothers than their fathers. She begins to relax. The conversation turns to college.

"I went to Howard," Cal tells Laina in response to her inquiry. "Despite getting into schools like Penn and Princeton. My father was not happy with me."

"Why?"

"He went to Howard. But he wanted something different for me."

"And why was it your choice?"

"Truth? When I visited, the tour was led by the most beautiful girl I'd ever seen." Cal gives her a smile. "Not the most mature reason to choose a college, but hey. Of course, by the time I got to campus, she was an upperclassman and never gave me the time of day."

Laina erupts with a full-throated laugh. "Poor you."

"Yeah, poor me."

"So." Laina pauses, toying with her wineglass. "What else can you tell me about that tape you mentioned? The one you implied might have triggered Peter Hutchinson?"

"Whoa. That was an abrupt turn."

Laina lowers her voice and leans in so she can speak to him more intimately. "Just between us, it's torturing me that I missed something with Peter and Clare. I pride myself on being observant about my patients, and I never in a million years saw this coming."

"Hey, hey, people are whack, you know that, you're a shrink. You can't take personal responsibility for every nut-job." Cal sneaks a grin at her, letting her know he's teasing.

Laina laughs in spite of herself. " 'Whack' and 'nutjob' are hardly clinical diagnoses."

"I'm just saying that you can only help people so much, so don't take the burden of someone else's actions on yourself. Particularly that nutjob Peter Hutchinson. What was it you said to him to get him to release Clare, anyway?"

"Why are you so obsessed with the specifics of what I said?"

"Who, what, where, when, and why are the fundamental questions of journalism. I've never met a 'what' I didn't want to unravel."

"Okay, then. I'll say what I can within the bounds of confidentiality. I reminded him of all they both had to live for, principally their two sons. I'll be honest, it was a hunch, drilling in on the boys, but it got through to him and I'm more relieved than anyone. I thought he was going to kill me for a moment there."

"You were very brave."

"I didn't feel like I had a choice." Laina shrugs off the compliment. "So what about that tape?" She's given him something he wanted and figures she's owed a favor in return.

"And men are accused of having one-track minds," Cal cracks. "But I can't tell you much more than I did already. I've got a friend on the force who told me there's some kind of a tape and a hell of a lot of downward pressure to make sure it never sees the light of day. That's all I know."

"Off the record?" Laina meets Cal's gaze and holds it.

"Okay. Off the record."

"I went to see Clare Hutchinson," Laina confides. "I don't know what you heard about a video, but she didn't have any idea what I was talking about. It was the pressure of the campaign that got to Peter. It was all just too much for him. He wanted to livestream his withdrawal from the race. Clare asked him to reconsider. He'd been drinking. One thing led to another. It's all sad but hardly salacious. And no mention of any kind of video. She didn't know what the hell I was talking about."

Laina raises her eyes to meet Cal's, hopeful that the lie has landed, that her expression is guileless.

"The next time you give me something off the record, can it at least be juicy?" Cal asks, smiling.

"No promises." Laina smiles back, relieved. *Mission accomplished.*

Dinner had been delicious, the bottle of white wine, selected by Laina, crisp and pleasantly grassy. Their conversation flowed easily; Cal found himself surprised by the many parallels in their lives and beliefs. They'd even dissected the similarities in their professions, such as having to rapidly assess people, make quick decisions, follow instinct as well as rely on research and training, and delved into some of the surprisingly similar pitfalls that came with that territory (a wrongly played move could shut down a patient as quickly as an interview subject).

Cal had ordered a second bottle of wine, but they hadn't been able to finish it. Now it dangles from Laina's hand as they stroll along the beach path; giggling, she'd snagged the open bottle from its cooler as they'd left the restaurant.

Cal steals a glance at her, admiring her profile in the moonlight. He's enjoying this night more than he'd expected. He doesn't want it to end. He wants to kiss her.

Laina takes a swig of wine and wipes her mouth with the back of her hand once she's gulped it down. Cal finds the gesture astonishingly erotic. She hands the bottle to him, and he takes a swallow. When he hands the wine back to her, their fingers brush and Cal feels an electric spark. Before he can even register what's happening, his hands are entangled in her hair and his mouth is pressing urgently onto hers. She moans and wraps her arms around his neck, pulling his tongue deeper into her mouth.

They kiss, long, probing, tender kisses that leave them both breathless.

Laina breaks away first. "Well," she says. "There's that."

"Right you are," Cal answers, his thoughts swimming. "There's that." He wants to kiss her again, but Laina starts to walk, undulating hips and legs calling him along.

They fall into a companionable silence as they continue to walk along the shore. Cal feels excited, nervous, fuzzy from wine, yet sharp as a tack with anticipation. He doesn't want this evening to end. Their hands brush and he links a single long finger around one of hers, startled by the power of their attraction.

"I should head home," Laina says, drawing to a stop. "Full day tomorrow. But thank you. This was lovely."

Cal's both disappointed and relieved. Truth be told, he's still feeling more than a little burned by his last relationship back in Savannah, where, as it turned out, a girl Cal was genuinely into was dating him mostly to piss off her white, conservative parents.

Besides, Laina's part of an evolving story, the biggest one he's hit on since landing in San Diego.

But damn, that kiss.

CHAPTER TEN

Laina's patient Michelle Marshall is happier than she's been in the months Laina's been treating her. The young, blond teacher is a tricky client; she tends to answer questions in monosyllables, and isn't open to much self-revelation. She's sat here in this office, week after week, clearly wanting to talk about *something*, but giving Laina very few clues about what that something actually is. Despite that, Laina's parsed and processed enough of Michelle's evasions to have formed a few educated guesses.

Today Michelle is bouncy, her blond ponytail swinging high; she can barely stay still in her seat. Laina wonders if the scale has finally tipped; has she earned enough trust to hear the secrets Michelle is carrying?

"I met someone." Michelle blushes. "I really like him."

"Do you want to tell me about him?"

Michelle does want to tell Laina *all* about him. How they met (church singles mixer), their first date (an Italian dinner downtown), their second date (surfing), and third date (kissing). He seems perfect on paper, never married, age appropriate, has a good job as a mortgage broker, is athletic (a runner and a surfer, just like her!), also loves tacos!

Tugging her hair free from its ponytail, Michelle shakes

the strands loose around her shoulders. She's always been an exceptionally pretty girl, but one whose life force seemed to have been tamped down by the weight of something unseen. Now she's light, golden, glowing.

Michelle leans forward, hands on her knees, and a shadow crosses her lovely face. "But even better than all that," she confides. "He brought me home to my place a couple of nights ago and there was the most horrible thing left on my front doorstep. . . ." She trails off. Twists her hands in her lap.

"What was it?" Laina prompts.

Dropping her voice to a whisper, Michelle admits, "It was an embryo, a human fetus. In a jar. With a note."

"How awful!" Laina exclaims. "Do you have any idea how it got there?"

"None at all."

"Did you call the police?"

"No!"

"Why not? Didn't it worry you? Who might have left it? And why?"

"Of course, at first, I was totally freaking out."

"And yet you didn't call the police?" Laina presses again.

"No. I came to realize it was a gift from God and that the human hand that put it on my doorstep was irrelevant."

Laina's deeply intrigued. "Tell me more about that. Why did you come to that conclusion?"

"Sam helped. He was amazing; he just took the whole thing in stride as a prank that some of my students had played and tossed the jar. He thinks the fetus might have even been plastic! Although, I admit, I didn't want to even look close enough to be sure. Anyway, the message that came with the jar was what was important, not the contents."

"What did it say?"

"Just two words. 'Watching You.'"

Laina can't keep the incredulity from her voice. "And you're not afraid?"

Laina's astonished by Michelle's composure, but the young woman continues her story in an even, happy tone. "Just listen, hear me out," Michelle says, twisting a lock of her blond hair around a finger. "Sam and I went inside—it was the first time I'd had him in my place—and he was so incredibly kind that we ended up talking all night. And finally, I told him my biggest secret." Michelle pauses and looks at Laina with wide, cornflower blue eyes.

Laina allows the admission a moment to breathe. Now that Michelle's acknowledged harboring a secret, the specifics are likely to follow.

"I had an abortion," Michelle confesses. "Right before I started seeing you. It's why I came, even though I never talked about it!"

Laina had suspected as much from all the things Michelle had talked *around* in the preceding months. "Why didn't you talk about it?" she asks. "If it's why you came to therapy?"

"Isn't it obvious? I'm Catholic. I teach at a Catholic school. I thought I was going to hell."

"But you told your friend Sam about the abortion?"

"Yes! He was unbelievable! He said he didn't know why I was punishing myself. That true faith requires forgiveness. That we all make mistakes, but that we are not our mistakes."

"And how are you feeling now?"

"So much better! I've been carrying that secret around like a stone. No one knew. Not even the . . . father."

"Why not the father?"

Michelle's golden glow dims a notch. "The one time I step out of bounds, the one time! I've been a good girl my whole life!" She fingers the purity ring on her left hand. Slides it off her finger.

"I went to Vegas for a friend's bachelorette party, against my better judgment I might add. I had too much to drink and lost my virginity to some guy named Joey, no known last name, never seen before or since."

Laina assesses Michelle. She might have expected this sort of confession to come with a torrent of tears, but Michelle leans back in her chair with a peaceful look on her face. She pulls her hair back up into a ponytail as she continues. "I told Sam everything, and it's all cool. We live in modern times, he said. A woman has the right to choose."

"And you can reconcile that with your faith?" Laina probes. "You don't think you're going to hell anymore?"

"That's the beauty of it!" Michelle exults. "It's Sam's faith too. We're just choosing to respect that we can have faith and also live in the modern world, with all the medical and other advantages that gives us. See? That prank became a gift. From God. Maybe it even *was* God. Watching over me. Like the note said. Allowing me to heal."

Laina leans back in her seat and contemplates Michelle's radiant transformation. It seems proof of the power of liberating secrets, as if the young teacher had been sipping on a poison of her own making, and speaking her truth provided the antidote. Michelle seems positively euphoric, the grotesquerie of a fetus in a jar left on her doorstep along with an ominous note somehow conveniently shunted aside.

People are fascinating. It's why Laina was drawn to this work. After Michelle departs, she takes the time to jot down some handwritten notes. Today's session had been so unexpected, and Laina's mind is racing with theories and ideas. This is the kind of moment she lives for, when she feels herself on the brink of a new insight or understanding, one that could help many, not just the one patient who may have been its inspiration. The young woman faced her truth and was liberated. If only Carmen (not to mention many of her other patients) could do the same.

Laina can admit to herself she has another cause for excitement. It had been a *real date*, and if he began it with an agenda, so what? So did she. The passion they'd felt on the beach had been agenda free.

He'd been tempted by the cherry red, but in the end decided on classic shiny black with a cream leather interior. The Mercedes GLB can seat seven, but Cal flips all five rear seats down and plans on keeping them neatly folded away. In his line of work, he's learned the value of a vehicle large enough to stow gear or even sleep in, in a pinch.

Cal snaps a photo of the SUV and shoots it out to his agent. They'd had a furious text debate on the merits of the Mercedes versus the BMW X3, with Ryan firmly on the side of the Beemer, so Cal's expecting some shade in response.

When his phone rings, he sees it's the man himself. Or at least his assistant rolling calls.

"Hello," Cal answers cheerfully.

"Hold for Ryan." It's the assistant. Something else Cal had to adjust to. He knows the kid's name is Charlie, but never gets in even as much as a *"how are you?"* before Charlie disappears in service of his boss.

"Cal, my friend, I have a question for you." Ryan leaps right in without any preamble. "You think that the shrink you interviewed is interested in representation? I sent some clips around, selling you, of course, but a couple of people sparked to her. Knowledgeable *and* hot but in an approachable way. She could be a natural as an expert commentator."

"I have no idea," Cal replies, somewhat taken aback. "But the interview hasn't even aired yet. . . ."

"Yeah. My assistant made a supercut of some of the footage you shared. Would you lay some groundwork for me? See if she'll take a meeting? Seemed like you two had some chemistry."

Something squeezes at Cal's gut, an uncomfortable, ill-defined unease. He bats it away, keeping his reply neutral. "Sure, next time I speak to her."

"Good man. Thanks. And the Mercedes? Piece of crap. You should have gone with the Beemer."

Ryan clicks off the phone before Cal can reply. He turns over Ryan's request in his mind. He's confident he'll see Laina again, and Lord knows he wants to, but he's less sure that he's comfortable with the idea of brokering this introduction, for reasons he can't quite name.

Cal decides to file the request away for now. He's meeting the other Cal Murray for breakfast and doesn't want to be late.

When Cal arrives at Kate Sessions City Park on Pacific Beach, he spies his namesake sprawled out across a bench next to a picnic table, fair hair and freckled skin damp with perspiration. He wears shorts and a T-shirt, his large feet are jammed into sneakers, and a plastic water bottle is clutched in one hand. Cal tosses him a foil-wrapped burrito, which is caught with lazy ease.

Cal drops down next to the cop, unwrapping his own burrito. "Barbacoa," he announces as he chomps down into the fat, fragrant wrap. The two men eat in contented silence, staring out over a vista of lush green lawn dotted with sturdy, leafy trees. Past the park, the blue sea ripples and sings. The warren of buildings clustered together on the other side of the cove provides a stark man-made contrast to all this natural beauty. A scrawny girl, maybe twelve or thirteen, zips by on a skateboard, all tough attitude and scraped knees.

Cop Cal releases a belch. "I hear," he drawls lazily, "that you used to run track in college. Broke some records too."

A startled laugh escapes Cal's lips. "Gunning to make detective?" he parries. "What else you dig up on me?"

"Nothing too damaging," Cop Cal replies with a grin. "But I need a favor. And you owe me at least one."

The request to help coach the high school track team Cop Cal's nephew is on takes Cal by surprise, but pleases him as well. Creating a network of sources in any new community is key, and this will be a way for him to meet a broad swath of locals. He agrees to show up at a practice next weekend to give the team a once-over before making a final decision, on the theory that it's never good to look too eager.

These arrangements made, Cal shifts to his own agenda.

"Anything more on that video you heard about?" Cal can feel Cop Cal shift on the bench next to him, an instinctive drawing away from the easy camaraderie the two have had since their first encounter. It had been more than their almost identical names; they'd shared a sense of humor, a love of sports, and a mutual sense that they could be useful to each other.

Every prickling instinct tells Cal to proceed delicately. "You know," he continues, "the one you mentioned was connected to the Hutchinson meltdown."

Cop Cal drums his fingers against his thigh. "I shouldn'ta said anything to you about that."

This is the kind of admission that Cal couldn't love any more. It's a validation of his instinct that there is more to the story and also an indication that more information is yet to flow. If he's careful, if he's deft.

"Yeah? Why's that?" Cal asks with a casualness he doesn't feel. If Cop Cal really didn't want to share what he knows, he would've just said there was nothing new. But the officer is also fully aware he has information he *shouldn't* share with a journalist, and he might still get skittish and bolt.

Cop Cal drums that nervous tattoo into the widening silence between them. Cal lets the silence expand until Cop Cal finally breaks. "You didn't hear it from me, right?"

"That's our deal. Everything's off the record. So, there is a video? What of?"

"Some kind of sex tape. I don't know more than that. The brass clamped down fast and furious." He laughs. "But in this day and age, it's gotta be something pretty fucking out there if they're trying to pretend the damned thing doesn't even exist."

Cal gets that feeling again, the delicious, enticing sense he's following a path that will lead to something larger than himself. The confirmation of the video is all the more interesting since Laina definitively told him no video existed. Cal's pulse quickens. "So why exactly are you telling me?"

"Peter Hutchinson's an entitled prick."

Reason enough, Cal thinks. "Any directions you can point me in?"

"You're the badass investigative journo. But if it's true it's a sex tape, I'd think about who might be starring and go from there."

"You might just make detective, after all," Cal jokes. "See you next weekend. And that nephew of yours better be every bit as good as you say he is."

CHAPTER ELEVEN

"You won't believe this." The agitated words fly out of Franny Goldstein's mouth before the office door is even closed behind her. She flops into a chair opposite the armchair Laina occupies and sprawls out, flinging her long legs in front of her.

"Is it something about your mother?" Laina asks calmly.

"Yes!"

"What have we discussed regarding stories about your mother?"

Franny stares balefully at the therapist. "That no story about my mother should begin with 'you won't believe this' because her behavior is unfortunately completely believable in its predictability," she replies begrudgingly.

"Right. She's consistent and will do or say things that will hurt you. Our task here is to help you feel less injured. So what happened?"

Franny squirms. She's always been a skinny girl, but she's too thin now, brittle-looking, hollows carved under eyes.

"I called her right after I called Dad and Benny. Her first question was if I'd talked to Dad before her."

"What did you tell her?"

"The truth! Yes, I called Dad and my boyfriend before I

called her. Big fucking deal! I'm the one with fucking cancer! Can't I call who I want?"

"Of course you can."

"Then I told her the doctor recommends a complete hysterectomy. I thought she'd be upset that meant no grandkids."

"And?"

"Didn't even come up. But she did suggest I get implants and maybe a nose job while I was under. She even offered to pay."

Franny smolders in outrage, but Laina is not a bit surprised. Franny's mother, Ruslana, a former model from the Ukraine who'd used her looks to marry well, was a plastic surgery addict now barely recognizable when compared with her early photos. Franny got her mother's tall, lanky build, but her father's bumpy nose and rectangular chin, something Ruslana seems to take as a personal affront.

The divorce between her parents had been bitter, and another frequent lament of Franny's is Ruslana's ugly resentment of her daughter's close relationship with her dad. Often stuck between her parents, Franny is now also dependent financially on her father, who's not only supporting her during her treatment but is also sparing no expense on the best doctors and every experimental option he can find.

"And then she said that Dad was buying me and I should be ashamed of myself, without recognizing the irony of her literally just offering to pay for plastic surgery! I mean, what planet are we on? I'm fucking dying and this is what she's on about?"

"Let's reframe this. You're not dying, you're fighting. And you need to keep up that fight. Ruslana is who she is, and you need to stop needing her to be someone else. It just saps your strength."

They've had versions of this reframe before. Franny shrugs in defeat. "I know. She just crawls under my skin every fucking time."

"Both your father and Ben have been amazing, right? Focus on that."

Franny shifts uncomfortably. Avoids eye contact.

"Franny? Is there something else? Ben?"

"No! Ben's great."

"Something with your dad?"

Franny's lanky limbs curl up into the chair. "I don't want to talk about it."

This body language is interesting. "You don't have to, of course," Laina reassures Franny. "But this is a space to be brave, right?"

"Right," Franny replies uncertainly.

Laina waits patiently and Franny does not disappoint.

"I think my dad might be in trouble," she whispers, eyes lowered.

"What kind of trouble?"

"I don't know!"

"Then what makes you think he's in trouble?"

Franny tugs her oversize shirt over her hunched knees and hunches her neck. *It's as if she's trying to disappear into herself.*

"He dropped a safe deposit key off with me. Said it was my insurance," Franny admits in a low tone, her eyes darting all over the room, except directly opposite her where she would have to meet Laina's steady gaze.

"What's inside?"

"I'm afraid to look!" Franny blurts, her eyes finally meeting Laina's. "I don't want to know. I have enough on my plate."

"But what if you're just causing yourself unnecessary worry? The box could hold a literal insurance policy with you as the beneficiary. Don't you think knowing has to be better than whatever it is you're imagining?"

"That's what Ben said," Franny concedes.

"Smart man you have there," Laina cracks, eliciting a small smile from Franny. "You're braver than you knew, we've seen it again and again since your diagnosis. Keep it up. You're getting stronger all the time."

"Sometimes I just feel like giving up," Franny admits.

"That's completely natural. Allow yourself to feel that when you do. But remember that no emotion is permanent. Despair or happiness, hurt, anger or joy—they're all temporal. The one constant is change. You'll feel like giving up one day, but the next you'll have your fight back, and it's important to remember that when you're down."

Franny nods. "I'll try. So you think I should just check out the safe deposit box?"

"Yes. It's always better to face things head-on. We humans have imaginations that conjure danger; envisioning catastrophe is partly a survival instinct. By imagining the worst, we're prepared for it. I know you feel betrayed by your body, but don't imagine disaster or disappointment where you're actually receiving support."

Franny departs composed and resolved, and Laina makes her post-session notes with satisfaction. Although of course she has no control over Franny's medical progress (or regression), Laina's certain their work together is helping Franny with the aspect of the battle tying a positive psychological outlook to beating cancer.

Laina's cellphone flashes to life. It's Cal. Her heart gives an involuntary little lurch. Their interview had aired and Laina had been pleased with how she came off, and despite Harley's fears, the response so far has been largely positive. But more than that, Laina likes the way Cal is with her, how he makes her feel, the promise of those kisses on the beach.

"Hi there," she answers, aiming for the right balance of pleased and nonchalant. "How's your day?"

"Hello yourself," he replies with a warmth in his voice that makes her stomach turn to jelly. "I don't know if this is anything that would interest you, but my agent asked if maybe you would have a conversation with him? He thinks he can book you. You know, as an expert."

"Oh god," Laina says with a laugh. "Doing that interview with you was nerve-wracking enough."

"Would you at least think about it? He's a pretty persuasive guy. And his ideas might surprise you."

"All right. I'll think about it."

"That's all I can ask. And, Laina? I think you should know. Rumors are still floating around."

"About what?"

"The Hutchinsons and a secret tape."

Laina swallows back the flutter of fear suddenly pulsing in her throat. "Where are you hearing this?"

"A journalist can't reveal his sources," Cal replies lightly. "But I heard it's some kind of a sex tape. And if that's true, then somehow, somewhere, somewhen, it's going to come to light. I wanted you to know because I can tell you care about both of them."

"As I do about all my patients," Laina replies automatically, her stomach and mind both churning.

"Lucky patients."

That gets a small smile. "Are you hunting for the tape?" she asks, trying to keep her tone casual.

" 'Hunting' might be a strong word."

"But don't you care about the damage it could do if it was released? I mean, if it even exists. But theoretically, if it did. Peter destroyed his life and his marriage. Clare's already traumatized, as are both their sons. What good comes out of finding this alleged tape?"

"It's not about good, Laina. It's about the story. If I don't chase it, someone else will."

"You'll let me know if you learn anything more?"

"Sure. And let me know what you decide about meeting Ryan."

"Will do. And, Cal? Thanks for keeping me in the loop." Laina hangs up the phone and sets it down. Cal is probably right. *Someone* will lay their hands on the recording eventually; she tried as best she could to point Cal away, but she can't control this.

Anyway, when has hiding the truth done any good? Bright, cleansing rays of light can chase away secrets, along with their dark stains on the soul; it's only then that true healing can begin. Laina knows this firsthand, just as she knows Clare may have to learn it now.

CHAPTER TWELVE

Upon opening her front door, Elizabeth Vanderbilt Hancock, known to one and all as "Bootsy," looks completely flustered to see Cal. Her eyes scan him quickly, noting, no doubt, his Italian shoes and well-cut sports jacket and Tom Ford glasses (no prescription, just clear glass). Cal likes to look flash, but he's also playing to his audience. He looks respectable, professional, and just the right amount of expensive.

"Mrs. Hancock," he charges in before she has a chance to speak. "Cal Murray, Channel Five. I met you and your husband the night of the Hutchinson tragedy?"

Cal sees the light shift in her eyes as she recognizes him. She hesitates and he suspects she might shut the door right in his face. He doesn't give her the chance, continuing seamlessly, "I don't want to bother you, and I promise I don't want to put anything on camera." Cal gestures back behind him to show he's alone. "I really just hoped to ask you one or two background questions for a follow-up story I'm working on. But first, how are you feeling? I know the night we met was very stressful."

Bootsy doesn't invite him in, but she cracks the door open a little wider. "You just never think someone you actually *know* could do something like that, do you know what I mean?"

Cal knows he's got her on the hook. "I absolutely understand," he replies in dulcet tones. "You said you lived next door to them for nineteen years, right? Were you good friends?"

"We were friendly, of course. They're lovely people. . . ." Bootsy trails off, catching herself. "Were lovely! Something terrible must have happened to poor Peter for him to lose his marbles like that!"

"Any idea what that could have been?"

Bootsy glances back inside her house, then turns back around and steps out onto the elegantly proportioned front porch, pulling the door firmly shut behind her.

"My husband wouldn't like me talking to you. He saw you keep recording us with your phone, you know," she says with a surprising slyness. "You're just lucky none of that made it on the air. Phil can be litigious."

Raising his hands in the universal gesture of surrender, Cal replies, "Like I said, no cameras, just me. And I'm just looking for background."

Cal knows she wants to spill. This delicious moment of suspended animation when he knows a source is about to deliver is a kind of nectar to Cal, sweet, nourishing, and divinely satisfying. He stays patiently silent, knowing that Bootsy's desire to share whatever gossip she knows about the Hutchinsons will trump her better instincts about talking to the press, as well as her husband's disapproval.

"I don't want to get anyone in trouble," Bootsy protests. "And I certainly don't want to rain down any more pain on poor Clare. But in trying to puzzle this out—how a man like

Peter Hutchinson can be brought so low, so fast, one has to wonder about the factors! Am I right?"

"Indeed, you are," Cal assures her. "So, what *did* you wonder about?"

"If you want to find the trouble in that family look at the younger son, Drew," Bootsy intones confidentially. "He was a mess before his brother was in that car accident and he really acted out afterward. Poor Clare was at her wit's end with him."

"What's Drew's particular kind of trouble?"

"Drugs, mostly."

"Mostly? What else?"

Bootsy lowers her voice. "He also got into trouble with some girl who cried rape."

"Cried rape? Did you think the allegation wasn't true?"

"Who knows? She wouldn't be the first girl who got carried away and then blamed the boy."

With some effort Cal restrains himself from asking Bootsy if she's heard of the #MeToo movement. "Were charges filed?" he asks instead.

"I don't think so. We would have heard if that was the case. But it was messy. I heard the whole incident might even have been filmed on an iPhone."

Cal's pulse quickens. Could this be the elusive video Cop Cal tipped him to? "How old is Drew?" he asks Bootsy.

"Teenager, fifteen or sixteen. Some kids just get lost at that age."

"You're right about that, Mrs. Hancock," Cal affirms, his wheels spinning.

In this day and age, exposure is easy, keeping things hidden is the much harder task. A sex tape involving possible rape at worst, and two minors at best, would completely align with the pressure to keep the video a secret as reported by Cop Cal. And a man on the brink of a political career could easily have been undone by a video of his son allegedly raping a girl. But would the existence of the tape alone be enough to cause Peter Hutchinson to crack? Could blackmail also play a part in this sordid tale?

Hutchinson's political career may be shot and his marriage may be in tatters, but he's still a member of a prominent local family. His brother, Tom Hutchinson, has been front and center in an attempt to control the narrative in the days since Peter's arrest, and successfully too. Cal's heard a plea deal is in the works, one heavy on anger management classes and therapy sessions and short on jail time. But what if Hutchinson is still a lit fuse?

"You've been incredibly helpful, Mrs. Hancock," Cal says. "I appreciate your candor."

Her bright blue eyes dart away from his brown ones. "That boy is trouble," she sniffs. "Ruined Clare and Peter's lives. It's disgraceful that they're protecting him."

Cal muses that if he had all the time in the universe, he still would not devote a minute to unpacking the contradictions that are Bootsy Hancock. Still, he got what he came for, so he thanks the woman and heads back down the path to his car.

It seems increasingly clear that there *is* a video at the twisted heart of the Hutchinson story. If Cal can find it, and break that story, his future will be limitless. His anticipatory glee quells a little as he recalls Laina asking him what possible good could come out of exposing a sex tape given the shattered lives of the family, but Cal reminds himself that he's not making the news, he's just covering it.

Cal has many cynical aspects to his nature, their edges hard-forged by a life lived balanced between multiple identities. But a central core of idealism glows hotly inside him, fueled by the ache to expose wrongdoing, corruption, and injustice. He loves what he does because he wants to make a difference. Powerful figures seem to be suppressing evidence. If he didn't chase this story, it would be a betrayal of self.

Pausing to look over at the Hutchinson house, Cal sees the outline of a figure, half-concealed by a curtain at an upper window. He takes a couple of steps closer, trying to discern more details. The curtain is abruptly pulled back and the figure comes clearly into view. A teenage boy, stocky and blond, with a round face contorted by a sneer. Their eyes meet. Cal suspects this is Drew Hutchinson. The boy gives Cal an aggressive middle finger salute before yanking the curtain closed, and Cal considers that act confirmation of his suspicion.

Cal shoots Laina a quick text asking if he can drop by her office. She replies that she has a break between patients in about an hour if he wants to come then. While Cal's pleased that she said yes so easily, he's also a little uncomfortable with the knowledge that his overture isn't a romantic one. He has to ask her about the possibility of a video involving Drew Hutchinson. He hopes she won't be disappointed by his agenda, and suspects she will be.

He squares his shoulders. What he told Laina is true. If he doesn't chase this story, someone else will. At least if he breaks it, he can give her a heads-up so that she's in the best position to help her clients. Uncomfortably aware that he's wading into the dangerous waters of self-justification, Cal climbs into his beautiful new car and heads over to Laina's office.

As he pulls into the underground garage in the small office complex that houses the BETTER LIFE clinic, Cal mulls over just how to broach the question of Drew Hutchinson's possible role in his father's meltdown. He pilots his Mercedes into a spot marked VISITOR, checks the time, and realizes he's got a few minutes before Laina will be free. He plays with the car's controls, tilting his seat forward and back, adjusting interior lights, getting a feel for his new ride.

Across the parking lot, he spies the elevator doors slide open. A man exits, white, thin, tall, with a receding hairline and a lined face, his hands jammed into the pockets of his windbreaker. After crossing the lip of the elevator, the man pauses and looks around as if he's uncertain where he parked his car. Then he pulls a scarf from one pocket of his windbreaker and brings it up to his nose, taking a deep inhale from within the folds of flowered silk.

Cal's stomach lurches. He's 90 percent sure that scarf belongs to Laina, that she wore it the night they met for dinner. He lifts his phone and takes a quick photo of the thin man just as he's shoving the scrap of silk back into his pocket. Cal checks the photo. *Damn.* Just a tiny corner of the pattern of pansies dancing across a cream background is visible. Still. Cal's going to have to say something to Laina; that was fucking creepy.

The BETTER LIFE clinic is hopping when Cal enters the waiting area. Several people are seated in the bright orange guest chairs; a receptionist checks in a mother and son. Cal gives his name to the receptionist when she's free, and moments later, Laina comes out from the inner sanctum to greet him. She's slightly flushed and Cal hopes it's with the pleasure of seeing him. As Laina escorts him down the hallway to her office, their hands brush, giving Cal an electric jolt. He reminds himself he has an agenda here, he can't get distracted by lust, or like, or whatever this thing with Laina is.

"So to what do I owe the pleasure?" Laina asks as she settles herself in one armchair and gestures that Cal should take the other. "Not that I'm unhappy to see you."

"Before I get to that, I just saw a kind of creepy guy in your garage."

"What kind of creepy?"

"The sniffing-a-scarf-I'm-pretty-sure-is-yours kind of creepy."

"Sniffing a scarf?" Laina laughs with a touch of incredulity. "What makes you think it's mine, anyway?"

"Purple pansies? I'm pretty sure I've seen it on you."

Laina's hand flies to her throat and comes up empty. "I was wearing that scarf today."

Cal raises an eyebrow and continues, "Anyway, tall skinny white guy? Maybe in his sixties?"

"Oh," interjects Laina, light dawning in her eyes.

"Someone you know?"

"A patient. Can't say any more than that. But he's totally harmless. Not creepy at all."

Cal looks at her skeptically. "You don't think it's creepy he was inhaling your scarf, which it appears he's stolen?"

"No." Laina crosses her legs and leans toward Cal. "He's also about to embark on a cross-country trip, so if you think he's a rival for my affections, you're mistaken. He'll be on the road next month." Her tone is light and teasing.

"If you say so," he says, deciding to drop it for now, distinctly pleased that she's flirting with him. "But that's not why I'm here. I wanted to let you know that there does seem to be a video involved in the Hutchinson case. One that might involve Drew Hutchinson?"

"Are you still looking into that?"

"I've told you. If I don't, someone else will."

"But why would you think Drew's involved?"

"Research." Cal catches Laina's frustrated eye roll. "I can't discuss sources any more than you can discuss patients. And I'm telling you because I know you're worried about the family. If and when that tape comes out, it could be devastating."

Laina looks him directly in the eyes. "I don't know anything about a tape involving Drew Hutchinson."

Cal wants to believe her. "Let me just ask you this: Do you think whatever Drew was up to could have been a factor in Peter losing his shit?"

"It's not ethical for me to talk to you about my clients!"

"Drew's not a client, though, right?" Cal presses further, knowing he's also pressing his luck.

Laina stands. Her hands anchor on her hips. "No. Therefore, I have no firsthand knowledge of anything to do with him, nor would I share anything with you that I learned from either of his parents, who *are* my clients. I wish you'd leave this alone," she admonishes as she strides over to stare out the large glass window.

Cal comes up behind her and lays his hands on her shoulders. "I'm not trying to piss you off."

"Well, you're succeeding at it, anyway," Laina retorts, but she lets his hands massage the tight muscles of her upper back.

"Have you given thought to joining me and Ryan for dinner?" he asks, redirecting the flow of conversation.

"I have. And I asked Vanessa to have a preliminary chat with him as well. She didn't disagree with your assessment that he can be 'kind of a dick,' but she also thinks there might be a human heart beating underneath all his bravado."

"I've always suspected as much! No wonder I'm not an anchor yet!"

Laina laughs. The tension finally eases from her shoulders. "So you'll do it?" he asks. "We could drive up together on Friday. Ryan suggested we meet at some place called Geoffrey's Malibu. Apparently it's on a cliff right on the ocean and you don't have to ever even step indoors. He says it's his go-to since the pandemic, where he's found, and I quote, 'Deals as limitless as the the sea and sky.'"

"Well, then. He's winning me over already." A wry smile crosses her lips. Cal finds himself thinking, *That's adorable,* before almost immediately clamping down and reminding himself to *slow the pace.* He likes this woman, but not enough to erase a lifetime of rigorous commitment to building trust slowly.

In Cal's experience, relationships in all contexts need a proving period. Friends, colleagues, lovers, it doesn't really matter. It takes time to see who someone truly is, particularly on the issue of race. Cal's learned the painful way what it's like to be a girl's temporary foray into exotic eroticism.

He inhales the scent of her, clean hair, lavender soap, cashmere. She turns around to face him.

"Okay," she agrees. "Friday. I can leave here by three; will that be early enough?"

"It'll have to be, you're the one he's trying to reel in."

"Promise me you'll give me a heads-up if you do come across some kind of a video?" Laina implores, looking up into his eyes. "I'd hate for poor Clare to hear about something like that on the news."

"I promise. You promise to think twice about creepy scarf guy?"

"He's just sentimental."

"Not the answer I was looking for!"

Laina laughs again. "Okay, I promise. But trust me, I'm a doctor."

Watching

Am I mad to think I can know the unknowable? I burn to unravel the mysteries of mind and heart, dedicate myself to it, yet find myself perpetually surprised, and even disappointed, by human behavior. For example, I can't fathom the chains that keep the vibrant young woman on my screen bound to her abuser. Is it just perpetuation of an ugly cycle? Or is she deriving a perversely satisfying pleasure from this marriage?

Her smaller body is curled within his, spoon fashion. His heavy and hairy forearm is flung across her narrow waist, locking her in place. He pulled her into that position and she stared listlessly into nothingness while he dropped off into sleep. Her eyes are closed now, but I think she might be feigning slumber.

I zoom in on her wrist, which is mottled an angry red-purple color. Bruises on the outside will heal relatively quickly, but the ones on the inside always linger; this I know from my own experiences. What will it take to liberate her from her captor?

I tap a couple of keys and my feed switches over to reveal another sleeping beauty, her face sweet in repose, her blond hair a soft tangle.

There are decisions to be made, preparations to be made, actions to be taken. My mind is a dizzy blur, but I slow my breath to match the soft swell and release of the girl sleeping on my screen. I release a soft sigh of pure satisfaction. She's angelic and her easy sleep soothes my agitated soul.

I think differently than other people and that makes it harder for me to fit in. But that hasn't made me any less ambitious or successful. Out-of-the-box thinkers are often condemned in our society, if not outright punished. I have no desire for either, which is why I keep to the shadows.

CHAPTER THIRTEEN

Laina always enjoys a drive. Not the piddling commute that takes her from her condo to her office and back again, but a real road trip, the thrill of heading out knowing that the journey may surprise as much as the destination. She also relaxes into being driven more than she expected; Cal's assured behind the wheel and she's surprisingly happy to relinquish control. They have a fine afternoon for it, and Laina glances over at Cal as he hums along softly with the music playing in his spanking-new car.

Cal's music of choice is solidly alt-rock. Foo Fighters and Death Cab for Cutie, twenty one pilots and the Arctic Monkeys. Laina's surprised and then a bit mortified by her own reaction to Cal's outright admission that he doesn't much like rap. She silently admonishes herself to check her bias, even as the devilish, self-destructive voice in her head wonders what ammunition this misassumption might give her to push him away.

Stop it, Laina admonishes herself. The more she and Cal connect, the more she feels compelled to seek out potential hand grenades, but she genuinely likes Cal, despite their hostile first encounter and her ambivalence about the press. And, well, her ambivalence about letting someone, anyone, in.

"What should I expect at dinner?" she asks, determined to fight her impulse to stay defended.

"Crazy amounts of charm and a hard sell," Cal replies with a laugh.

"But what exactly is he selling me? I'm a therapist, not a reporter or a TV personality."

"Dreams, he sells dreams. What are yours, Laina?"

"My new clinic is the big one—I've wanted to expand our work for a long time. There's so much need. But I'm dubious a Hollywood agent can do much for me."

"All you have to do is hear him out, eat some seafood, and enjoy the view."

Their conversation then drifts from the fairly prosaic (the beauty of the clouds playing chase over the glistening ocean) to the deeply profound as they discover a mutual interest in the theories of futurist Ray Kurzweil, which leads to their sharing views on bioethics and the very meaning of what it is to be human.

"I've always believed we are more alike than we are different," Laina observes. "And that if we can identify where we connect, then the ways in which we differ can be bridged."

Cal frowns. "Don't you think that's a little simplistic? It assumes everyone is equally invested in connecting and crossing those bridges. That's not been my experience."

"Fair enough," Laina concedes quickly, wanting to steer away from tricky territory and keep the glow between them simmering. "But you can't fault me for optimism."

Cal shoots her a quick grin. "I don't; it's kind of endearing. And optimism must be necessary in your line of work."

"And not in yours?" Laina queries.

"Not so much. You know, 'if it bleeds, it leads' and all that."

"Why were you drawn to journalism?" Laina asks and then adds, teasing, "Did you just think you looked sharp on camera?"

"All modesty aside, I do look sharp on camera," Cal replies, smiling again. "But the real reason is that I believe freedom comes from truth. Lies, corruption, injustice—if these things aren't exposed we all suffer."

Laina feels a rush of something warm, the tendrils of entwining connection. "That same philosophy, about freedom coming from truth, it's a big part of why I was drawn to psychology," she tells Cal with excitement. "So often we deny things to ourselves, when squarely facing the truth of one's history or circumstances is the real way to heal and move forward."

"Interesting," Cal observes. "Journalism allows that on the societal level, and therapy on the individual."

"The individual *is* societal," Laina adds. She feels emboldened to share the details of her patient Michelle Marshall's recent transformation (without disclosing any details that would violate patient confidentiality). She knows it's a risk, as Laina knows nothing of Cal's views about abortion and it's not necessarily a topic for what's essentially a second date, but while it's a bizarre story, maybe even grotesque, it's also such a hopeful one. So symbolic. An unexpected liberation achieved through Michelle facing a literal reminder of her deepest shame.

"She even interpreted the two-word note that came along with the fetus, 'Watching You,' to mean God was watching over her," Laina says, wrapping up the tale. "Supporting her. Remarkable, right?"

Cal shifts his eyes away from the road just long enough to

meet Laina's. "Yeah, sure, from a psychological perspective, but doesn't it worry you? What if someone *is* watching her? The whole thing is so creepy."

"Do you think I got so caught up in her breakthrough I ignored a real threat? Of course not. If she tells me there's another incident, I'll advise her to go right to the police. But they tossed the jar, so all they have is a story of a possible prank." Laina shrugs. "I admit it's worried me some, but I haven't known what else I could do."

"You have to carry the weight of a lot of other people's pain and troubles, don't you?" Cal asks.

"Part of the training is learning how to compartmentalize the work," Laina replies, even while thinking, *How right he is*.

"Sure, but it still must come with a cost."

"Sometimes, of course," Laina admits. "But that side of it is far outweighed by seeing patients survive and thrive despite the hard things they grapple with."

It's been a very long time since Laina's felt this *seen* by a man. So much like *herself*. Or felt *protected*, the way Cal makes her feel protected. His concern about poor, silly George Holden, for example. So caring of Cal to be so fierce. She'll raise the issue of the scarf with George in their next session, of course, but that's hardly the point. Her heart beats a bit faster. These feelings she's experiencing are new, unformed, almost painful, a sweet and sour ecstasy.

"So tell me, Dr. Landers," Cal asks, his voice light and teasing. "Why are you . . . ? I mean, you're great; why haven't you been plucked out of the dating pool long before this?"

Laina knows she and Cal will have to talk about past relationships eventually, but the wound caused by the man whose identity she'd kept so solid a secret Bex and Vanessa had dubbed him Mr. M, short for Mr. Mysterious, still throbs just below her thinnest skin. Mr. M betrayed Laina horribly. How can she trust that Cal won't do the same?

She answers Cal's question about her single status carefully, neutrally. "There are a number of reasons, all mutually impactful. I devoted most of my time first to my education, and then to building my practice. It's not like I don't date, I've even been in a few longish relationships, but I'm discriminating, some might say picky, about who I choose to spend my time with."

"I'm glad I made the cut."

"Don't get ahead of yourself." Laina smiles. "Jury's still out."

"Yes, Your Honor."

Laina struggles again with that deep-rooted instinct to push Cal away, flee, hide. Men have invariably failed her. Her last relationship was so laden with lies, secrecy, and deception that just thinking about it makes her stomach cramp.

Cutting questions designed to make Cal back away from her begin to form in Laina's mind, unwelcome stormy clouds threatening the sunny horizon of her happiness. *Where can I best needle him? What knives can I twist?* To escape her mounting feelings of alarm at her own thoughts, she reaches out and turns up the radio volume.

"What are you thinking about?" Cal inquires, his long fingers tapping a beat on the steering wheel.

"Music," Laina lies.

Cal turns the volume up another notch. "I love this song!"

He joins in on the chorus with a surprising velvety alto. Laina can't help but sway to the beat. She can't remember when a man made her feel lighthearted like this, so full of possibility. She beats back her anxiety and joins in for the last chorus, singing along with Cal at the top of her lungs.

"It's nice to feel happy, isn't it?" Cal asks as the song concludes.

It's as if he's reading my mind. "Yes! I mean, yes." Laina feels the blush color her face and turns the conversation away from herself. "What about you? I know you're new in town, but surely you left a broken heart or two back in Savannah?"

"The other way around, actually," Cal replies with a grimace.

"Do you want to talk about it?" Laina asks, conscious of slipping into a professional mode of questioning, even as her heart thrums at this intimacy. *We've both been hurt in the not-too-distant past, another thing we share.*

"I'll spare you the sordid details," Cal reassures her. "But don't worry. While she took my heart, impaled it on a spike, and paraded it around the neighborhood, I'm totally over it."

A startled little laugh escapes Laina. "Very vivid imagery," she says. "How long ago did this barbaric act take place?"

"Almost a year. I'm thinking of celebrating with champagne and cake."

"You are a surprise," Laina says appreciatively. "The rare man who talks about his feelings."

"You know what they say about time healing all wounds, etc. Besides, nothing for getting over an old heartbreak like the possibility of a new one."

Cal sends that killer grin her way and Laina suddenly feels lost, overwhelmed. *Reciprocity.* It's an exciting sensation after Mr. M's torturous convolutions to keep her at arm's length, his version of what was "best" for Laina.

Am I ready for this? Laina wonders. *What is this, anyway?*

As if somehow sensing her unease, Cal reaches a hand for one of hers. His skin is warm and dry. Laina stares down at their entangled fingers, pale pink against brown. "Recent times have kicked the shit out of all of us," Cal says, stroking his thumb against hers. "I don't know about you, but I feel sharper about what I want out of life, clear about my priorities. Not just what I do want, but also what I don't. And one thing I don't want is to waste time. It's a cliché, but life's short."

The GPS announces that the turn for the restaurant is upcoming. Cal maneuvers his Mercedes into the turning lane that stripes the middle of the Pacific Coast Highway, makes a U-turn, and doubles back into the restaurant's steeply pitched driveway. At the bottom is a wide parking lot and sweeping ocean views.

The car is handed over to a valet, along with Cal's stern admonishment to treat his new car with the respect it deserves. The kid looks unimpressed, and Laina sees why as she gazes around the parking lot: Teslas, Porsches, Maseratis, and Lamborghinis abound, along with Jags, Beemers, and Benzes.

The restaurant is, as promised, entirely outdoors, strung along a patio that hugs the side of the rocky shoreline. Waves crash below and they are led past a sign that points the way to a path leading down to the beach. Laina allows herself to solidly luxuriate in that feeling of genuine happiness that had started in the car; god knows it's an elusive emotion.

A shortish man with bristling energy leaps up from his

seat at a prime table as Laina and Cal are led over by a hostess. "Cal, brother," Ryan exults. "Great to see you." Turning his brilliant blue eyes on Laina, Ryan turns his smile up a notch. "And, Dr. Landers, a real pleasure. Ryan Greenspan. I've done my homework, and you are one impressive woman. Allow me to also introduce a colleague. This is Adedayo Musa, a newly promoted agent in our division."

"Call me Ade. Good to meet you, I'm a fan," Adedayo greets Cal. "Good meeting you too," he adds with a nod at Laina.

Ade is young, mid-twenties, with closely cropped hair. He's dressed in imitation of his boss (either deliberately or unconsciously), both wearing expensive jeans and soft cashmere sweaters along with aggressively impactful designer sneakers.

"Cal, my man, I have excellent news!" Ryan announces as they take their seats. "Your latest reel got some attention at CNN Newsource. We're starting to taste national, baby!"

A broad smile splits Cal's face. "That *is* good news!"

"You bet your sweet ass it is. In San Diego you get paid in sunshine, in L.A., the sky's the limit!"

"What's all that mean, exactly?" Laina queries.

"It's the L.A. local affiliate for the network," Cal explains.

Ryan expands on the explanation. "It's CNN's news hub. They'll use Cal to cover a local story that can then be shaped so it can be dropped into newscasts around the country. An important next step in our quest for world domination!"

"Or at least an anchor job," Cal jovially responds. "I'll settle for that. You can have the world domination, Ryan."

"You see how I make dreams come true?" Ryan turns the full power of his baby blues on Laina.

What follows is pretty much what Cal had predicted. A hard sell on "the future you never knew you wanted," accompanied by four bottles of expensive Sancerre, much of which is consumed by Ryan. He gets bigger, more expansive, as he drinks and the evening wears on, ebulliently greeting acquaintances and lobbing ribald jokes at their pretty waitress.

Laina's not feeling particularly swayed toward signing with Ryan. He seems a bit of a cliché, as if he'd watched satires about agents and modeled his persona on an exaggeration. She can tell even Ade is quietly amused by his boss, although he conscientiously engages Cal in conversation that shows he's done his homework, on both Cal's career and his personal interests.

"Oh my god!" Ryan suddenly exclaims, distracted by an alert on his phone. "Satchel Goldstein's been arrested!"

"Who's that?" Cal asks.

Laina pales. She knows all too well who Satchel Goldstein is—the financier father of her cancer-stricken client, Franny Goldstein. The emotional and financial rock of a young woman struggling for survival.

"Arrested for what?" Laina's voice comes out a squeak. She clears her throat.

"Fraud and embezzlement," Ryan replies, staring down at his phone as he scrolls through the story. "Well, that's a whole house of cards that's going to come tumbling down. He's got his fingers everywhere in this town."

Laina forgoes coffee and dessert, hoping Cal will take her lead so they can get out of there. She's antsy, no longer patient with Ryan's glitzy bonhomie. But Cal wants a coffee before their three-hour drive back to San Diego, and she can hardly fault him for that, although her mind thrums with anxiety about what this arrest will mean for Franny, not only psychologically but physically.

The foursome gather at the valet stand after dinner. Ryan's car, a sleek black Lambo, is ready and waiting. Laina worries about Ryan driving until she realizes he has a driver, an equally sleek young woman dressed in head-to-toe black who slides behind the wheel. Ryan bumps fists with Cal and air-kisses Laina exuberantly on both cheeks. "We'll talk soon!" he exclaims as he climbs into the passenger seat of the low-slung car.

Cal's Mercedes and Ade's Chevy Volt arrive simultaneously, with both valet drivers waving away proffered tips. "Mr. Greenspan took care of it," one of the valets announces.

As they're pulling on their seatbelts, Cal turns to Laina with a questioning smile. "So what did you think?"

"He's pretty much a walking cliché."

Cal laughs. "Granted. But he gets shit done. And like I said, I have no more time to waste."

"I feel like that too, sometimes," Laina agrees. "Like I want my dreams to happen fast, because I know all too well the impermanence of things."

Laina twists her fingers in her lap and tries not to think about Franny.

They speed south along the PCH in silence for a bit, the sky now an inky black cover over the seething gray sea to the west, the flash of northbound headlights sweeping across their windshield in a regular rhythm.

"What do you know about Satchel Goldstein?" Cal asks. "He hasn't come across my radar yet."

"He's a money guy. As I understand it, he has a lot of different investments: energy, tech, hospitality. He's also played around in the entertainment sector, movie co-financing, that kind of thing."

Laina can feel Cal's sharp glance, like a laser piercing the night. "Do you know him?"

"No," she answers truthfully. "But he's a San Diego native, and ultimately, it's a big small town, so I've heard about him."

"Too bad. I'm going to need some kind of angle if I want to get in on this story, now that I'm late to the break."

Laina doesn't respond. She winces thinking about some of the vitriol Franny's mother has spewed in the past about her ex-husband, imagining the assault that must be coming Franny's way in the wake of his arrest. Poor Franny kept her father on such a lofty pedestal and now he's toppled to the ground. Her mother, Ruslana, will no doubt find gleeful vindication in pouring salt in that wound.

Laina fervently hopes that Franny's with her boyfriend, Ben, who from all of Franny's accounts is a sweet, stable young man with a knack for peacefully navigating the battles that frequently erupt between Franny's parents.

Cal's thinking about the story, and Laina can't blame him. After all, he's a journalist and has no personal connection with anyone involved, but all Laina can think about is the human cost.

CHAPTER FOURTEEN

Determined to find a way into the Satchel Goldstein story, Cal enlists Mike to meet him early. The shooter climbs into Cal's Mercedes and accepts the coffee offered him without a word.

They take a swing past Goldstein's mansion in La Jolla, only to find it gated, with guards from a private security firm stationed out front, obnoxiously open in their swagger. It's an easy decision to keep on driving after stealing a little B-roll.

Now they pull up in front of Goldstein's daughter's place, a surprisingly modest faux Spanish condo complex closer to the city center. Cal's done his homework on Satchel Goldstein and knows the man not only has beaucoup bucks but is sparing none of it to fund his only daughter's cancer treatment. He'd expected to find more of what he'd seen at her father's house: opulence and ostentation, gates and guards.

He parks the Mercedes and he and Amis go through their routine, setting up to record. Cal has no idea if they'll find Francesca Goldstein at home, but no matter who or what they find, he wants to be ready. He scans the street but sees no other reporters lurking. *Good.*

"Unit 16," Cal confirms as they enter the building's interior courtyard through an unlocked gate providing only dec-oration, no security. A series of attached two-story units ring the perimeter of a courtyard paved with Spanish tile. A spar-kling aqua pool sits in the center, surrounded by chaise longues and sun umbrellas. A heavily tattooed couple relax on adjacent chairs, holding hands and passing a joint back and forth. The acrid-sweet scent of weed floats in the air. The smokers take no notice of Cal and Mike as they make their way around the courtyard looking for number 16.

The unit is tucked into a corner, a mezuzah affixed to the doorjamb. Cal mentally reviews his first question, counting on the element of surprise to hopefully get at least a sound bite. He presses the doorbell. *Here goes nothing.*

The door swings open. A white guy with brown hair and a well-maintained, luxuriant ginger beard stares at Cal. "Yeah?" he says skeptically.

"Francesca at home?" Cal asks. "Cal Murray, Channel Five. I'm hoping she'll be willing to speak to me about the charges against her father."

"What the fuck?" Ginger Beard retorts. "Get the hell out of here!" He moves to slam the door in Cal's face, but a thin hand reaches out to stop him and the pale face of a woman comes into Cal's view. Francesca Goldstein. Cal recognizes her from his deep dive into the internet last night. He knows she's ill, but even so, the gaunt hollows of her face are star-tling.

"You're the reporter that Dr. Landers did an interview with," she states flatly.

"Guilty as charged," Cal affirms, turning on his warmest smile in order to counter his concern about where this might be headed. "Francesca, right? How're you doing?"

"How do you think I'm doing?" Franny spits back. "I'm battling cancer, the experimental treatment that was supposed to save my life is on hold because my father's assets are frozen, and all of it is playing out in the tabloids."

"I promise you—" Cal begins, but Francesca cuts him off.

"Come in," she orders to Cal's surprise. "But turn the camera off. That's nonnegotiable." To Ginger Beard she adds, "It's okay, Ben."

Cal and Mike exchange a glance that eloquently communicates pleasant surprise, and Mike does as she asks; the camera's red light dies. Ben glowers at them, but he yanks the door open.

They follow the couple into a comfortable, open-plan space, meticulously clean and precisely arranged. It would look like a model apartment, designed to soothe all and offend no one, but for the messy profusion of fresh vegetables heaped next to a Vitamix on the white granite kitchen island.

"I'm juicing, I hope you don't mind," Francesca says as she takes up her station next to the machine.

"Franny," Ben interjects, "I don't think this is a good idea."

"I need to talk to someone," Franny replies, feeding celery into the juicer. "He was good with Dr. L." Turning to Cal and Mike she adds, "I'll talk to you. But off the record. Or not at all. Okay?"

Cal nods. He'll take it. But "*Dr. L.*" The shorthand doesn't escape Cal's notice. "Okay, deal. So. What can you tell me about these allegations against your father?"

"Total bullshit," Franny rages, adding carrots through her processor at a furious pace.

"No disrespect"—Cal raises his voice over the whir—

"and I appreciate your loyalty, but at this point it's not looking too good for your dad. You need evidence that helps him. If you have any."

Franny lifts damp eyes to meet Cal's. Silences the juicer. "I don't have evidence," she says in a strangled voice. "But I know my dad. He might skate near the edge on financial stuff. In fact—" She breaks off to stifle a sob and leaves the sentence unfinished.

Cal holds his breath waiting for Franny to elaborate.

A long-haired cat with gray-tipped black fur and a glorious fluffy tail pounces onto the coffee table and hisses emphatically at Cal, back arched, teeth fully on display. Cal recoils.

"That's Larri McSherry," Franny says. "Don't mind her."

"She doesn't like anyone except for Franny," Ben adds, clearly taking some amusement in the cat's aggressiveness. "Don't take it personally."

Cal tries not to, but the cat continues to bristle at him with hostility. "How much did you know about the financial side of your father's business?" he asks, trying to take back control of the interview.

Ben interjects again. "Franny, babe, you don't have to talk to this guy."

"I'm trying to help," Cal says. "If Francesca can help me find the truth and that truth helps her father, everyone wins."

"Call me Franny," the gaunt girl announces as she walks over and picks up Larri McSherry. The cat immediately stops hissing and begins to purr. "Only my mother calls me Francesca."

"What can you tell me that can help your dad, Franny?" Cal asks softly, keeping his eyes fixed on her.

"I know his character," she replies simply. "He's a bit of a cowboy, sure." Her voice cracks again. "And I know he *loves* me. I know that's not much help. . . ." She trails off with a shrug. "But if everyone's only looking for the bad, they'll find it, right? Maybe you could look for the good?" Her voice is childlike in this last appeal, and she buries her face in Larri McSherry's soft fur.

Cal pities her, which makes him a little angry at himself. Journalism can't be clouded by sympathy. Plus, it's clear Franny actually has nothing to contribute to this particular story but her sorrow.

"Do you know Dr. Landers? Laina Landers?" he asks abruptly. *"Dr. L."*

Franny looks startled. "Of course. She's my therapist. That's why I let you in in the first place. If she trusts you, I figured that I could too."

Cal's head jerks. Laina never said a word to him about treating Franny Goldstein. He knows he shouldn't really be surprised as she's been quite clear about her professional boundaries, but he marvels at the poker face she kept during their three-plus-hour drive back from Malibu after hearing about Satchel Goldstein's arrest. He makes a note to self about that ability before turning his focus back to Franny.

"Good instincts," he assures her. "I'm definitely a fan and friend of Dr. L."

Franny looks visibly frailer than when they arrived, which is not lost on Cal. Or Ben. He puts one arm around his girl-friend to support her and motions toward the front door with the other. "She's tired. Please go."

Cal reluctantly gestures to Mike. *A dead end.* As they gather up their gear, the sound of a key is heard in the front door.

A woman enters the apartment. She's a gazelle, six feet tall at least, with a luxuriant mane of expertly highlighted hair in tones of honey and platinum. The planes of her face are symmetrical and angular, anchored by wide-set emerald eyes and a lush, rosy mouth. She wears a silk leopard print shirt tucked into skintight white jeans and pair of brown suede high-heeled boots.

Larri McSherry leaps from Franny's arms and flies at the woman, fangs bared.

"Francesca," the woman purrs in an accent flavored with the Ukraine as she expertly sidesteps the hissing cat. "You have package." The woman hands Franny a small box wrapped in brown paper. A red ribbon firmly holds a square of white note card in the box's center.

The woman turns her brilliant green eyes on Cal. She must be in her fifties, but she wields her sexual magnetism like a club. "I'm Ruslana Kovalenko Goldstein," she introduces herself imperiously, offering a limp hand to shake.

"Cal Murray and Mike Amis from Channel Five, Mrs. Goldstein," Cal introduces himself and his shooter. "Any comment on your ex-husband's arrest?"

Ruslana shrugs with eloquent fatalism. "My ex-husband is capable of anything, despite Francesca's ridiculous insist he some kind hero. You don't really know man until you divorce man."

"Amen," Mike pipes in unexpectedly. Cal shoots him a look, and Mike adds, "I feel the same about my ex-wife, what can I say?"

Ruslana laughs, a full-throated expression of pleasure. Mike stares at her, transfixed, and Cal lifts a hand to cover his own grin. Amis has a crush!

"These gentlemen were just leaving," Ben asserts, gesturing them toward the door.

"Sure, sure." Cal is quick to back off; a soft touch now is more likely to garner access later. He hands his card to Ruslana, who's engaged in picking a couple of stray cat hairs from her tight white jeans. "But I'd like you to call me. It must be shocking to learn of these allegations. I promise I'll be sympathetic to your side of the story."

Ruslana accepts the business card with an enigmatic smile. Cal turns to Franny and his sharp glance rakes over the package held in Franny's bony fingers. The white card in the center has just two words, written in heavy block print: WATCHING YOU.

An uneasy prickle runs down Cal's spine. "What's that, then?" Cal asks, nodding at the box and struggling to feign nonchalance. It can't be a coincidence that two of Laina's patients have received packages with identical ominous notes.

"How do I know? It just came," Franny replies.

"Doesn't that note seem a little creepy?" Cal presses.

Franny seems to focus on the package in her hands for the first time. She turns even paler, which Cal didn't think was possible. She gingerly puts the package down on the counter and looks to her mother.

"I found it there, outside. On mat," Ruslana says with a touch of defensiveness.

Cal's interest is piqued. "No idea who it's from?"

Franny shrugs. "Look, my family's rich, sometimes that attracts shitheads no matter how hard I'm just trying to fucking *live*. You wouldn't believe some of the crap that's gone on since Dad's arrest."

"Like I said, it's time to go," Ben reiterates firmly as he backs Cal and Mike toward the front door.

Cal hands Ben a card and leaves one for Franny on the counter next to the irate cat. "A journalist with a sympathetic ear can do a lot to shape perception," he pitches. "I get that trust needs to be earned, but keep us in mind if any of you change your mind about going on the record."

As the front door closes behind them, Cal and Mike both stop to pull on their sunglasses, momentarily blinded by the glare.

"What d'ya make of all that?" Mike asks.

"Not entirely sure yet. That note was fucking weird. I wonder what the hell's inside the box?"

Mike grunts noncommittally but gestures that Cal should follow him. They creep around the side of the unit to a window that looks into Franny's open living space. Keeping low to the ground, they can't see much, but the window is open and they can hear everything.

"You say you found it just sitting there on the doormat?" Ben challenges Ruslana.

"Yes!" she insists, her voice vibrating with indignation at an unstated accusation.

"Who does shit like this?" Franny whispers hoarsely.

"I don't understand," Ruslana quavers. "What is it supposed to mean?"

"It's a hundred dollar bill soaked in rancid oil," Franny spits. "What do you think it means? Someone funny is making a statement about dirty money."

Cal and Mike exchange a glance and wordlessly beat a retreat to the car.

"Hey, Mike. Let's keep this all on the down low, especially

that package and the note, until we can get more of a feel for things." Cal's mind is ricocheting in a dozen different directions. He needs to figure out what this means and how it relates to Laina before he shares any more with Mike—anyone else for that matter.

"All right," Mike says in his usual flat tone. "By the way, good work in there. I like being on your team. I bet we hear from one or more of them."

"Cool, man. Thanks. Feeling's mutual," Cal replies.

It occurs to Cal that even as L.A. beckons with her siren call, he's building a life here in San Diego. There's his solid working partnership with Mike. And the woman he's more than a little intrigued by. Dr. Laina Landers is proving more layered all the time. He likes her ability to be discreet, on top of her smarts, wit, and the numerous common touch points they've already discovered. Despite his innate caution, Cal knows he's on the brink of *something;* he's poised on the edge of an abyss, one more step and he will likely topple. The astonishing thing is that he doesn't feel afraid. Only excited.

CHAPTER FIFTEEN

Cal asks her to meet him at an apartment he's thinking of renting before they go to dinner, which comes as no surprise to Laina. He's mentioned several times now just how eager he is to get out of the temporary and "depressing corporate squat" in which the station had landed him upon his arrival in San Diego. She's excited to see him but also trepidatious. She knows her mood turned the night they went to Malibu; how could it not have after learning of Satchel Goldstein's arrest? She could hardly explain that to Cal for reasons of confidentiality, but also because she was too sick at heart wondering how the arrest would affect Franny. She knows Cal noticed her fallen spirits on the ride back and just hopes he doesn't think they were a result of meeting Ryan or, even worse, a reflection on Cal himself.

Laina knows the building Cal's designated for their rendezvous, tall, modern, gleaming, a fixture on the downtown skyline. She can't imagine living here in San Diego and not living near the beach, but she imagines a place like this has its perks.

She's not wrong. For starters, the building has valet parking for guests, the attendants hatted and gloved. Laina can't help but feel sorry for them; the day's been a warm one and while the purpling sky serves as a harbinger of night, the temperature has yet to cool. There's a pump jar of hand sanitizer on a little table by the entrance, as well as a complimentary basket of face masks. She makes use of the former as the front door swings open automatically at her approach. She's welcomed by a petite Asian man in a skinny black suit perched behind a slab of a desk.

"Good evening. Dr. Landers? Here to join Mr. Murray in 25C? We're expecting you. I'm Bennet Lau, senior concierge."

Laina affirms her identity and Lau directs her to an elevator. "Take number three. It's contactless. I'll control it from the desk and take you right to the twenty-fifth floor. Enjoy the apartment. It's a stunner."

The elevator ride is smooth and quiet. The doors open and Laina steps out, trying to determine in which direction apartment 25C might lie. She hears voices and instinctively turns to follow, indeed finding herself outside her desired destination. The door hangs halfway open and she pushes her way in, calling, "Hello? Cal? You in here?"

A smile warms her face, but halfway over the threshold it freezes. The concierge was right, the completely empty apartment is a stunner, well proportioned, freshly painted in a clean eggshell color, with vast windows showcasing mind-blowing views in every direction. Also a stunner is the young Black woman with a mass of looped and cascading braids laughing with Cal.

"Hey you," Cal affectionately greets Laina without missing a beat. She feels her frozen smile melt around the edges.

"This is Janelle Dunham, my real estate agent. Janelle, this is my friend Dr. Landers."

"Nice to meet you, Doctor," Janelle greets Laina with a friendly smile.

"Oh. Hi. Call me Laina. Wow! I have to admit this is pretty amazing." Laina kicks herself for her momentary stab of insecurity. Not for the first time she wonders how she can see others' problems and foibles so clearly but continue to wrestle with her own.

"Right?" Cal's enthusiastic. "Look around. Two bedrooms, two and a half baths, and look at this kitchen!"

The kitchen is sleek and elegant, with top-of-the-line appliances and a respectable amount of storage. The adjacent dining area features a curved floor-to-ceiling window; it makes Laina sway with a bit of vertigo. She edges away to inspect the gas fireplace along one wall of the main living space.

"The building has twenty-four-hour concierge service, a gym and spa, an outdoor pool, a conference center, and a no-contact Amazon hub. Two underground parking spaces come with the apartment." Janelle pours on the sell. "But you're so close to so many cool downtown spots right here, you could also easily walk."

"What do you think?" Cal asks Laina. "I think I'm going to take it."

"It's gorgeous," Laina affirms.

Cal turns to Janelle. "Okay, then. Send over the lease! Thanks for all your help."

"Of course," Janelle replies.

Cal continues, "Do you mind giving us a minute? We'll pull the door closed on our way out."

"No problem," Janelle agrees. "Take your time. Get a feel for your new home!"

She says goodbye to them both and then heads out, shutting the door softly behind her.

Cal kisses Laina lightly on the lips. "Thanks for coming. Glad you approve."

"What's there not to approve of?" Laina asks. "It's gorgeous."

"Look, there's something I want to tell you. But I'm a little hesitant to bring it up."

"No turning back now, is there? What's up?"

"I went to see Franny Goldstein today."

Laina can't help herself; a tiny shocked gasp escapes her throat.

"I know she's your patient. I didn't know before I went to see her, but she volunteered it while I was there."

"Can't you leave Franny alone?" Laina asks. "The poor girl has enough going on."

Cal's phone vibrates.

He takes a quick look. "Do you mind if I take this?" he asks before answering.

"Go for it." Laina folds her arms against her chest, conscious of an irrational sense of *violation* in the wake of Cal's revelation.

"Hello, my friend!" Cal greets his caller cheerfully. "What've you got?" He listens before continuing. "You are good to me, brother. But I'm with someone and kind of in the middle of something. . . . Right. Talk soon."

Cal clicks off the phone.

Laina looks up at him. "Work?" she asks.

"Yeah, a buddy of mine on the force."

"What's happening?"

"Some whack job pinned an ex to the side of a building with her car. And get this, with her two kids in the backseat."

Laina punches him on the arm with a little more force than she intended. "'Whack job' is not a term we use in my profession. I thought you were learning to respect my work."

"Well, I don't know what else to call her. She's apparently yelping loud enough for the whole neighborhood to hear about getting an email with a link to some nude photos he had taken of her—"

"Wait," Laina interrupts. "Did you say she had two kids in the car with her?"

"Yup. Why?"

"Shit. It can't be."

"Can't be what?"

"Do you have a name? Of the woman?"

"I passed on the tip," he reminds her. "You know as much as I do."

They take Cal's car. Laina's face is pinched and pale. A quick return call to Officer Cal Murray had revealed that it was indeed Laina's patient Daisy Sullivan who'd rammed her car into her former friend and lover, the despicable, nude-photo-taking Mark Victor.

Daisy is now under arrest. Mark Victor is in surgery, with two broken legs and a fractured pelvis. Daisy's two small children, Kylie and Kevin, ages five and six respectively, are with child services while a public appeal is being made for their father, Brad Sullivan, to come forward to claim his children.

This level of violence in Daisy is unfathomable. And with

her children in the car! Laina's horrified but also turns over the events with her clinician's perspective.

Not for the first time, Laina wonders how much pain and grief and loss people can bear before they break.

They're headed to the police station. Daisy's attorney has requested Laina interview her to help establish state of mind at the time of the attack. Laina feels queasy. She has the suffocating sense that things are slipping wildly out of control, much, she imagines, like the very last moments before knowing one will drown, gulping water, fighting uselessly, watching that fine line between life and death erased before your very eyes.

Laina looks over at Cal, grateful that he offered to drive, appreciative that he's maintained a respectful silence since the revelation.

"I admire your restraint," she says finally.

"How do you mean?" Cal responds, taking his eyes off the road just long enough to shoot her a surprised glance.

"The reporter in you must be dying to pump me about Daisy."

Cal laughs. "That much is true. But I figured I'd better keep my mouth shut for the time being. If I ever want you to have dinner with me again. Priorities."

Laina releases a small laugh, surprising herself. "Thank you," she says. "I appreciate that."

Once they arrive at the station house, there's some internal controversy and a spirited discussion about parameters before Laina is allowed to talk to Daisy. Their conversation is protected by privilege, and it's not like the police need a confession to seal their case; they have cellphone video footage from multiple onlookers clearly showing Daisy's vehicle striking Victor and her subsequent leap from her car to scream a diatribe at him while he was pinned to the wall. As the negotiations go on, Laina realizes they're less about substance and more just about two peacocks jockeying for power and positioning.

Once all the BS is out of the way, Arthur Fallon, Daisy's attorney, a tall angular man with a prominent Adam's apple and a sweep of silvery hair, corners Laina for a quiet sidebar. He says just enough to "encourage" Laina to invest in his forming defense: temporary insanity based on some kind of a psychotic break caused by the actions of the victim. Laina learns that while Daisy unleashed a torrent of well-formulated rage at Mark Victor, since being arrested her statements have been reduced to jumbled sentence fragments.

"Maybe she's dissociative?" Fallon wonders out loud.

"Why don't you do your job and let the medical professionals do theirs?" Laina rebukes him.

Fallon backs off, but in doing so makes it clear that his priority is to use Laina to help create that narrative. With a clench of her jaw, Laina realizes *her* priority is to see if Daisy knows where her children's father might be. Those kids deserve better than Child Protective Services.

When Laina enters the interrogation room, she can't help but shudder at the oppressively dull gray-green paint, the lack of windows, and the general air of despair that permeates. Daisy's hunched into herself on a hard-backed chair, chewing on a corner of her thumb, her face blank, her blue eyes unfocused, her pale blond hair limp.

"Daisy," Laina greets her softly as the door to the interrogation room closes behind her with an ominous, solid *thunk*. "Hi. How're you doing?"

Daisy doesn't reply or even look in Laina's direction. Taking the seat opposite her patient, Laina continues, asking gently, "Do you want to tell me what happened?"

She pauses to give space for Daisy to respond in some way. She doesn't.

"It's just you and me, Daisy," Laina tries again, gesturing to their bleak surroundings. "Our conversation is as protected as if we were in my office. You can speak freely."

Daisy retains a stony silence. Laina wonders if she's even aware of her presence.

"I know you must be really hurting right now," Laina presses, "and worried about Kylie and Kevin too."

A low sound escapes Daisy's throat, guttural and primal. She chews on the corner of her thumb with renewed vigor.

"The kids are fine, Daisy," Laina assures her, leaning in, urgency in her tone. "But they need to be with Brad now. You know that would be best. I know how angry you are at him, but your kids need their dad now."

"He posted the pictures." Daisy's voice is so low Laina isn't sure she heard her correctly.

"Tell me, Daisy. Tell me what happened," Laina probes, lowering her tone to match Daisy's.

Tears slip from Daisy's eyes as she continues in a whispery voice, her eyes determinedly avoiding Laina's. "I got an email, just as I was loading the kids into the car. I didn't recognize the address. I thought it might be Brad, but . . . it was a link to a pornographic website." Blood trickles from the corner of Daisy's thumb where she continues to worry it between her teeth.

"I just drove straight to Mark's. I didn't even think about the fact that the kids were in the backseat. I didn't have a plan, but when I saw him outside his place, his arm around another woman . . ." Daisy trails off and Laina waits quietly.

"I had to stop him. He was going to do it to someone else. Oh god, what have I done?" Daisy wails, dropping her head down on the cold metal table.

"It's like I blacked out," Daisy continues between sobs. "One minute I saw him standing there with that girl and the next he was up against the wall. And I was screaming and the kids were screaming. . . ." Daisy's face slackens. Her blue eyes dim back to a vacant stare.

"You've been under an enormous amount of stress and he did a horrible thing to you," Laina reassures Daisy in a gentle tone. "I can't say what'll happen to you legally now, Daisy, but certainly all of that will be taken into account."

Daisy lifts her head from the table but only to resume her dead-eyed chewing of her thumb.

"Daisy, have you heard from Brad? Anything? I don't want Kylie and Kevin to go into the system while we try to sort this out. If you have any idea about his whereabouts, now would be the time to tell me."

For the first time since Laina's entered the room, Daisy looks her directly in the eye.

"I have no fucking idea where that bastard is. This is all his fault. All of it. He can rot in hell."

CHAPTER SIXTEEN

Cooling his heels in the lobby of a police precinct is not how Cal envisioned this night going. He'd anticipated it would not be wholly easy, as he'd planned on telling Laina about the "gift" Franny Goldstein received with its ominous two-word note. This, of course, was interrupted by the awful news about Daisy Sullivan.

Cal innately doesn't like or trust coincidences, and there are too many mounting up to ignore. Is someone with intimate knowledge of Laina's patients harassing them? If so, to what end? Could Daisy Sullivan be a part of that pattern? Cal feels that flip of excitement he's come to associate with being on the right track when sniffing out a lead.

Cal hurries outside and calls Cop Cal. "Quick question. Any particular note or message attached to that email Daisy Sullivan received?"

"Do you have anything to offer in return? This relationship is starting to feel one-sided."

Cal hesitates, then says, "I might. It depends on the message."

"The subject line of the email was 'Watching You.' That hit the jackpot?" Cop Cal replies.

"Bingo. I might have a couple of linked incidents. Same message."

"Interesting. Tell me more."

A man in a hurry brushes past Cal as if he were invisible. White, tall, spiky black hair—Cal's eyes snag on the man's watch, a Patek Philippe Nautilus in an ostentatious rose gold rimmed with diamonds. Cal's a fan of a nice watch and knows that one probably cost a cool $75K. Everything about the guy screams privilege, from his expertly coifed spiky hair and trimmed salt-and-pepper beard to the soft cashmere sweater thrown casually over his shoulders. Then Cal realizes who it is: Harley Weida, Laina's partner in the BETTER LIFE clinic, recognizable from the research Cal did for their interview.

"Listen, man, I've got to go. Talk soon." Cal hangs up before Cop Cal has a chance to react and follows Weida into the fluorescent-lit lobby.

"I'll just wait here, then," Harley says testily to the desk sergeant. He turns away from the desk and his eyes lock on Cal.

"You're that reporter, right? Who interviewed Laina?" Harley asks in a friendly tone. He approaches Cal with his right hand extended for a shake.

"Yes. Cal Murray. Nice to meet you, Dr. Weida," he replies as he accepts the doctor's hand.

"Call me Harley. But can I ask what you're doing here?" Harley asks. "I hope it's nothing to do with Laina." He smiles. "No offense, but I'm not really a fan of press for the practice."

"I'm not here in a professional capacity," Cal reassures

him, matching Weida's affable smile with his own. "Can I ask what you're doing here?"

"I heard Laina was with a patient from our practice who was involved in an incident. I came to offer support."

Once again, Cal finds himself surprised. *Did Laina call her partner?*

"Harley," Cal says tentatively. "Do you think someone might have it in for you and Laina? For the practice?"

The smug confidence exuding from Harley evaporates in an instant. "Why do you ask that?"

"Answer the question first," Cal presses, taking advantage of Harley's momentary fluster.

Laina emerges from the bowels of the precinct, and Harley uses her arrival to hastily abandon Cal. She seems surprised to see her partner, and they exchange a few sentences in hushed tones. Cal's disturbed by how wholly flattened Laina looks. He can tell that it's taking effort for her to forestall whatever it is Harley is proposing. Finally, the two of them walk over to Cal.

"I understand you've met my partner, Dr. Weida," Laina says.

"Yes," Cal affirms.

"See, Harley? It's quite all right. Cal will drive me back to my car. You go on home to Megan and the girls. Thanks for coming, though," she adds firmly, as if putting an argument to bed.

Harley bids them both good night and departs, but Cal has the sense he's not happy about it. He ushers Laina back to his Mercedes in silence, a supportive hand on the small of her back.

"How's Daisy?" he asks once they're settled in and under way.

"As well as could be expected," Laina answers quietly. "It's a very painful situation all around."

"Of course. Look, Laina, I don't know how to say this but plainly. Is there someone that might want to hurt you?"

She gives him a look of astonishment. "Why would you ask that?"

"You told me about that patient of yours who got that fetus in a jar, right? With the note that said 'Watching You.'"

"What's that got to do with anything?" Laina exclaims.

"When I was at Franny Goldstein's place, a box was left outside on her doorstep. Inside was a hundred dollar bill coated in rancid oil. Dirty money. And the note attached to the box also said 'Watching You.'"

A small gasp escapes Laina's throat.

"And my cop friend, the one who called about Daisy? He just told me that same message was in the subject line of the email Daisy was screaming about."

Laina stays very silent and still.

"That's three of your patients. And maybe Hutchinson too, for all we know. It's too much evidence to ignore," Cal asserts. "Is there anyone who'd want to hurt you? Or Harley? The practice? Take a minute. Think before you answer. I know it's not a pleasant thing to contemplate."

"You're scaring me."

"Who has access to your files?" Cal presses.

"Me. My electronic records are all protected and I keep additional written notes in a locked cabinet in my office or locked in my desk."

"Same for the other practitioners?"

"I assume so."

"So anyone's written notes might conceivably have been accessed?"

Laina looks doubtful. "I suppose, although we would've noticed if the locks had been broken or anything like that."

"If someone is clever enough to manipulate your clients through their secrets, they are surely smart enough to get past your locks undetected. Or to hack into your network."

"There's a happy thought," Laina replies grimly.

Another moment of silence envelops them. Cal breaks it. "What about creepy scarf guy?"

"I consider him one of my success stories, honestly; it would kind of break my heart if he was behind anything hateful."

"Laina, if you have an idea about who might be doing this, you have to tell me."

"I wish you would stop. This night has been upsetting enough."

"I'm going to dig further, Laina. It's what I do." Cal places a hand over hers. "I need to be sure you're safe."

Laina looks into his eyes and Cal feels a rush. *There I am, one step closer to the abyss.* "Is there anything else you should tell me? Anything at all?" he asks.

"We did have to fire someone a few months ago. Our last receptionist, before Abi," Laina confesses.

"Why?"

"She was an alcoholic, in recovery, but she kept relapsing. We tried to support her. We even got her into a thirty-day residential treatment center. But when she came back to work, she showed up drunk, caused a scene, fell, and cracked her head open. Blood everywhere, with patients in the waiting room . . ."

"Do you think she could be vindictive like this?"

Laina looks him straight in his brown eyes. "I'd hate for it to be true. I felt sorry for her more than anything and hoped we left on terms that were going to allow her a fresh start. But she did leave more than one threatening message when we were trying to settle with her, and one thing I've learned is not to be surprised by what people can do. We're ultimately capable of anything under the right circumstances, all of us, no matter what else we'd like to believe."

They sit in silence in the driveway of Cal's towering future home for a few moments before Laina asks Cal to drive her back to her condo. She's drained from the ordeal with Daisy as well as Cal's suspicions, and doesn't feel like she can be alone with all the jumbled thoughts cycling through her head. He takes immediate action, swapping his car with hers, telling her he'll drive her home and then Uber back. She's grateful for his effortless command of the situation; it allows her to sit quietly with her restless thoughts.

They park outside her condo, with the windows of her car rolled down, both of them silent and still, breathing in the smell of the sea. Overhead, scudding clouds play hide-and-seek with the moon and stars.

Laina feels tears threaten. Pushing back the torrent of emotions threatening to overwhelm her, she puts a hand on Cal's arm. "Come inside with me," she invites.

She climbs out of the car and strides toward the entrance

of her condo without looking behind her to see if he's followed. But she hears the slam of a car door and the beep of the automatic lock. She feels reckless, not an attitude Laina allows herself very often. Her life is controlled, planned, organized; that's what makes it work. That's what keeps her safe.

But tonight, she doesn't care. When she pauses by her front door to insert her key, she feels Cal behind her, the warmth of his body, the electricity coming off his skin. She shifts her position slightly, "accidentally" backing her ass up into him, grazing what feels like a very promising erection. A low groan escapes Cal's throat as she shifts away again.

Once they are inside, Cal takes her hand and the lead, kicking the door shut behind them. He kisses her, releasing her hand to cup her jaw between both of his palms, raining a shower of delicate kisses along her eyelids, the bridge of her nose. It's Laina's turn to moan. Cal's hands move up and twist into Laina's hair, their mouths find each other, their kisses become probing and deep. Their bodies press into each other, desperate with the need to merge.

Laina pulls Cal toward the bedroom, shedding her clothes as she goes, tugging at his, past caring about anything beyond her need to have this man inside her.

The sex is hungry but also languorous. Cal takes his time, making Laina slow her urgency with repeated soft kisses, capturing her hands, making her squirm. She thinks she will lose her mind as he explores her body. She urges him inside her and he resists, murmuring, "We have all the time we need."

When they finally do come together, it's fireworks and

cartwheels. Mouths and hands and piercing thrusts. Cries and moans and muttered obscenities. Calls to god as if they are both praying. Maybe they are. The release when it comes is shattering. Laina pants, trying to regain her breath, struck by the moonlight reflecting off their intertwined bodies, hers so pale, his so dark.

As the tide of pleasure ebbs, Laina has a flash of unease. *Oh my god. What did I just do?* While one half of her doesn't give a fuck, the other half is terrified. And the terrified half is devilish and can't help but probe for trouble. Aware that she is trespassing into the dangerous territory of self-sabotage, Laina plunges in.

"Is it your first time with a white woman?" She asks the question nonchalantly, even though her heart is pounding.

Cal's closed eyes flick open to meet hers, wariness evident in his gaze. "Uh, no, does that matter?"

"This is the first time I've been with a Black man," Laina whispers.

"Well, you know what they say," Cal replies lightly, although his body stiffens. "Once you go Black . . ."

"Which do you prefer?" *Why am I doing this?* But she can't stop herself. "It's a simple enough question," she continues. "Which do you prefer, Black women or white women? Or something else altogether?"

Cal pulls away from her and props himself up on one elbow. His face is carefully composed as he replies, "I like to think of myself as equal opportunity in that area."

"I bet I can guess. It's why you went to Howard; you told me as much."

"Why are you doing this?" Cal asks. "I don't get why

you're going down this road. Unless you're the one who's done something you're uncomfortable with?"

While cursing herself for having embarked on this path, Laina also feels compelled to double down. "You're the one who told me you chose Howard to chase a girl. I'm just infer-ring your preference from that," she continues tartly, squelch-ing the inner voice silently pleading with her to *stop trying to wound him! Why? Why do I do this?*

Cal takes a moment before he replies and Laina holds her breath. *Have I succeeded in pushing him away? Is that what I want?* She realizes with a terrible jolt that that's not what she wants at all.

"I lied to you about why I went to Howard," Cal tells her. "I chose Howard because I grew up in a mostly white area. Upper middle class, my parents are both professionals. But I got tired of being the only Black guy in the group, sick of how the parents of girls I'd known my whole life suddenly got different around me—and different about me being around their daughters—as we hit adolescence. I went to Howard because I saw a sea of people who looked like me. I went to Howard to better understand my identity."

Laina wishes she could bite back her words. *Why did I try to push him away? What is wrong with me?* "Thank you for sharing that with me," she says, flushed with shame.

"You're welcome. But as long as we're here, *is* my race an issue for you? 'Cause Black is the only color I come in."

"Absolutely not," Laina replies emphatically. "I was ner-vous. Trying to push you away because . . . I was afraid this is a mistake. Is it? Are we?" She raises her eyes to meet his.

Cal cups her jaw. "I don't want it to be."

"I apologize," Laina says. "It's been a while since I've been . . . intimate with someone. And sometimes when I get scared, I get prickly and lash out. I'm sorry. Really."

Laina runs a hand up along his inner thigh and Cal's breath quickens. "Will you forgive me?" she whispers.

He will.

CHAPTER SEVENTEEN

Vanessa Calabres stares across her polished oak conference room table with a look of concerned disbelief. Laina sits opposite her, flanked by her partner on one side, and Cal Murray, or as Vanessa would call him, the cub reporter, on the other.

"Say what, again?" Vanessa stalls, obviously trying to process the information the three of them have just shared with her.

Laina flicks a quick glance at Cal before responding to her attorney. "I know it seems far-fetched. . . ."

"It's clear as day to me," Harley exclaims. "There have also been a total of three anonymous messages threatening me left on our voicemail. I'm afraid to ask my patients if they've received any weird notes or gifts! God knows what else we'll turn up."

"People have been hurt," says Cal. "More people could be hurt."

"What do you want to do?" Vanessa asks. "Go to the police?"

"God, no!" Harley erupts. "Someone with access to our fucking patient records? If this goes public, Laina and I are screwed, our careers are over! We have to figure out how to shut this down. *And* keep it quiet!"

Laina puts a steadying arm on her partner's biceps. "Harley. Sshh. We're all on the same side here." She directs her attention back to Vanessa. "Remember the employee we had to terminate last year?"

"Of course," Vanessa replies drily. "A very memorable character."

"I know we signed an NDA about the termination. But Cal thinks that person might be behind all this, and I have to agree, it makes some sense; I can't think of anyone else with a grievance against the practice."

"I agree!" Harley says emphatically. "She's the only person I can think of who would do something this vindictive."

"What exactly are you asking?" Vanessa queries.

Harley's answer is prompt. "We want Cal to investigate, get a sense of whether we're sniffing in the right direction."

Vanessa deliberates for a moment, fiddling with her exquisitely balanced mother-of-pearl inlaid pen. "You face a stiff financial penalty if you discuss the grounds for the termination, a term, which as you may recall, I advised you against accepting."

"There's no point rehashing old ground, V." Laina has a tinge of weariness in her voice. "We were trying to help get her a new start; she was moving out of state, and we never thought we'd have any reason *to* discuss it."

"Why was there an NDA in the first place?" Cal asks, a puzzled look on his face. "I mean, if she came into work intoxicated, surely you had grounds—"

"Oh, great," Vanessa interrupts, tapping her pen in exasperation. "You've already told him."

"That's why we're here." Laina turns back to Cal. "She threatened to sue us for the head injury she sustained when she fell. We felt sorry for her, of course, losing her sobriety, her job, incurring medical expenses on top of that, but we also didn't want a lawsuit."

Harley chimes in. "Damn right! It would have been messy, expensive, time-consuming. And public! It was extortion. And as a reminder, Laina, you were the one who felt sorry for her, not me. I suspected she'd make more trouble."

"Hush, Harley, let me finish." Laina again lays a restraining hand on her partner's arm. "We gave her a hefty lump sum to help her start over. And all sides agreed the past was best left in the past, hence the NDA."

Harley snorts indignantly.

Cal looks thoughtful. "Well, maybe she doesn't agree with that sentiment anymore. Maybe the money's run out and she's looking for trouble. Or more cash. Could be that some kind of demand comes next."

"Let's not get ahead of ourselves," Vanessa interjects. "Neither of you has had any kind of extortion attempt, correct?"

"Right," Laina affirms. "And I can also see both sides. What if she's *not* involved? She's fragile, I don't want to risk jeopardizing her recovery or her mental health."

Harley leaps up from his chair. "Are you kidding me, Laina? If this bitch is fucking with us, we need to know!"

Cal stands, instinctively moving toward the agitated Harley, but it's Vanessa who takes control of the situation, sharply commanding, "Sit down, Harley. And watch your tone. I won't be shouted at."

Harley slumps back down into his chair and fiddles with

his watch, today a Panerai. Cal folds himself back down as well.

Vanessa addresses Cal. "So, cub reporter, what's your plan?"

"I'll go see her," he replies. "On a pretext. Get her talking. It's amazing how many people open up to someone taking even the slightest interest. I'll try to get a sense of her."

"And if you think she's innocent of involvement?" Vanessa probes.

Cal shrugs. "I'll leave her be and report back."

"And if you think she's guilty?" Harley demands.

"Much the same. Look, I'll approach this deftly. It's what I do for a living, get people to open up to me."

"I think we should let him do it," Laina says. "She'll never have to know Cal has anything to do with us. He can at least get a read on her."

"As your attorney, I'm telling you that we never had this conversation. You've never spoken to Mr. Murray about your former employees. I know nothing about anything. Nice to see you, Harley. Good luck, Mr. Murray."

Vanessa stands, signaling the meeting's end. "Laina, will you stay back a minute, please?"

The two men file out and Vanessa closes the door behind them. "Shit, girlfriend," Vanessa says softly.

"I know," Laina responds. "I'm not sure what to think."

"Harley seems like he's having trouble keeping his cool."

Laina laughs, but her laughter has a hollow chime. "That's an understatement."

"What's your gut tell you about what's going on?"

Laina takes her time before answering. She weighs what she knows for certain and what she doesn't. She ponders the unknowability of the human mind and heart, even for those who have made the study of the same their life's work.

"I would hate to think that I impacted someone so harmfully that that person felt compelled to try and wound me and Harley, or anyone else for that matter, in return," she says finally.

Vanessa tucks her mother-of-pearl pen into the breast pocket of her immaculate tailored suit. "Okay, then. Let the cub reporter do a little recon."

Laina beams a smile at her. "Who? Should do a little recon about what? I don't know what you're talking about."

"Speaking of the cub reporter, what's up with the two of you?"

"I don't know what you mean," Laina demurs.

Vanessa laughs. "Come on. The heat was coming across the table in waves."

Laina finds herself blushing. Vanessa raises an eyebrow. "I see. It's like that, is it? Okay. Just be careful, honey. I know Mr. M roughed you up—"

"Let's not talk about him anymore."

"Well, that's healthy! I'd just hate to see you get hurt again."

"I'm pretty sure I know what I'm doing," Laina replies.

"Pretty sure. Now, there's a standard for the ages," Vanessa shoots back.

Before she departs, Laina assures Vanessa she's got it all under control, but a little piece of her wonders, a sharp, shiny knife edge pressing against the thin membrane of her happy anticipation.

CHAPTER EIGHTEEN

Kelsey McKendrick. The name feels clunky on Cal's tongue, the hardness of its anchoring *K*'s making him feel like he's swallowed a thistle.

He's headed to Phoenix, Arizona. A city named for a bird that reincarnates in fire and rises from the ashes. A fitting place for BETTER LIFE's former receptionist to reinvent herself, if she in fact has done so. In Cal's experience, most addicts relapse regardless of any and all good intentions, and even with "settlements" to help "get them started on the path to a new life." Grimly, Cal remembers a sometimes-source of his back in Savannah, Bettina Godreaux, a junkie he tried to get clean. After her stint in rehab, Bettina came home and promptly checked in with Cal. She looked healthy and seemed well, told Cal a friend had hooked her up with an interview for a job on one of the riverboat cruisers that tourists favored. She couldn't stop thanking him for taking a chance on her and Cal was a little gruff with her, uncomfortable with the effusiveness of her gratitude. She was found dead of an overdose the next morning.

Cal knows Kelsey is reportedly a drinker, not a junkie, but to him all addicts seem depressingly similar, desperate liars who lie to themselves along with everyone else. He accelerates to flee these dark reflections, enjoying the powerful thrust of the Mercedes, the traction with which it hugs the asphalt. This road trip to Phoenix is a chance to flex his new car, really feel her purr. But it's not only the pleasure of the car, this road trip is also a chance to sift through the elusive, shifting puzzle pieces that dance tantalizingly before him.

What solid facts does he have in hand?

There's Daisy Sullivan. No doubt about the existence of the nude photos; Cal saw them on the porn website with his own eyes, before Daisy's lawyer got them taken down. There's also no doubt about the painful result of her receiving them. Franny Goldstein's "gift" seems to have done no more than irritate her; Laina's other patient actually considered the "gift" a gift!

But if Kelsey McKendrick is behind the harassment, what did she think would be the upshot of her actions? Cal chews his bottom lip. Surely she couldn't have predicted Daisy would run over Mark Victor? So what *was* the anticipated or desired outcome?

And what about the Hutchinson tape? It's unconfirmed, but could that have been the first of the pattern? Was there also a "Watching You" message attached to whatever kicked Peter Hutchinson over the edge? Cal makes a mental note to look into that possibility.

He considers the accusations against Harley next. Laina had described him as one of her earliest friends in San Diego, a man who'd taken a chance on her and with her when she was just starting to build her career, a steadying force in her life. In Cal's estimation, however, Harley is anything but steady. He seemed ready to pop off when they all met up at the lawyer's office. Could that mean there's truth to the allegations against him? Is Harley unnerved because his behavior is actually at the root of this?

Cal shakes his head and adjusts his visor against the glare. *Some of these rabbit holes I'm falling into seem just too damn crazy.*

The landscape out the window is a blur of dusty greens against sandy grit. The sun beats hotly through the window. The road is flat, the horizon endless. The occasional tall, prickly cactus stands sentinel on the side of the road. It occurs to Cal that he's not a "desert person." This arid, unforgiving *sameness* is making him itch.

The city itself comes into view: a cluster of tall buildings set against an impressive mountain backdrop, dotted throughout with a luxuriant green foreign to the natural terrain. As Cal continues on into town, he sees man-made irrigation has allowed for a profusion of plant life: emerald green lawns and parks, explosions of flower beds, creeping vines heavy with colorful blooms. He checks the outside temperature on the Mercedes's thermometer: 109 degrees.

Thanks to the modern miracle of the GPS, Cal finds Kelsey's place easily. It's a condo in a squat complex of dull design, brightly hued panels in shades of orange and yellow affixed to the exterior in an attempt, Cal supposes, to give it a little flair. The outdoor parking spaces are covered by a carport, which at least affords some shade in the face of this relentless heat. Cal pulls in underneath and parks the Mercedes in one of several spots marked VISITORS ONLY.

Cal expects Kelsey will be at home, as a result of running some numbers, namely the amount of money BETTER LIFE had paid her minus the full cash purchase price of this place. He figured it left Kelsey with no rent to pay and enough money that she didn't have to work, an alcoholic's dream cocktail.

The searing sun bakes Cal's head as soon as he clears the carport. He jams on a baseball cap hastily purchased in a gas station convenience store on the edge of the city. The cap sports the logo of the Arizona Diamondbacks. Cal's learned that the tribalism of sports can at a minimum create a kind of wary acceptance, sometimes even an enthusiastic embrace.

The grandly named Desert Palms Luxury Estates is not particularly grand on close inspection. The brightly colored panels are sun faded, and the doors to the units themselves are made from cheap, battered wood. Cal finds Kelsey's apartment, composes his face into a pleasant smile, and rings the doorbell.

The door opens to reveal a woman who is to Cal's eyes surprisingly fresh and attractive. He'd expected a slovenly wreck, but Kelsey McKendrick is neatly dressed in a pair of khaki capris and a crisp white sleeveless blouse. Her honey-streaked blond hair is caught up in a messy bun and her gray eyes are lashed with mascara. She can't be more than thirty.

"Can I help you?" she asks politely. She holds an ice-and-liquid-filled glass dripping with condensation.

Cal keeps careful watch for an indication of alarm or suspicion, but Kelsey's face remains neutral. She raises her glass to her lips and takes a sip. Cals licks his own lips, suddenly desperately thirsty.

"Ms. McKendrick?" he launches in. "My name is Cal Martin; I'm a private investigator here in Phoenix." Cal gives her a quick flash of bogus credentials which he then tucks back into his blazer pocket before continuing smoothly on. "Your late aunt, Patricia Hodges?" He pauses for an infinitesimal moment while a flicker of recognition hits Kelsey's eyes. "It appears she owned a property that's been left to you. I just need to ask you a few questions in order to authorize the transfer."

The flicker of recognition gives way to the unmistakable flash of greed. "What kind of property?" Kelsey challenges with narrowed eyes.

"A single-family home. In Bakersfield. Purchased in 1997?"

Cal's done his homework. A little social-media stalking had revealed a wealth of information about Kelsey, including the fairly recent demise of her beloved aunt Pat. While at the time of her death Aunt Pat lived in Rancho Mirage, near Palm Springs, she had lived in Bakersfield for seven years in the late 1990s with her second husband. Cal's counting on Kelsey's greed coupled with his assumption that she probably doesn't know much about Aunt Pat's life in that long-ago era. He's proven right.

"You'd better come in and have a drink, then," she announces. "Hotter 'n hades out there."

Cal steps into the cool, welcoming blast of central air-conditioning. The apartment is otherwise unprepossessing: cottage cheese ceilings, cheap nylon wall-to-wall carpet, a galley kitchen with cabinetry constructed from white MDF panels. Despite the blasting AC, a ceiling fan in the center of the living room spins lazily overhead. Cal takes off his cap.

"You a D-backs fan, then?" Kelsey asks.

"Uh-huh!" Cal replies enthusiastically.

"Hmmpf," Kelsey snorts, a sound ripe with disapproval. "I'm die-hard for the Giants. Grew up in the Bay Area." She moves a basket of laundry off the sofa with a grimace. "Sorry," she apologizes vaguely as she sets it on the floor and reclaims her glass. She takes another hearty swig. "Can I offer you something?"

"I'll have whatever you're having," Cal agrees. He has a rule to always accept a drink if one is offered by an interview subject. He figures that if the subject gives him a beverage, more is sure to follow. Cal accepts the cocktail she pours him and takes a refreshing sip. He then precisely lays out the ruse he's concocted: A review of Pat Hodges's estate has revealed the ownership of a house, a twenty-nine-hundred-square-foot beauty in a lovely part of Bakersfield, that's been left to Pat's favorite niece, Kelsey McKendrick.

"What's it worth?" Kelsey asks, getting right to the heart of the matter.

"Uh, between six hundred and fifty and seven hundred thousand dollars, I believe, according to comps."

"Aunt Pat hasn't lived in Bakersfield for a long time," Kelsey offers skeptically.

"I don't know about that," lies Cal. "But I believe your aunt was using it as a rental property."

Kelsey rises to refill her glass with more rum and Diet Coke. "Is it occupied now?"

"I believe so," Cal replies.

"How much rent they paying a month?"

"Uh, around four grand, I believe." Cal shifts position on the sofa; he'd thought he was prepared for this scenario but the questions are flying at him fast and furious. He turns on his killer smile and lowers his tone to a confiding tenor. "But I only have an idea about the values because I did a little of my own research on Zillow. You're a lucky woman. With a very generous Aunt Pat."

Kelsey contemplates that information. "How about if I sell it? Is there a mortgage on the property?"

"You'll have to talk to the lawyers. I was just hired to locate you," Cal demurs.

Kelsey takes another long pull on her drink. "Okay. That was fun. A nice story. But what's *really* going on? What do you want?"

"Excuse me?"

"Do you think I'm stupid?" The pretty blonde's face contorts with venom. "Using Aunt Pat? You ought to be ashamed of yourself!"

"I'm not sure what you mean," Cal responds. But his protest sounds weak even to his own ears.

Kelsey drains her glass. "I *wish* my dead auntie was leaving me a windfall. But I recognize you. You interviewed my old boss on TV."

Cal nearly drops his glass in surprise. He debates denying her charge but decides to come clean. He shoots her another charming smile. "You got me. Sorry. But if you recognized me, why did you let me in?"

"Curiosity," Kelsey replies. "I still keep tabs on those two, but I had no idea they were still keeping tabs on me. Why are you really here?"

Thinking fast, Cal pivots. "After I did that interview with Dr. Landers, I felt a little like she was too good to be true and

I began to do some digging." He shrugs. "And that landed me here."

Cal falls silent, wanting to divulge no more information than is demanded of him. He feels disloyal, but his lovestruck brain seized on the first reasonable lie he could come up with. Laina does sometimes seem too good to be true; his ruse is somehow rooted in truth.

"Surely if you found me, you also know we have a mutually binding NDA?" Kelsey asks, making herself a fresh rum and Diet Coke. "You certain you don't want another one?" she inquires, hoisting her glass aloft.

"I'm good, thanks," Cal answers. "And I don't want you to say anything you're uncomfortable with—"

Kelsey cuts him off. "What do you think you're going to find, exactly?"

"I'm just looking for some background. Your impressions of Dr. Landers. Of the practice."

"I think you're sniffing the wrong clover patch," Kelsey says.

Cal has absolutely no idea what she means by that statement and his confusion must show on his face, because Kelsey chortles with pleasure. "Oh my," she continues. "You don't get it at all, do you?"

She comes over to where Cal is sitting on the sofa and sits so close to him that he can smell her, a dry, papery scent laced with rum and spice. He shifts away, uncomfortable, and she laughs again. "Don't worry, I'm not going to hurt you, I'm just going to tell you a secret."

Kelsey leans over and whispers in Cal's ear. "Dr. Landers is one of the good ones, but take a look at Dr. Weida. He was the one who pressed for the NDA. He threw in some extra cash at the end too."

"Why?" Cal can't hide his shock.

Kelsey settles back, deep into her corner of the sofa, and sips at her drink. "You'll have to ask him that, won't you?"

Watching

It's still dark when I leave my warm bed and head out on my planned mission.

I reach the Spanish-style condo complex with its ornamental gate and drive past, parking a block and a half down. I realize my jaw is clenched tight, and I stretch my mouth open wide. Roll my neck. My last gift to the poor little rich girl didn't create the result that I wanted. A useless squib. I need to gather more information about her.

I slip from my car and pull up the hood of my black sweatshirt. I've got black sweatpants on too, and a pair of running shoes. A scarf around my neck is pulled up high in order to obscure my features. I pull on a pair of black gloves and strap a tummy bag around my waist.

Jogging casually down the street, I keep alert for any other early risers. Glancing down to the left, I see a couple of women power walking, pumping their arms and legs as fast as their mouths. They don't even look in my direction.

I'm inside the ornamental gate in a snap. Why this girl lives here, in this unsecured complex, is yet another puzzle. Particularly since her father's arrest. I can understand the impulse to "live a normal life," but not at the risk of one's personal safety. Still, this makes my aims easier to achieve, so it would be churlish of me to complain.

I keep my pace slow and casual as I loop around the pool at the center of the complex and head for unit 16. As I pretend to stumble and then catch myself, I affix a discreet spy camera in a niche where it will catch all comings and goings to the rich girl's home. Motion activated, picture only, but virtually undetectable, it can run on its battery for up to three months. It's a delightful piece of new technology I've been looking forward to putting to the test.

With that camera in place, I move to a window on the unit's ground floor. The floor plans for the complex were all too easy to find online, another reminder of our constant exposure. A few days of observation netted me the knowledge that the unit's occupant rarely locks her windows, even though she has double locks installed on her front door.

That may appear odd, but as a student of human nature I've observed that people have distinctly different requirements for a sense of basic safety. I see this over and over again. These personal requisites can be inherently contradictory (like the double-locked door and unlocked windows), charmingly odd (one woman I watched who couldn't leave her house without planting three kisses on the top of a favorite childhood stuffed toy), or downright painful (the teen girl who believed that by cutting herself she would magically protect her little sister from their stepfather's abuse).

That girl turned out to be living proof that those who appear the frailest are often actually the toughest and the girl living here in this complex is no exception to that rule. Sometimes the mere fact of having to battle can provide strength.

I pull a screwdriver from my tummy pack and use it to

pry away the edges of the window screen I've targeted. The screen comes loose and I lift it carefully, placing it gently down on the ground. I slide open the window and it rises smoothly and quietly, my last barrier to entry. I'll be in and out in mere moments with any luck, leaving behind another camera to provide me with an inside view.

I lift one black-clad leg and swing it up on the window ledge. A blurry, hissing mass comes flying at me. I wince back a yelp as claws penetrate my sweats. Swiftly I detach the furious cat from skin and cotton and toss it back into the condo.

I didn't mean to be rough. My throw was pure instinct. Yet the cat lands with an outraged skid and howl. I can't help but feel a small thrill of victory at the cat's injured fury. Blood for blood.

Retreat seems the prudent option. Particularly when I hear sounds of stirring from the far recesses of the condo. I leave the screen where it lies, but slide the window firmly closed before casually resuming a slow jog, taking me out of the property and back to my car. I got the one camera in place, but I'm frustrated I lost the second opportunity to a fucking cat.

As I drive away, dawn breaks with a surprisingly sharp golden glow, promising a warm day ahead. I quell my vexation by reminding myself that we are all capable of surprising ourselves. I'll find another way into that condo (and into that girl's mind if I need it). My resourcefulness is no surprise to me, but I know that it might shock other people. The people who know me don't think me weak necessarily, but they don't know what I'm capable of either.

Sometimes even I wonder.

CHAPTER NINETEEN

Every single one of Laina's nerves feels like it's on red alert. She's been jumpy all day, and actually lost her temper with an agoraphobic patient who insists on being treated via Zoom. Her momentary loss of control will cost her weeks of work with the girl, and Laina's annoyed with herself.

Her sense of disquiet only intensifies when she checks her schedule and realizes her next appointment is with George Holden. She's going to have to confront him today about stealing her scarf, in what was supposed to be their last session before George hits the road in his RV. Laina had hoped for a warm, closure-providing session in which they could both acknowledge how much George had healed and she could wish him well on his next adventure. Laina has no small amount of pride in what she perceives as her contributions to George's return to a state of emotional strength and she dreads having to confront him about the theft.

She sighs. Thinks of Cal meeting Kelsey McKendrick. Sighs again.

Kelsey is an odd duck, that had become clear to Laina pretty early on in her employment. The drinking, of course, is a disastrous component, but Kelsey is peculiar in other ways too, tricky. Laina suspects Kelsey always had a bit of a crush on her—not sexual, but more that she viewed Laina in an idealized way, as if Kelsey saw in Laina the woman she wished she could be. It was flattering initially, but as time wore on and Kelsey's erratic behavior intensified, Laina had to keep her at arm's length. She has no idea what Kelsey'll serve up to Cal.

George arrives right on time for his session, bearing a bouquet of flowers as a thank-you gift. Laina's touched by the gesture but she watches George carefully as they ease into the session, on the alert for any signs that her assessment of his progress might be off. She'd summarily dismissed Cal when he raised the possibility of George as a potential "enemy," but she can't lie to herself. She missed something with the Hutchinsons. She didn't know Daisy Sullivan was so close to cracking. It's conceivable she's wrongly assessed George Holden too, despite how uneasy that realization makes her.

The discussion about the scarf goes well enough with George, better than Laina had anticipated. With a bright blush that colors him from neck to forehead, he admits to impulsively lifting the scarf when it slithered from Laina's neck to the floor as she was escorting him out of their last session. He'd intended to hand it back to her right there and then, but, as he says with an embarrassed shrug, "A bit of me thought it might be helpful to have a bit of you with me on my travels."

He offers to return the scarf or pay for a replacement, gestures that Laina declines. When Laina finally escorts him out of her office with enthusiastic wishes for safe travels (Laina) and promises of postcards from the road (George), she feels her tightly plastered smile deflate like a punctured tire. It's not that she reevaluated George and came out concerned, as she'd feared, but more that she's shocked at her gut's simple, pure relief that he will no longer be a patient.

She snacks on a granola bar while she makes some final notations about George Holden, grateful she has a short break in between patients. There's a knock at her door, and irritated by the interruption, Laina barks a peremptory "What?" in response.

Abi pokes her head in. "I thought you'd want to know. Brad Sullivan turned up. It's all over Twitter. He was in Maui but flew back to get his kids."

"Thanks, Abi! That is good news!"

"You'd think, but apparently Daisy's parents want to contest his custody on the grounds that he abandoned the family."

"What a mess," Laina observes, anger throbbing underneath her words. "Those poor kids could be bounced around for years because of this bullshit."

"Future clients, I guess."

Abi's attempt at a joke hits Laina dead wrong. "For fuck's sake, Abi! It's not funny," she explodes. "Those kids are already traumatized."

"Right. Sorry."

Laina softens, looking at Abi's tense face. "Me too. We're all under too much stress. Sorry I snapped at you."

Abi backs away, waving off the incident. "It's okay," she reassures as she closes the door behind her.

Why is nothing simple? The Sullivan family mess is just one example. Her conflicted feelings about George Holden are another. Not to mention the complicated powder keg of emotions and connections she's forging with Cal Murray, cub reporter.

Laina's sense of disturbance only rises with the arrival of her next patient, Carmen Hidalgo. A purplish bruise is visible on the angle of collarbone exposed by Carmen's open-necked blouse. When she swings her hair, Laina can see the bruise extends up the side of her neck. The more Carmen talks, today dissecting an argument with a colleague, the edgier and angrier Laina becomes.

Finally, she can take it no more. Blasting past the specifics of Carmen's work-related tirade, Laina goes right for it. "Carmen," she interrupts. "What happened to your neck? Your chest?"

Carmen tugs at her neckline defiantly. "I have nothing to hide. I could have come in here with a turtleneck or a scarf and you'd never even have noticed. I *fell*. We hadn't been biking in a while and we took them out for a spin. I tried to show off, got cocky, and took a spill."

"So that's your story and you're sticking to it?" Laina says.

"Of course I am. Listen, if you keep making these insinuations about Ricky, I'm going to have to find another therapist."

Dragged down by the events of the day, Laina wishes she could show Carmen to the door and tell her she should do just that. Laina's more convinced than ever that Ricky is hurting Carmen and overcoming her denial about it will be a monumental task, one that in this moment in time seems entirely too daunting. Instead, Laina backs off and parses the argument with the colleague instead. The hollow of Laina's throat pulses. She catches herself biting her lip, and forces her face and her breathing to relax. She doesn't *want* to counsel more couples, but is concerned enough about

Carmen to offer up a joint session with both Hidalgos if Carmen thinks that would be beneficial.

After Carmen leaves, Laina examines the shots of her client she surreptitiously snapped with her cellphone as they scheduled their next meeting. She expands a corner of one pic, zeroing in on the ugly marks discoloring the skin over Carmen's breastbone. *Are those finger marks?* They look like it.

Today has left Laina raw, throbbing, depleted. Rubbing her eyes, she straightens her spine. She needs a lift. A friend. She shoots off a text to Bex asking if he's working tonight and if she can come lurk around his bar later.

The response, a cheerful thumbs-up emoji, gives Laina enough mojo to get through the rest of her day. When it's time to go, she secures her patient notes, double- and triple-checking the locks before gathering her bag and jacket. She sees Harley in the corridor as she steps out and purposefully ducks back into her office. She just *can't* right now.

Laina makes it out of the office and to the restaurant without incident. She wanders over to the outdoor bar, debating wine or something stronger. She passes the table where she first met with Cal and feels a little thrill deep in her core. She realizes she *misses* him, an astonishing thing given both that she barely knows him and that he's only been gone a day. Laina orders a margarita in celebration of (or possibly dread at) this revelation.

Bex joins her at the bar, telling her she should try the scallop special. "I can't hang out long," he explains. "We're jammed, as you can see. But if you can stay until we close, that's another story."

Laina demurs. She already feels the effects of the margarita, and while it's succeeding in its mission to cheer her spirits, she also suspects it will have her crashing in an hour. Despite his protestations of being too busy to socialize, Bex spends enough time with Laina at the bar to get her howling with laughter. She orders a second margarita, and the scallops as recommended.

She's feeling much better, slightly inebriated, full of energy, when Bex finally does excuse himself, ordering her a third drink on the house. The scallops are just placed in front of her, fragrant with lemon and sage, when her phone pings from the depths of her shoulder bag with the telltale sound of a news alert. Laina ignores it, but the pings of other phones and the slowly growing, roiling murmur of the patrons on the deck make the back of her neck prickle with alarm.

Laina fishes her phone from her bag and swipes it on. There is indeed a news alert:

FORMER CONGRESSIONAL CANDIDATE PETER HUTCHINSON ARRESTED IN SHOOTING DEATH OF BROTHER THOMAS HUTCHINSON

The fairy lights strung throughout the deck swim before Laina's eyes. She closes them and sees instead the spatter of blood that haunts her recurring nightmare, bright red droplets exploding onto slate-gray tile. Laina pops open her eyes and finishes her third margarita in a few convulsive gulps.

Peter murdered his brother, Tom. Actually shot and killed him. *Fuck. Yet another thing I never saw coming.*

CHAPTER TWENTY

Cal heard about Peter Hutchinson murdering his brother from Mike before the news hit the airwaves, and a strategic call to Cop Cal had turned up a few not-yet-known-to-the-public details. As much as he loves his new car, after almost eight hours out to Phoenix and then the same back to San Diego (all for an interview that lasted a total of maybe thirty-five minutes), Cal can't get out of the Mercedes and to Laina fast enough.

His entire body is pulsing with a combination of stress and the long-term buzz of the Mercedes's engine vibrating up through his leather-upholstered seat. He checks his phone again. Still no reply. He's texted Laina and called her repeatedly since he spoke to Cop Cal and received no response. It occurs to him as he barrels through the darkest hours of the night just how little he really knows about her. She lives alone; she hasn't talked many specifics about her family, and they don't live locally. He knows she has friends, of course, he's met Bex and Vanessa, and colleagues at the office, but who would Laina call in an emergency? Cal wants that person to be him.

Oblivious to the perfect SoCal night with its soft, caressing sea air, and a cloudless sky in which a hangnail sliver of moon hangs rimmed by stars, Cal finally pulls up to a parking space near Laina's condo. He races over to her front door, unsure where the burn of his urgency lies; he just knows that he has to be sure Laina is okay.

He presses the doorbell. Nothing. He tries to call her again. Voicemail.

Frustrated, frightened, desperately reassuring himself that this fear might be completely irrational, Cal pounds on Laina's door. "Laina," he shouts. "Are you in there? Are you all right?"

A persistent, shrill yapping pulls Cal's attention away from his futile knocking. He turns to find himself staring into the frightened-looking face of a middle-aged Asian woman and the agitated snout of a small white dog clutched under the woman's right arm. The animal's outfit, a purple polka-dotted jacket with matching booties and bow, is incongruously whimsical juxtaposed against the dog's bared teeth.

"Move away from that door and off this street," the woman orders, raising her voice above the dog's frantic barking. "Or I'm calling the police." She raises her left hand to show him her cellphone is poised and ready.

Cal raises his open hands to show he means no harm.

Just another night in America for a Black man.

Laina wakes up to find herself bound, her mouth covered with duct tape. She tries to wriggle free, but her arms are locked behind her back, her ankles and knees also wrapped in tape. Pins and needles prickle her heavy, immobile limbs. Images swim past her eyes, blurry and indistinct. She strains to see. Is that her brother being dragged by his hair? Her mother with a gun at her temple? There's the sound of a gunshot. A splatter of blood on slate-gray tile. She screams but the tape over her mouth means her cries are muffled and ineffectual.

Laina bolts awake in her bed, gasping. As the sanctuary that is her bedroom here in her La Jolla Shores condo swims into focus it registers: *I'm safe! I'm safe. I just had the dream again.*

Then in the next instant something else registers: *Someone's pounding on the door.*

Throwing a robe around her naked body, Laina hurries to the door. She glances at the clock set in the kitchen microwave as she passes: 4:37. She realizes she barely remembers getting home last night. *Did Bex drive me?* She's disoriented, groggy, hungover already, with the sickly sweet taste of the morning after sticky on her tongue. The shouting voice on the other side of the door becomes identifiable to her. It's Cal.

My god. What is Cal doing here at this hour?

She knows her hair is matted, her skin slick with sweat from her nightmare. She doesn't care. Laina pulls open her door. She's startled to see not only Cal but her neighbor Pam Takeshita, clutching her little dog, Pepper, with one arm and brandishing her cellphone like a weapon with the other. The dog's high-pitched yelps land like a hammer on Laina's aching head.

"It's okay, Pam," Laina says feebly as she takes in the tableau. Cal looks at her with unmistakable relief.

"Are you okay, Laina? For sure?" Pam asks warily. Pepper lets loose with a whine.

Jumbled thoughts slip through Laina's sluggish brain, even as her thick tongue struggles to find the words to express them. *Please. Go. Just go away. Why are you even walking your damn dog at this time of night? Fuck, my head hurts. I'd give anything to get that dog to be quiet. I'd give anything to be alone with Cal.* Laina's shocked by the wild and reckless urgency of this last desire.

"Yes. Thank you. Good night, Pam," Laina says firmly. She takes Cal's hand and leads him inside, shutting the door behind them.

Even in her blurred state, Laina can feel the powerful currents of Cal's agitation. Laina's been motivated to help others process their pain since she was a teenager, but she's never wanted to ease someone's suffering as strongly as she does in this moment. The urge to heal Cal usurps her sour stomach and achy head. She feels clear and calm and welcoming.

Laina cups Cal's face with one soft hand. "I'm so glad you came," she says simply.

Cal sweeps Laina into his arms. She wraps herself around him; their mouths meet. Her body is warm, feverish almost. The nape of her neck is damp with sweat, her mouth tastes sour, but her nipples are hard against his chest and when she moves his hand between her legs, she's wet. Cal lifts her. Carries her over to the kitchen island and deposits her on top. With strong hands, he pushes her thighs apart. Laina gasps when he leans to put his warm mouth between her legs.

It's like a fever dream, the touching, the exploring, the

fantastic, passionate kisses. With an unspoken agreement, they delay his full entry into her body until neither can stand it any longer. When that moment finally comes Cal looks deeply into Laina's eyes and both cry out, animal noises, deep and urgent.

Afterward, when they are both spent, Laina takes Cal's hand and walks him into the bedroom. They collapse on the bed, Laina curling on her right side and Cal spooned up against her back. As they drift into sleep, Cal thinks, *I'm too happy.*

When Cal wakes, he's alone in the bed and he can hear the shower running. He stretches luxuriously, enjoying the feel of his body, *which performed to perfection last night, if I say so myself.* Climbing from the bed, he does a little cursory "investigative reporting." He slides open the top drawer of the dresser. Underwear, both lacy and feminine and no-nonsense and practical. He rummages around, but only finds more of the same. He tries the second drawer. Pajamas, T-shirts, leggings. He runs a hand underneath and through the stack of neatly folded garments but comes up empty. The bottom drawer contains neatly folded jeans in an array of different washes.

With a glance toward the bathroom, from which he can still hear the running shower, Cal opens the door to the walk-in closet. He jumps in shock, startled by his own reflection. A full-length mirror hangs on the far wall, surrounded by a heavy wooden frame. With that minor fright resolved, Cal can appreciate the spacious order and symmetry of Laina's wardrobe. Neat, just like her drawers. Clothes are organized by color, shoes displayed in clear plastic boxes stacked on shelves, accessories hang from a pegboard, an array of neck-laces, ribbons, and scarves. There's even enough room for a small pink velvet pouf, which, Cal assumes, Laina uses as a place to sit when she puts on her shoes.

He's dated women who are slobs, and it's been an issue, as Cal prides himself in treating his possessions fastidiously. Just another thing to like about Dr. Laina Landers.

"I don't think you're my size," Laina says from close be-hind him, causing Cal to jump for the second time in two minutes. He stumbles out of the closet, busted, embarrassed, and sorry he gave way to his nosy impulses.

"Did you go through my drawers as well as my closet?" Laina challenges him, her voice tight.

Cal's heart sinks. He thinks he might be falling for this woman, and he knows he fucked up. "I won't deny it. I'm sorry. Habit, I guess. Professional hazard."

"Did you find what you were looking for?"

"I wasn't looking for anything. Laina, really, I'm an idiot, I'm so sorry. I'll tell you what, you can come over to my place and root through all my drawers. Even my medicine cabinet. Tit for tat."

Cal sees a tiny smile tug at the corner of Laina's lips.

"What do you say I cook you breakfast?" Cal proposes in order to divert attention from his snooping. "I make a mean boiled egg. I even know how to use a toaster."

"Trying to win me over with your culinary prowess? Okay, go to it, I'll be right out."

In the kitchen, Cal sets about boiling eggs. He finds a loaf of bread on the counter and pops a couple of slices into the toaster. Rooting about in the refrigerator, he finds a jar of fig jam and a dish of butter. He puts both on the kitchen island, and then pops a Nespresso capsule into the machine.

He's just making a second espresso when Laina emerges from the bedroom in jeans and a white T-shirt, her feet bare, her hair damp, face clean of any makeup. At the sight of her, Cal's entire being throbs with a longing that startles him.

She accepts the tiny cup of espresso he offers her. "I'm so sorry about Peter Hutchinson," Cal consoles her. "I know it must be awful for you."

"Yes," Laina agrees, sipping at her coffee.

"But you're also going to want to know . . . I heard . . ." Cal pauses.

"What? Just say it."

"The tape that tipped Peter Hutchinson over the edge was a sex tape of Clare with Peter's brother, Tom. That was his motive."

"No!" Laina gasps, and Cal understands her shock. For weeks Tom has played the role of his brother's greatest defender, demonstrating his commitment to his brother's defense and mental health through both talk and deed. He'd posted Peter's bail and taken him into his home. On television interviews, Tom talked "family solidarity," and "the burden of loss," and "mental health reform." He'd even taken to publicly criticizing Clare for not being more understanding of the "stress" that had led to Peter's "episode."

"You're sure?" Laina asks.

"I have it on good authority," Cal confirms. "It'll hit the news soon enough. You had no idea?"

"No. God. What a mess." Laina sets her cup down and busies herself pulling out plates, cutlery, and napkins.

Cal sees Laina's face has paled; she seems to be avoiding his eyes. She prides herself so much on her work, it must be a blow to learn this couple she believed she'd helped hid so many secrets from her as well as each other.

"Do you want to hear about my meeting with Kelsey?" Cal asks.

"Of course," Laina answers, keeping her hands and eyes busy elsewhere.

"First a question: Was Harley the one who pushed for the NDA?"

Laina looks at him in surprise. "Well, yes. He thought Kelsey was a loose cannon. But he wasn't wrong."

"Did you ever think there was something in particular about Harley that Kelsey might have known? Something he wanted her to keep quiet about besides the fall that led to her head injury?"

"Where's this coming from, Cal?" The toast pops and Laina extracts the slices, dropping them onto plates.

"Kelsey observed the terms of your NDA, but she also intimated that Harley might have been trying to keep something else quiet."

Laina slathers her toast with fig jam but sets it down without taking a single bite. "I can't think what," she replies. "And I don't know, she's not exactly a reliable narrator, is she? Sure, Harley was worried Kelsey might make some trouble for us, but her behavior up to that point had already proven his suspicions weren't unfounded. I'm more interested in what *you* thought after meeting her. Do you think she's behind the harassment?"

"I just don't see her for it, truthfully." Cal suspects Kelsey

McKendrick doesn't drive anywhere much besides the hair salon and the liquor store, and that the latter probably blunts her aspirations for long distance mayhem. He explains his thinking to Laina, who nods in agreement. "I think maybe she dripped a little poison in my ear when she was presented with the opportunity," Cal continues, "but I don't think she has the capacity for an organized campaign of . . . anything."

"That makes sense," Laina replies. "It's sad, but she seemed pretty determined to drink herself to death."

Cal knows he ought to proceed cautiously in floating his next supposition. "What if the harassment is a smoke screen for one true target? What if it's designed to look like a campaign against you and Harley, but you and your other patients are really just collateral damage?"

"What are you suggesting?"

"That I ought to take another look at the Goldsteins."

"Why?" Laina asks, her body stiffening as if she's poised for flight.

"The Goldsteins have a lot of money," Cal explains. "And money—"

Laina interrupts. "Is the root of all evil."

"I was going to say, it's one of the primary motives for all kinds of bad behavior."

"Like murder. Although money isn't the only motive, is it?" A dark shadow crosses Laina's eyes and Cal can tell she's thinking about the Hutchinsons again.

Cal comes around the island and gathers Laina up in his arms. She's tense at first, but she doesn't push him away. Gradually, her body softens. She nestles her head into his chest and returns his embrace.

They cling to each other in silence for a very long time.

The water boils away in the pot with the eggs until they scorch, setting off the smoke detector. It's only then that they break apart, laughing at this small self-created calamity.

Ignoring the cold toast and scorched eggs, Cal takes Laina's hand and leads her back to bed.

CHAPTER TWENTY-ONE

With Kelsey McKendrick eliminated from suspicion in his mind, Cal is as eager to keep investigating a possible culprit as Laina is adamant about not disclosing any more information about her clients than she already has.

But Cal can't let it go. Not while he believes someone is out to harm either Laina through manipulation of her clients, or one of her clients with no regard for the collateral damage to Laina and others along the way. He's convinced there's a threat *and* a story, and he can't let either of them alone. He doesn't dare go near Clare Hutchinson for fear of antagonizing Laina. Daisy Sullivan is in custody. But Satchel Goldstein. Franny. That box with the red ribbon. That note. The oil-soaked bill inside.

Cal remembers Laina saying that San Diego is essentially *"a big small town"* when talking about Satchel Goldstein. Nowhere is a big town smaller than within the tight-knit circle of its elite, and this realization gets Cal thinking. He decides to pay another visit to his voluble new friend Bootsy Hancock.

Cal's in luck; Bootsy's home alone, and after a quick glance in the direction of both of her widely spaced next-door neighbors, she practically pulls Cal into her foyer. "Is it true about Tom and Clare?" she asks, her eyes dancing with the gossip. "And I thought that boy of theirs was the problem! When all along, Clare was the wild one! I guess the apple doesn't fall far and all that."

"I actually wanted to ask you about someone else," Cal replies.

"Oh yesh?" Bootsy asks with unmasked delight in her eyes and just the slightest slur to her words.

Cal's eyes drift to the highball glass clutched in her hand. A faint whiff of gin, tonic, and lime drifts past his nostrils. "Want one?" she asks, clearly eager to have a drinking companion.

"Sure," Cal agrees. Bootsy leads him into a comfortable and spacious room. An oversize L-shaped leather sofa cradles a square coffee table constructed out of a heavy, dark wood. A large TV is mounted over a gas fireplace; the sound is off, but images flash on the screen: a gruesome crime scene being combed by a forensic team. A logo promoting the show tags the right-hand corner of the screen: It's an episode of Investigation Discovery's *Evil Lives Here*.

Bootsy walks over to the impressive carved wooden bar that's built into one corner of the room, highly polished and long enough to accommodate five stools. "G&T okay?" she inquires.

Cal nods. Bootsy pours him a drink and freshens up her own. She takes a long swallow. "So, who d'ya wanna ask me about?"

"Francesca Goldstein or her father, Satchel. Do you know either of them?"

Bootsy sniffs. "Why, of course I know them. They were members of our club. Not anymore obviously." She lowers her voice and leans in closer to Cal, creating an air of boozy confidentiality. "Now, Franny, that's a sad story there. Poor girl."

"She's out too?" Cal asks. *The sins of the fathers.*

"Well." Bootsy pauses to take a sip. "There was some controversy when he was even admitted, you know. New money and all for one thing, and of course . . ." Bootsy trails off abruptly and takes another gulp of her cocktail. "Anyway, no one was too sorry when they were voted out. We can't have *criminals* mingling with our grandchildren."

"Completely understandable," Cal agrees equably, in the interest of keeping the conversation flowing. "Do the Hutchinsons belong to the same club as you as well?"

"Yes, they do. Did. I feel sorry for Clare," Bootsy asserts in a tone that implies just the opposite. "But they'll all be voted out too at the next board meeting. Morals clause. It's not the kind of thing we can be associated with."

"Which thing?" Cal asks pleasantly.

Bootsy slurps from her cocktail. "You know, all of it," she prattles happily. "I mean! Sex tapes. Adultery with the in-laws. Murder. It's just not our kind of thing."

Suddenly sickened by Bootsy's greedy glee in her neighbors' distress, Cal shifts gears. "Do you know someone named George Holden?"

Bootsy frowns. "I don't think so."

"You're sure? You never heard that name. Not in connection with the Hutchinsons, for example?"

Bootsy shakes her head. Cal continues, "How about Daisy Sullivan?"

"Isn't she that crazy girl who rammed an ex with her car? I know her from the news." Bootsy gestures at the TV. "She'll be her own TV special soon enough." Eyes glinting, she presses on. "Have you seen the Clare and Tom tape?" she asks. "I heard some members of the media saw it before the lawyers got busy."

"I haven't seen it," Cal answers truthfully, grateful that's the case. Otherwise Bootsy would no doubt be pressing him for a play-by-play.

She peers at Cal over the rim of her glass, seemingly irritated by his reticence to gossip. "I don't know how you do it," she states ambiguously.

Cal replies cautiously. "Do what exactly?"

"Spend your days sticking your nose up other people's assholes."

His shock at her sudden crudity must show on his face, because Bootsy, loosened by gin, releases a very unladylike cackle.

"I believe showing people the truth of things is for their benefit," he replies succinctly before putting his untouched drink down on the square wooden coffee table and bidding Bootsy a good afternoon.

Cal buckles himself back into the driver's seat of his car and contemplates his next steps. His encounter with Bootsy makes him long for a shower, maybe a hazmat suit. His phone rings. Cop Cal. "My man," Cal greets him. "I'm glad to hear from you; you were on my list for today."

"And here I am beating you to it, proving once again that I'm the superior Cal Murray," Cop Cal needles with good humor. "But Satchel Goldstein?"

"I'm listening." Cal perks up. He needs a break on this story whether it ties back to Laina or not.

"You were asking me about the daughter? Well, my

brother Dave's an agent in the local FBI office that's been investigating Satchel."

"You're full of surprises, aren't you?" Cal says. "How did I not know you had a brother in the bureau?"

"Whose kid did you think you were coaching at track?" Cop Cal parries back. There's a pause. Cal can sense how much his namesake is enjoying drawing this out.

"Come on," Cal says. "Don't make me beg for it."

"They're going to raid the daughter's place today. The FBI."

"When?" Cal's surging with excitement. He throws his car into gear.

"Half hour from now."

"I owe you," Cal promises.

"Don't worry, I'll collect."

Cal clicks off. He heads to Franny Goldstein's place, calling Mike and telling him to meet him there. Cal's just found street parking when he spots Mike pulling up in his black Toyota. He scans the street quickly. No sign of the Feds. With luck they'll get to Franny before they arrive.

"Let's go, go, go," Cal entreats Mike as they push past the complex's ornamental gate and into the courtyard. With quick steps, Cal and Mike circle around to unit 16 and Cal rings the bell.

The wait seems interminable, but finally the front door is pulled open and Cal finds himself looking into Franny Goldstein's gaunt face. Somehow she doesn't seem surprised to see him.

"Now what?" she snarls, her eyes sparking with anger.

Taken aback by her venom, Cal hesitates and Franny forges on with her attack, her fists balled, her skinny frame tense. "Were you responsible for that fucking 'present'? You sick fucks."

"Absolutely not. I give you my word."

"Yeah, right. You two show up right when that fucking thing does! And then someone tries to break into my place! Was that you too? I should call 911 right now."

Conscious of the irony inherent in the fact that the Feds are about to descend, Cal moves to reassure her, "I promise you that we had nothing to do with any of that, Franny. I'm a friend of Dr. Landers, as you know, and I promise, Mike and I, we'd never do anything like that. We report the news, we don't try to make it."

Some of the fight leaves Franny's rigid, bony frame. "What do you want, then?" she asks, poised to shut the door.

"Boss."

Mike's single word draws Cal's attention. He twists his head to see half a dozen suited individuals marching through the gate and into the complex.

"Thank you, Franny, we'll talk again soon," Cal says hurriedly, realizing he and Mike better get out of the eyeline of the agents if they want to get unimpeded coverage of the raid. He gestures to Mike and the two of them retreat behind the shed housing the pool equipment, leaving Franny staring after them in astonishment. Her bewilderment morphs to dismay as she takes in the agents' purposeful progress across the courtyard. Cal thinks she might slam her door shut, but then she slumps against the doorjamb, looking utterly defeated. Ben comes up behind her and puts an arm around her shoulders.

"You're rolling?" Cal mouths to Mike from where they've taken cover.

"Since we got here," Mike mouths back. Cal gives him a thumbs-up.

"Francesca Goldstein?" asks a crisp-edged woman with short hair and big eyes as she approaches the entwined couple at the door of unit 16. "I'm Special Agent Lucy Nemeck, from the FBI's San Diego Field Office. I have a search warrant for these premises."

Franny sinks deeper into Ben's embrace, her limbs so brittle they look like matchsticks.

Cal feels queasy. He doesn't often let his thirst for a story be curtailed by sympathy or pity. It's a mistake, and he knows it. But he can't help but feel sorry for Franny Goldstein, fighting the cancer ravaging her body while also battling the fallout from her father's arrest.

His attention is caught by the imposing figure of Ruslana Goldstein striding through the ornamental front gate. Ruslana wears a clingy rib-knit top tucked into cinched trousers. Her spike heels must be at least six inches high. She also wears a fierce expression on her expertly made-up face.

How did she get here so fast? Franny didn't have time to call her even if she wanted to.

What if Ruslana didn't find that beribboned box on Franny's doorstep? What if she brought it with her? Maybe she isn't a mama bear racing to protect her cub. Maybe she's more like the mama quokkas of Western Australia, known for tossing their cubs at predators in order to escape being prey themselves.

Cal guiltily remembers he's overdue calling his own mother and resolves to do it this Sunday. If he catches her after church and in a good mood, she might not even give him grief for how long it's been.

A sudden shout pulls him back from his thoughts. Ben emerges from unit 16 carrying a limp Franny in his arms. Ruslana strides next to them, shrieking curses at Agent Nemeck, who trails behind her.

"Where are you taking her?" Agent Nemeck demands.

"The hospital, you vulture," snaps Ben.

Mike gestures to Cal. *Should we move closer?*

But Cal can't do it. He can't film this girl's collapse. "Cut," he says.

Mike looks at him in surprise as Ben hurries away with Franny in his arms.

"We have enough of that. Let's wait and see what the agents carry out," Cal says.

Mike does as Cal asks and doesn't say a single word in protest. *This is a better partnership all the time.*

But Cal's mind is spinning out with questions. *What would Ruslana have to gain by tormenting her daughter? Is she also responsible for the FBI tip that led to this raid? Is that how she knew to show up? What motivations could be informing her decisions? Could she somehow have accessed BETTER LIFE's patient records?*

Cal feels at sea. Despite his deeply rooted instincts to "follow the money," and his fierce determination to find answers that will protect Laina, nothing makes sense.

CHAPTER TWENTY-TWO

As unsettled as she is, Laina knows she must go see Clare Hutchinson. She's been summoned and didn't feel she could say no. This time, the door to the Hutchinson home is opened by a helmet-haired, hatchet-faced woman that Laina recognizes as one of the family's attorneys. They've never met in person, but Laina's seen the lawyer on the news, making comments on the family's behalf, comments that have been, more often than not, "no comment."

Laina struggles to pull up the lawyer's name, but this need is obviated when the woman thrusts out a thin, cold hand for Laina to shake and announces, "Thank you for coming. I'm Fee Reynolds."

Right. Fee (short for Phoenicia) Reynolds. How could Laina have forgotten? A partner at her law firm, she probably billed something like eight hundred dollars an hour. Laina had wondered if any of her clients saw the dry humor intrinsic in Fee's nickname when she'd first seen her on the news.

Fee ushers Laina into the house and directly to the room where Laina had last met with Clare. The comfortable, well-appointed space has grown more chaotic since Laina's last visit. Newspapers are heaped on the floor; the driftwood coffee table is littered with candy wrappers and empty mugs.

Clare is curled up in the same corner of one of the two navy sofas, once again wrapped in wispy cashmere. Her face is puffy and pale. Gray roots spring up along her hairline. Dark purplish circles rim her red-veined eyes. Laina's shocked by how much Clare appears to have aged.

Seated on the other sofa are two young men. Laina recognizes Drew, who wears the same contemptuous sneer he aimed in her direction the first time they met. The other boy must be James. He's a leaner, more athletic, better-looking version of his brother, despite the fine spiderweb of scars sprawled across his forehead and right cheekbone.

"Hi, Clare." Laina greets her before nodding at her sons. "Boys. I'm so sorry. I know you must all be in enormous pain right now."

Laina's not quite sure what's expected of her here. She looks over to the doorway where Fee Reynolds stands with her long fingers steepled, hoping for some guidance. To her surprise, Fee announces, "I'll leave you, then. Take a walk through the garden, get a bit of sunshine. You can text me when you're ready, Clare." Fee crosses to the doors opening out to the patio and adjacent garden and disappears.

"How can I help?" Laina asks into the ensuing silence.

"Please tell the boys that Peter and I loved each other. That we both made stupid mistakes that had unintended consequences, but that our whole marriage wasn't a sham." Clare's eyes are pleading.

Laina knows this request thrusts her right onto the sharp horns of an ethical dilemma. But she also knows this request is costing Clare dearly; she was held at gunpoint by a man who has now murdered his brother, but for the sake of their children she is trying to construct some repaired version of their family that will allow those boys to still love him. Laina looks into Clare's ravaged eyes and picks out a careful answer that she addresses to the two young men.

"As I guess you know, your parents came to me for help with working through some marital issues. That's not uncommon; it's actually a healthy sign in a relationship, especially if both parties are equally invested in doing the work. It shows that despite the fact that a couple may be having a difficult time, they recognize their history and shared long-term goals can carry them through."

"Fucking bullshit," Drew snarls.

"One of the things that brought your parents to see me was their shared love and concern about you two boys," Laina presses on, undaunted. "James's accident took a toll—"

Drew interrupts. "I am so fucking sick of hearing about James's accident!"

"Drew!" Clare gasps. "Stop that!!"

"Let him say it, Mom!" James shouts. "You're such a fucking idiot, Drew! It's like you think I wrecked the car on purpose to take attention away from you!"

"Somehow it's always about you, you piece of shit!" Drew yells back.

Laina strides over to confront Drew, who's still seated on the sofa. "James's accident took a toll, as did your forays into drug addiction and petty theft," she admonishes him. She looms over him, hands on her hips, and some of his bravado fades. She sees the frightened little boy concealed beneath the surly demeanor of an enraged teenager.

Laina steps back and softens her tone. "But, look, all of you are still probably in shock, and it will take a little time to process what's happened. Be kind to one another. I know you're all angry in different ways and about a host of different things; taking it out on one another is not helpful."

"Fuck this. I'm out of here," Drew announces. He bounds out of the room and into the hallway. Laina can hear him clumping up the stairs.

James struggles to his feet. For the first time, Laina notices the cane propped next to one of the sofa's end tables. The boy leans on it for support. "Thanks for coming," he says bleakly to Laina. "Nice try. I've got to finish a paper, Mom," James adds. "I'm going to go up too." He limps away as Laina and Clare remain enfolded in silence.

Once the sound of his labored, cane-assisted ascent up the staircase has faded, Clare finally speaks. "He's so conscientious, James. Of course, he could have gotten extensions on everything—Lord knows, Drew did—but he says it helps him to have things to focus on."

"How's he healing physically?" Laina asks.

"Slow but steady. He won't get plastic surgery for the scars on this face, though. Says he wants a reminder that life can change, or end, in an instant." Clare's eyes grow damp. "Like we don't have enough reminders already."

Laina sits next to Clare and takes one of her hands in both of her own. "I'm glad you reached out. That was a brave thing you did for your kids. You're going to have to keep on being brave."

They sit in silence for a few minutes. Occasionally, sounds drift in: Fee Reynolds talking on her cellphone in the garden, the hiss of a sprinkler turning on, the tuneful song of a bird, the distant buzz of a lawnmower.

"I have a confession," Clare whispers.

Unsure of how she'll respond to yet another shock from this family, Laina steels herself for what's to come. The pulse in her throat announces itself, and Laina's right hand drifts up to cover it.

Clare continues, "That's why Fee is here. I'm going to tell the truth to the police."

"The truth about what, Clare?" Laina can't imagine what will be worse than the now public knowledge that she'd cuckolded her husband with his brother, leading to fratricide.

Clare ducks her head. "I know it's all going to come out. That's why I need to set things straight. Why I needed you to talk to the boys."

"Go on."

"I knew Tom filmed us. We both had copies. It was his idea, a kind of mutual insurance." Clare laughs, a bitter sound that turns into a cough.

"Why Tom?" Laina can't help but ask. "Of all people."

"Maximum impact," Clare says simply.

Laina waits a beat before deciding she needs to press Clare further. "You know, I've been doing my best to try to keep the video under wraps, using press contacts, denying its very existence. I took you at your word. Why did you lie to me? You told me the filming wasn't consensual. And you never mentioned Tom was your partner!"

Clare shrugs with a helpless fatality. "He'd been after me

for years. But I always sidestepped, and I never said anything to Peter. He worshipped Tom and I didn't want to wreck that. But I was so angry! Not just that Peter had cheated but that he was able to lie about it so seamlessly for so many years! Birthdays and Christmases and anniversaries and graduations, and all the while, his smug, smiling face knew what he had done. And if—and that's also a question—*if* she was the only one, what would happen if he got elected? Women are attracted to that kind of power. I was a closed door to Peter, and Tom played it just right, knew just what to say, just how much wine to pour, to get me to finally open up to him instead."

"But why would Tom share the video with Peter? Surely he had as much to lose as you did?"

Silence fills the room again and Laina lets it, suspecting further revelations are to come. She's not wrong.

"You don't understand. I'm the one who sent the video to Peter."

Laina's heart races. She realizes she needs to entirely rethink her perceptions of Clare Hutchinson. "Why?" she manages to ask. "Why would you do that?"

Clare lifts her eyes to meet Laina's. "Did you know Peter was responsible for James's accident?"

"*What?*"

"The night he crashed his car, James was at dinner with his father and some golf buddies at the club. James was drunk. He never should have gotten behind the wheel. Peter let him. Peter got him drunk in the first place. 'I was just treating him like one of the boys,'" she mimics bitterly. "That was his excuse. And then there was the incident with Drew."

"What incident was that?" Laina asks softly, dreading the answer. *How did these two conceal so much from me? How could I have missed all these underlying tensions and issues?*

"He got into trouble with a girl. Peter laughed it off. 'Boys will be boys,' he said. The same old bullshit excuse. He couldn't see that Drew needed help. He needs it even more now." Clare laughs hoarsely. "I wanted to hurt Peter, but not just because he fucked other women. I'd had enough of the whole toxic *thing* that was my marriage. That's why I sent him the video."

Clare pauses to take a sip of tea. "But I knew Peter, or thought I did. I believed the thing he'd want more than anything would be to keep my betrayal a secret. I thought it would hurt him enough to get him to pull out of the race and let me go. That he would burrow inward. I never thought he'd threaten me. And even though Tom told me that Peter's resentment of him grew the more Tom stepped up for him publicly, neither of us ever dreamed that he'd . . . he'd . . . he'd . . . kill him." Clare shakes her head. "He worshipped him," she whispers.

Clare seems to become frailer and less rooted to the earth with every word. For a fanciful moment, Laina imagines a weightless Clare wafting out of the room and into the garden, away from her tragedies and up into the brilliant blue sky.

Laina remembers that the last time she'd been in this exquisite room Clare had felt *liberated* despite the terrifying event that led to her freedom. While Clare had been furiously angry at Peter, and rightfully afraid of him, she'd also *reveled* in the finality of their marriage. Peter's future was clearly bleak after the assault, but Clare, while traumatized by the event, had already been crafting a new life with relief. The worst had happened but she was free.

Unfortunately, Clare hadn't realized that the worst was yet to come.

Sadness carves a lonely, hollow feeling in Laina's heart. "What can I do? How can I help?" she asks. The pulse in the hollow of her throat flutters rapidly, an insistent, threatening reminder of Laina's powerlessness.

"You came today," Clare says serenely. "Thank you. That's all I wanted. I don't expect we'll be seeing each other again."

Laina feels dismissed. She rises to her feet uncertainly. Her cellphone vibrates. Grateful for the distraction, she pulls the phone from her bag. It's Cal. Laina shoots him a message letting him know she'll call right back.

"Clare," Laina says hesitantly. "Why didn't you ever talk to me about all those things that were going on with the boys? Or within your marriage? Why did you come to therapy if you were going to conceal your most challenging stressors and struggles?"

Clare looks at her with mild surprise. "We don't talk about problems or emotions. Not in this family, nor in the one I grew up in; you just zip your lips and soldier on." She shrugs. "I just wasn't used to it, I guess."

With a hasty goodbye, Laina hurries out to her car, glad to encounter neither the Hutchinson progeny nor Fee Reynolds as she departs. As soon as she slams the door of her Jeep, she calls Cal back. He picks up right away.

"Listen, Laina, I just left Franny Goldstein's place," he says without preamble. "She was raided by the FBI."

"What!"

"Yeah, I know. They had a warrant and everything. But

more to the point, I'm worried about Franny. I think Ben and Ruslana took her to the hospital. Maybe you can reach out?"

The flutter in Laina's throat announces its return with gusto. She swallows hard to fight back her rising feelings of panic. "Of course I will," she finally chokes out. "Thanks for letting me know."

"Of course. Are you okay?"

"Sure I am. Just busy. Talk to you later." Laina clicks the phone off and drops it on the passenger seat. She folds her arms over her steering wheel and drops her head down into their cradle. A tear slips from her eye.

Laina prides herself on her composure. On her ability to support others while needing little support herself. It's her very self-definition. She's a woman who's resilient. Self-reliant. Who can be encouraging and empathetic while staying self-contained and in control. It's a necessary quality in her choice of profession, of course, but one borne of a long-time personal preference that has kept her safe.

Until now.

She's grateful Cal called her about Franny, although heartsick at the news. When she pulls herself together, she'll follow up and arrange a visit. But right now, in this one fragile moment, Laina's afraid she herself might shatter.

Even Mr. M didn't leave her feeling this vulnerable. And after that fiasco, Laina swore she would never *need* anyone again. Can it be she needs Cal Murray? The thought is thrilling but also terrifying. She's pushed herself way out of her comfort zone, and in this sick, sorrowful moment, can only feel dread.

CHAPTER TWENTY-THREE

Scripps La Jolla is a state-of-the-art facility, nationally ranked in treating adult cancers. Whimsical sculpture dots the grounds along with flowering trees and bushes. A burbling fountain topped by a joyous, leaping stone child takes pride of place in a hardscape courtyard. Despite all the charming details, a hospital is a hospital. Illness lives here and death lurks just outside.

Laina finds a spot in visitor parking and exits the cool of her air-conditioned Jeep. The sun is hard and sharp, but icy fingers tickle her spine as she crosses the hospital's asphalt lot. Laina squares her shoulders and forces herself to step inside.

She finds Franny easily and learns that Ben and Ruslana have gone to the cafeteria to get some snacks and coffee. Laina's simultaneously relieved and disappointed. On the one hand, she's been hearing about Franny's dynamics with both of them for years now and seeing them in the flesh would no doubt be revealing. On the other hand, she's glad to talk to Franny alone and maintain the purposeful veil dropped between a therapist and her patients outside of the treatment room.

"What do the doctors say?" Laina inquires.

"Nothing good," Franny says limply. A thin sheet covers her skeletal frame. "I don't want to talk about it."

"Okay." Laina pauses. "How about your dad? How's he doing?"

"Not well. Better now that he's out on bail. But he's wrecked." Tears fill her eyes. "Mostly because my illness led to him cutting the corners that got him in trouble. And now it's all blown up, anyway! He's ruined and I'm going to die."

"You don't know that." Laina rushes to reassure her patient.

"But I do" is Franny's despondent reply. "I've stopped fighting it. I'm making my peace with my situation. At least if I'm going to die, I die knowing my dad is still my hero. He did everything he could for me, even if it led him to break the law."

"You knew, didn't you?" Laina probes. "Before Satchel's arrest? You said some things in session, nothing direct, but when it all came out, I suspected you knew something beforehand."

Franny looks frightened. "He told me to never admit to it," she whispers with wide eyes. "But anything I say to you is protected, right?"

"Yes. But more important, if you're making your peace with things as they are, you have to accept that reality too."

"I feel like it's all my fault!" Franny wails.

"Your father made his own choices, Franny. He could have fought in every way possible for you that *didn't* include breaking the law. You are not responsible."

"Aren't I?" Franny narrows her eyes. "No cancer, no crime. I deserve to die."

"Do I need to remind you of the importance of a positive

attitude in fighting cancer? You're a fighter; don't give up now."

"It's so hard," Franny whispers.

"It is. But it's also what your dad would want. It's what *you* want." Franny's angles seem to soften, encouraging Laina to continue. "None of us are saints, Franny. Your dad included. Do you think you can learn to look at him as a man with his flaws and foibles like the rest of us? You're so hard on your mother all the time, and I get that she can be a pain in the ass, but don't you think by deifying your father you inevitably polarize against your mother?"

Franny scowls at her.

"I mean," Laina continues, "Ruslana may be 'hovering,' but she's also trying to help. The best thing you can do for yourself at this point is put your strength and energy into getting well. Fighting with your mother just exhausts you. Stop battling her. Nod along and let it wash over you. You need support right now, so try to accept the kind she can give."

That comment at least elicits a wry smile. "I think I need to sleep now," Franny says drowsily.

"You do that," Laina says. She resists the impulse to give the wasted-looking girl a kiss, and instead strokes one open palm across Franny's forehead in a swift caress.

Behind Laina's desk chair hangs a large painting, hued in blues and grays, tones that coordinate with the soothing colors of her office décor. It could be an abstract, but is that a man and a woman entwined? Maybe. That's definitely a pillowy pink heart tilting off-center. It's the first piece of art

Laina ever bought, a tangible symbol of her hard-earned success after years of student loans and pasta dinners, as demonstrated by the simple fact that she had money to spare for anything as frivolous as a painting she adored.

Night's gathering outside her window, but Laina hasn't switched on any of the lights. She came to the office after seeing Franny and had Abi cancel the rest of her appointments for the day. She closed her office door and collapsed into the chair usually reserved for clients, the one with clear sight lines to the painting. Its beloved brushstrokes are fading now in the gloom of the evening and she tells herself she should go home, but she can't seem to move. She stares at the artwork, which now feels like nothing more than a rebuke of her youthful optimism.

She thinks about calling Cal, but she knows he's working tonight; the man has to do his job. And it's definitely not his job to "fix" her (as if anyone could). Still, she finds herself longing for his embrace.

Should she text? Ask him to check in when he can? *No,* she firmly decides. She's gutted by this day, Clare's revelations, Franny's deterioration, but Laina recognizes she must bear this grief privately. In this state, Laina might be tempted to tell Cal everything, and the very last person to whom she should relay a patient's confidences, or her own for that matter, is a journalist.

She also can't quite bat away the squelch of uneasiness that hits her gut every time she remembers she caught him poking around inside her closet. What was he looking for?

Of course, she's lied to him too, or at least *withheld* knowledge that she possesses about George Holden and Daisy Sullivan . . . about herself. Laina stops herself from slip-sliding down this path, which is only leading her to a feeling of deepening inertia and despair.

Trust is so fucking difficult.

Laina's ears prick up at a muffled sound coming from outside her office. She frowns. These rooms are soundproof, whatever that noise is, it must be *loud*. She rises and flings open her door to see Carmen Hidalgo squirming on the floor in the corridor. She's yelling and clawing to get away from Abi, who's braced against a doorjamb, holding the furious Carmen back by clinging to one booted foot.

"What the hell?" Laina can't muzzle her shocked response.

"The police came to interview him, you fucking crazy bitch!" Carmen screams. Her face mottles red and spittle flies from her mouth. "For hurting me. Which he has never done! At his fucking job! Do you know what kind of shitstorm you started?" Carmen makes a lunge for it, but Abi holds tightly to her ankle.

"Call 911!" Abi shouts over Carmen, who's cursing in English and Spanish.

"Wait!" cries Laina. "Let me try to talk to her." She addresses Carmen, who's still wriggling on the floor, attempting to elude Abi's valiant grip. "Carmen. The police don't arrest people without evidence."

"The hell they don't!" Carmen fires back. "You ever been a brown face in America? I know this is your fault! You're the only one who had this crazy idea that Ricky could hurt me."

"If he's innocent, nothing will come of it."

Carmen stops struggling. She looks at Laina with a look of genuine, bemused astonishment and then laughs, sour as vinegar. "You are so fucking naïve. How could you *ever* possibly help *anyone*? And don't think I didn't notice that you didn't deny you were behind it either." Disdain paints Carmen's every word.

Abi relaxes her grip momentarily and Carmen twists from her grasp, pulling her foot free and leaving Abi clutching an empty boot. Carmen leaps up from the floor and comes at Laina, roiling with fury. Laina tries to stand tall but can't help but flinch as Carmen advances. To Laina's surprise, Carmen doesn't hit her or tackle her.

Instead, she rears her head back and spits, lobbing a loogie directly into Laina's face. It's somehow worse than a savage blow. "If I can prove you had something to do with this, I'm going to sue your ass," Carmen hisses. Then she spins on her heels and hobbles out, cursing loudly, grabbing her errant boot from Abi as she passes by.

"Should I call the police?" Abi asks.

"No," replies Laina. "I think she's gone. It's all right." She aims for a tone of reassurance but is aware that her legs are shaking, as is her voice. Abi hands her a tissue to wipe her face.

"That was fucking nuts," Abi says. "Good thing I stayed late to do some insurance filings."

"Wasn't the door locked?" Laina asks. "It's after hours."

"Of course it was, but I recognized her. It was only after I let her in that I realized she was so out of control."

"You did well," Laina says to Abi. "Thank you."

"Are you okay?" Abi asks sympathetically.

Laina's not okay; she's heartsick and reeling and reevaluating virtually every assumption that has guided her life to this point. If she was to answer Abi honestly, she would shout *"No! I'm not okay! I'm bone weary and confused and afraid."* But she lies. "Of course. I'm fine."

"There was no truth . . . I mean, did you . . . know what she was talking about?"

Laina looks into Abi's distressed eyes. "Not a clue, Abi," Laina replies firmly.

There is absolutely no reason Abi needs to know Laina made an anonymous call about Ricky Hidalgo. As a survivor of the damage a man's fists and boots can inflict, Laina couldn't in good conscience let poor Carmen suffer without trying to help.

Laina touches Abi's shoulder. "It's been a day. Why don't you go on home? I'll do the same."

Watching

Of course, I've been outside this condo many times, but today I study its façade as if I've never seen it before. Good advance planning requires looking at a place with fresh eyes; one can't afford to get complacent.

Fog hangs low and heavy, cloaking the sunset with gray. The harsh cry of a swooping gull draws my eyes. The ocean glints and rumbles downhill to my west.

Twisting my head back eastward, I again turn my attention to the condo's exterior. I take notes on both the placement of the security cameras and where their lenses are pointed. I examine the front door with its double locks. The next-door neighbor emerges from her unit, her overdressed dog on a leash, and heads off for a walk.

Glancing back at the wide window facing the street and the ocean, I note how many details can be seen when the curtains are left open; sage-green throw on white sofa, wine-glass on kitchen island. The open-plan living space is open indeed, another instance where even those of us who should know better expose ourselves to prying eyes.

CHAPTER TWENTY-FOUR

His piece had aired on the eleven o'clock news, slickly edited, angled sympathetically toward Franny, but still exploiting the delectable drama of an FBI raid on the deathly ill daughter of a fallen business titan. Cal and his producer ended the segment with a tease: What might that raid reveal? What fresh hell could be blasting toward the formerly invincible Satchel Goldstein?

Cal's adrenaline is pumping. His tip from Cop Cal gave them an exclusive, and he has some juicy footage for future use safely logged in to an editing bay. He knows his finished piece is good. He also knows it's likely to piss off Laina.

It's late, but he wants to call her. Whether she saw his piece tonight or not, he wants to get ahead of her reaction by talking to her directly.

Just as he's resigned the call will go to voicemail, Laina answers. "Hello?" Her voice is scratchy with sleep.

"Did I wake you?"

"Just a little."

Cal hears the smile in her voice and his heart warms. "Look, did you see my piece tonight?" He gets right to the point, anxious to get the subject behind them.

"No. Sorry. I had a shit day and went to bed early."

"I hope this call doesn't make your day worse."

"Why? What happened?" Laina's voice is suddenly sharp, all traces of grogginess gone.

"Nothing. We ran a segment on the raid on Franny's place. It focused on Satchel, I promise. If anything, my producer beat me up because he thought I was too soft on Franny. You should watch it. I'm proud of it." Cal lets this hang there. She *should* watch it before she judges. And he's not going to defend his job to her, or any other woman, for that matter.

"Oh," Laina breathes, more of a sigh than a word. "Is that all?" She stays on the line, breathing softly into Cal's ear.

"Are you okay?" Cal asks, suddenly firmly convinced that Laina is not at all okay.

"I've let everyone down," she whispers.

"Who are you talking about?"

"I'm a failure," Laina continues. "Look at the messes my clients are in. The Hutchinsons. Daisy Sullivan in jail. Franny in the hospital. I really believed in what I was doing; that in helping people face their truth, I was helping to heal them. I've let everyone down. Most of all myself."

Cal hates hearing her this way. From the first moment he saw her striding across the Hutchinsons' lawn, he recognized this woman had a special kind of power, charisma, strength. It's not like he expected her to have no soft underbelly, he's just shocked at how much it hurts him to see it exposed.

"Hey," he says, "you can't carry the burden of all that. You can only do what you can to help your patients. You didn't pull that trigger or drive that car, or give Franny cancer, or make her father embezzle money. And you're not responsible for whoever it is that's sick enough to be playing these games with you and your clients."

"I have to confess something," Laina says in a low voice.

Cal's heart skips a beat. *What now?*

"I hate to say it, but I do have a suspicion about one of my clients."

"Who?"

Her voice is small. "He's said things in session. . . . I can't reveal the details. . . ."

"Laina." Cal's voice is stern. "I know enough about the law to know that the possibility of harm to others overrides confidentiality. If you think one of your patients is behind all this shit, we have to let the police know."

"But what if I'm wrong? An accusation like this could destroy him!"

"What *are* you able to tell me?" Cal demands.

A silence falls between them. Cal imagines Laina in her soft bed, a tangle of her dark hair spread across a white pillow. "Do you want me to come over?" he asks impulsively.

"No," Laina says emphatically. She leaves it at that and Cal swallows his disappointment.

"If you think you know who's responsible, you have to tell me," Cal presses. "Enough damage has been done. You know that it's something I say about the news: that we're showing people the truth for their own benefit. You're not wrong about the power of truth, even when it hurts."

"I didn't want to believe it," Laina says, her voice softer again. "I still don't. But I think you might be right about George Holden."

"Is that creepy scarf guy?"

"Yes. I'll just say this: He likes to watch."

Cal is once again grateful for the symbiotic relationship he shares with Officer Cal Murray. With the promise of a tip-off in the event of confirmed criminal activity, Cop Cal employs the resources of the SDPD to provide Cal with an address and a little background. (No record, not even traffic tickets.) Now Cal is on his way to pay George Holden a visit.

Cal's done his own independent research as well. Holden's a widower. A retired IT guy, with a penchant for astrophotography. The kind of man neighbors always describe as harmless and quiet. After the bodies are discovered in his basement. And the IT background seems a promising lead; maybe he hacked into the BETTER LIFE network to access patient records?

George lives in a nondescript beige house in an unremarkable neighborhood. An RV is parked in the driveway. Cal doesn't know much about RVs, but he can tell this one is new. He knocks on the front door.

Creepy scarf guy comes to the door wearing an old black T-shirt faded to gray and a pair of khaki green cargo shorts. "Can I help you?" he asks warily.

"Hi, there. Mr. Holden? Cal Murray with Channel Five News. I'm working on a segment about local amateur astronomers and your name came up as a good possible interview subject. Might I have a few moments of your time?"

Holden looks pleased and acquiesces, holding the door open for Cal and welcoming him into the cramped living room. Cardboard boxes are stacked everywhere, some open and waiting to be filled, others packed and taped up tightly. Gesturing to the boxes, Holden says, "Sold the house. Going cross-country in that baby out front."

"Wow," Cal says admiringly. "Sounds like the trip of a lifetime."

"It is! Something I've always dreamed of. But it didn't happen when I was a young man, and then, well, my wife and family came along."

"But no time like the present, right? When do you leave? Are the wife and kids going with?" Cal knows that Holden's wife, daughter, and grandchild are all dead, but he's here to poke the bear.

"Solo trip," Holden says as a shadow crosses his eyes. "So. What can I tell you about our local astronomers? This isn't about the board infighting, is it?"

Cal has no idea what he's talking about. "No, no, nothing like that. We're thinking about a piece showcasing outdoor hobbies, and of course, astronomy should be included."

After a truly dull hour, in which Holden meanders on endlessly about the very infighting at his local astronomy club that he hoped Cal *wasn't* focusing on, Cal claims another appointment. He can't imagine how Laina listened to this guy drone on for weeks on end. Cal asks to use the restroom before he leaves, and Holden gestures him down a narrow hallway. "Second door on the left," he specifies.

The first door on the left is cracked open. Cal's steps hitch as he takes note of the extensive equipment stacked everywhere: computers and monitors, headsets, and a profusion of wires and camera gear of which Cal can make no sense.

After using the bathroom, Cal casually reapproaches Holden. "Couldn't help but notice your office setup. Pretty impressive. What's all that for?"

Holden stares at him like he's an idiot. "Astrophotography. What we've been talking about for the past hour."

"Of course. Hey, by the way, do you recognize me at all? I'm new to the station and I'm trying to see if I'm making an impact."

"I can't say that I do."

"Really? Not even that interview I did with a local therapist. Dr. Laina Landers? That one seemed to hit home with a lot of people."

Holden shifts back and forth at the mention of Laina's name, but keeps his gaze steadily on Cal. "Sorry, no. I don't watch much TV. I will say this, though . . ."

"Yes," Cal prompts.

"You're very articulate, you know. . . . So, let me know if you want me for your astronomy story."

"Thank you," Cal replies, his voice cold steel. He knows all too well the answer to this fill-in-the-blank: *"You're very articulate for a Black guy."*

Cal excuses himself and gets out of there fast. Holden's a weirdo, no doubt about that. And a racist. But is he malicious and depraved enough to be wreaking havoc in Laina's life?

CHAPTER TWENTY-FIVE

She knows she's off-kilter. So much has happened, both good and bad, in the last few weeks. Laina reminds herself that she's been through harder times and she'll get through this, although the oft repeated self-reassurance feels empty. A little normalcy, that's what she needs. A day seeing patients, doing what she's best at.

The Itos are up first. Their challenges with fertility are totally forgotten as they are determined to gossip about Peter and Tom Hutchinson (while pretending it's the last thing they would pry about). The session has a bumper car quality; Laina can't find a rhythm to the conversation, and finds herself disconcerted by the couple's ghoulish interest.

Laina's agoraphobic teenage Zoom client is next. The girl's been down every social media rabbit hole there is and announces, "Clare and *Tom* Hutchinson! I don't know who the fuck wants to see those two wrinklies bang, but it sure gives the husband a motive! Did you know? You must have known!"

As she logs out of the Zoom session, Laina feels a pounding headache forming. She fervently hopes that her next client is not as obsessed with the Hutchinsons as the first three have been. *This is the downside of the press,* she realizes.

Because Cal filmed me that night, everyone knows I treated Peter and Clare. Maybe Harley wasn't wrong, after all.

When her cellphone vibrates, Laina jumps, startled out of her morose thoughts.

"How're you doing, baby?" Cal asks. It's the first time he's used an endearment with her outside of the bedroom and with a little thrill, Laina's spirits lift.

"Hanging in. Thank you for being so kind last night."

"Of course," Cal says gruffly. "I paid George Holden a visit this morning."

"You didn't!"

"I did, but don't worry, he bought my pretext. Definitely a weird dude."

Laina swallows against the sudden flutter in her throat. "Do you think he's behind the harassment?"

"I'm not sure. Can you give me a little more information about him?"

"Cal. I'm just not comfortable—"

"All right," Cal cuts her off. "I get it. But I'm going to keep digging."

"I'm so ashamed," Laina says softly.

"About?"

"I couldn't see it," Laina haltingly explains. "Or didn't want to see it. I thought I'd really helped him after the deaths of his daughter and grandson. His recovery was a success, but mine as much as his. I wonder if my ego got in the way of seeing him for who he truly is."

"I can't speak to that, but I know you well enough to know that your intentions were good. And I shouldn't have to be the one to tell you about the complexities of the human mind. Don't beat yourself up."

"Thanks for that. It's just that I can't help wondering what else I've blinded myself to."

Harley strides into her office without a knock and Laina tells Cal, "I have to call you back," as she takes stock of Harley's aggressive stance. She clicks off the phone.

"What did she say?" Harley demands of her without preamble.

What is with this attitude? "I'm fine, thank you. How are you?" Laina replies tartly.

"Cut the crap, Laina. Did Kelsey keep her mouth shut?"

Laina contemplates Harley's level of agitation, and feels a sense of intense *dislike* creep through her system. "Yes," she answers him calmly. "Kelsey apparently adhered to the letter of the law. But she also intimated that *you* might have had an additional reason to keep her quiet. Do you know what she meant by that?"

Laina tries to read Harley's face, but he remains opaque. She expected a glib denial, an easy dismissal, which she'd prepared herself to distrust and parse for hidden meanings. Instead, she gets silence.

"Anyway," she continues, "Cal doesn't think she's involved. He says she's likely drinking herself to death but she doesn't seem spiteful." Laina's on the verge of sharing Cal's suspicions about George Holden when Harley pipes up.

"Someone sure is," Harley says sourly. "And it's going to destroy this practice. You've only made it worse by inviting that reporter in."

Laina looks at Harley's face and all her reasons for wanting out of this partnership jumble in her head. *He always had the quality of an exuberant kid. It used to charm me, but now it's just irritating. He seems more like a spoiled brat than the ambitious, aspirational crusader he was when we met. Has Megan's family money quelled the fire in his belly? Vanessa's right. I've outgrown him, which is just a sad fact. I've had to drag him along for months to get the new center going! Then there's his volatility. He wanted me to kill the interview with Cal, but he was the first one to suggest using Cal to investigate Kelsey. And now he's laying blame for that back on me? And the bastard hasn't offered me even a single word of consolation in the wake of the Hutchinson tragedy.*

"I think we should dissolve the practice, Harley." The words are out of her mouth before she has a chance to really consider them.

"That might be best," Harley replies immediately, to Laina's surprise. She opens her mouth to speak, but Harley cuts her off. "If we can reach the right terms."

Is that a hint of menace in his voice?

"That'll be up to the lawyers," Laina responds, keeping her tone cool. "Vanessa will represent me. If you must know, it was she who first suggested it might be time for us to go our separate ways. You'll have to find someone else."

Harley's face cracks in a wry smile and he tugs a hand through his spiky hair. For a moment, Laina remembers meeting him, all those years ago, when she was new to San Diego and Harley, not yet married to Megan, showed her the town from his native's perspective. Then he represented *all the promise of the new.* Now looking at him makes her ill.

"Good thing Kelsey knows how to keep her mouth shut," Harley says softly. "For both our sakes."

"I don't know what you're talking about," Laina protests. "After I realized she had that girl crush on me, I kept out of her way; I barely saw her."

"It's not what you saw. It's what she saw." Harley pulls off his sunglasses and meets Laina's gaze head-on. "If you know what I mean."

Harley has been holding out on her, she realizes with a flash of anger. Kelsey had brought him something that he's now lording over Laina. It must have been pretty valuable if she got him to fork over extra cash. Or maybe Megan's pockets are just that deep. And Harley's hung on to this tidbit all this time. For what? To have leverage on Laina when he needed it. She's furious.

Harley continues to drawl on in his infuriatingly casual voice. "But sure, I'll hire an attorney and we'll figure it out. I want the BETTER LIFE name and trademark, though."

Laina feels her face flame red. The pulse in the hollow of her throat beats a rapid tattoo. "That's bullshit, Harley. I came up with the name, the whole concept!"

Harley shrugs. "I want what I want. But let's keep this friendly between us. Let the lawyers handle it, fair and square, and we'll agree to go our separate ways with nothing but respect and appreciation for each other. Good for everyone, right?" He smiles, wolfish and insincere.

"Nothing I'd like more," Laina assures him. But her mind is reeling. She thought Harley might be disappointed about her proposal or maybe even get angry; she never guessed he would be *manipulative*.

"After all," Harley adds with a cunning smile, "with your client taking out his brother and all. And on the heels of the Daisy Sullivan disaster. And now the Goldstein girl? You need all the friends you can get."

Is he threatening me?

That suffocating feeling descends again like a miasma; that

sense that things are spiraling out of her control, leaving Laina gasping for breath and fighting for survival. An image flashes across her eyes: *scarlet blood splattering on slate-gray tiles*.

"What is it you want from me, Harley?" Laina chokes out.

Megan and the two little Weida girls, ages three and four, burst into the office. The little girls are both clad in pink tulle ballet tutus; Megan is matching maternal chic in a pink tank top over a white denim skirt. The girls are arguing and Megan laughs as they descend upon Harley. "They've been fighting all the way here about who was going to hug you first." She sees Laina and continues, "Hey, Laina, sorry to interrupt. How are you? We've come to kidnap Daddy from the office."

"No problem," Laina says. "Harley and I were just wrapping up."

Laina takes in the family tableau. Harley is in a tickle fight with his two pink princesses. Megan fishes out her phone in order to film the tussle.

It occurs to Laina that she always thought she was the smarter, more ambitious one of the two of them, the long-term strategic thinker. She'd believed this gave her a bit of an upper hand with Harley. She still thinks those things are true, but she'd underestimated how determined Harley would be to protect himself, his family, his cushy situation with his wealthy wife.

A thorny knot of sadness clings to Laina like a barnacle. She used to feel so much pleasure and pride every time she was here in her office, but that sense of quiet accomplishment feels distant now, tainted and tarnished.

This conversation may have been interrupted, but it sure as hell isn't over.

———

Laina parks her Jeep and clambers out, weary and longing for a shower and a glass of wine.

A thin sliver of light shines from the inside of her apartment and cuts across her welcome mat. Her front door is hanging slightly ajar. Her heartbeat quickens.

She glances around, the street seems dark and quiet, deserted. A soft yelp alerts her to her neighbor Pam Takeshita walking her little scrap of a Yorkie-corgi mix, Pepper. The pair are suddenly illuminated by a pool of light cast by a nearby streetlamp. Laina hurries over to them.

"Pam," Laina says breathlessly. "I just got home and found my front door open."

"Call 911," Pam advises immediately, scooping Pepper up in her arms.

Laina keys in 911 on her phone and hovers her thumb over the SEND button, hesitating. "You think so? I mean, I think I remember locking the door when I left, but what if I didn't?"

"Of course! What are you waiting for? Look at Pepper! She knows something's wrong." Rigid with fear, Pam clutches the small animal too tightly, and the dog yaps furiously. "Sshhh, Pepper," Pam soothes her little dog, easing her grip. "It's all right. You're a good little puppy, yes, you are."

Laina's mind races. Things have been set in motion; things she has no control over. She feels unmoored. She's always been careful about the box she keeps herself in, but things seem to be spiraling in a way that's pushing her not only out of the box but into free fall.

She presses SEND.

CHAPTER TWENTY-SIX

When Cal arrives outside Laina's condo, he's simultaneously cheered and horrified by the presence of two police cruisers with their twirling cherry beacons. Cheered because "the cavalry" has arrived, but horrified that Laina's home was violated by a break-in, as she'd informed him when she rang him right after she'd dialed 911.

Four uniformed cops are on the scene, and Cal does a quick sweep for his namesake before coming up empty. Laina's talking to one of the uniforms, arms wrapped protectively around herself as if warding off a chill, despite the warmth of the night. The pleasure he felt in being so forward in her thoughts is eclipsed by how shaken she looks.

A gray-haired Asian woman stands a few feet away from Laina with a small white dog cradled in her arms. Cal first notices the dog is wearing a knit sweater made from wool the same creamy color as her soft fur, a tiny pearl-trimmed velvet bow, and a long-suffering expression. He then realizes to his horror that it's the same woman who threatened to call the cops on him the night Tom Hutchinson was killed.

"Hey," he says, walking over to Laina. "I got here as soon as I could. Are you all right?" The little white dog yaps and snarls at him and the Asian woman watches him warily. He aches to enfold Laina in his arms, reassure her, make her feel safe, but it didn't escape his notice that Officer Diaz landed her hand on the butt of her service weapon as he approached.

Diaz's gesture is also noticed by Laina, who jerks her head in his direction as she addresses the cop. "He's a friend," Laina chokes out, her teeth chattering. Cal pulls off his blazer and drops it over her shoulders. The little dog begins to yap furiously.

Laina snakes her arms into the sleeves of Cal's blazer and wraps it tightly around her. "This is my neighbor Pam Takeshita," Laina explains to Cal. "And that fierce little creature is Pepper. I think you met but weren't properly introduced. They waited with me until the police came. No one was inside. But someone had been."

Cal's stomach gives a lurch of anxiety.

Two people exit the condo. Assessing their wardrobe and wary, seen-it-all faces, Cal guesses they are detectives. One of them says something to his partner before splitting away and advancing toward Laina and Cal with hurried steps.

"You're not that news guy?" The detective seethes with overt hostility.

"I am," Cal replies with forced equanimity. "Cal Murray, Channel Five. But I'm here in a strictly personal capacity as a friend of Dr. Landers."

The detective's creased face is skeptical. "That right, Dr. Landers?"

"Yes," Laina replies tersely. After a beat, she continues, "Can I go now? I've given my statement, and I'd really like to get out of here, get some rest. It's been a hell of a day."

Once cut loose by the cops, Laina thanks Pam for sticking with her and turns to Cal. The look of naked suffering on her face is unbearable. "Where do you want to go?" he inquires. "I'd take you to my place, but I'm still in the corporate apartment and it's a dump. But tell me where you want to go, and we'll go."

"Let's go to the Del Coronado," Laina suggests.

"Done."

Cal's never been to the Hotel del Coronado, but he knows of the famous landmark. The red-roofed Victorian main building was constructed in the late 1880s, although the beach-hugging property has expanded over time. And, as Laina informs him, the hotel has been famously haunted by the ghost of Kate Morgan, who shot herself at the tender age of twenty-four after a five-day stay in the hotel pining for a lover who never arrived, all the way back in 1892.

Although Laina balks at first, Cal persuades her to accompany him to register. He knows she's in shock and exhausted, but he wants to be sure she has first-class treatment and he knows from sorry experience that a Black man checking in alone can often be shunted off to a less desirable room, the kind that's out of the way and features a glorious parking lot view.

They're in luck and have no problem booking one of the cabana rooms for the night (Laina's preference over a room in the traditional "haunted" Victorian). Cal appreciates her choice when he sees the room: large and clean-lined with pale blue walls, earth tone accents, and crisp white bedding on the king-size bed; sliding doors reveal a private cabana opening directly to a sandy beach and foamy waves.

Laina makes directly for the cabana and curls herself into one of the cushioned daybeds, so that the ocean is in her direct view. Cal sits by her feet and pulls them into his lap. "Do you want to talk about it?" he asks.

"Tell me a really good memory from your childhood," she entreats, leaving Cal a little stumped. "Something that made you happy." Her tone is earnest and Cal wants to give her something genuine.

He debates his answer. He had relative privilege and pleasure growing up, as well as his fair share of sports triumphs and academic distinctions. But *happy* is a different story. His life has always had a slow rhythm beating powerfully beneath the surface, a song composed of his pervasive sense of *not really belonging* and the relentless pressure his father always put on him to *be more,* despite any and all of Cal's achievements.

Happy. What is Laina really trying to discern with this question?

"When I was nine, my class went on a field trip to the natural history museum. I missed it because I was home sick with chicken pox, and I was heartbroken. There was a traveling exhibit about the human body I was dying to see and now I wasn't going to get the chance. A few weeks later my mom showed up and took me out of school on the basis of a 'family emergency.' I was pretty freaked until she told me in the car we were going to the museum for the very last day of the exhibition and that it was to be our secret, from the school, from my brother, from my dad. That was a happy day."

"Secrets are so hard to keep." A frown creases Laina's brow. "Were you able to keep that one?"

"My brother knows. But I don't think my dad does to this day."

The waves tumble and crash with their beautiful, inevitable swells and ebbs.

"Listen," Cal continues, "I can get my buddy on the force to recommend someone to up the security in your place. Put some cameras out in front, take a look at your windows and such, make sure you're taking every precaution."

"Sure," Laina agrees in the same odd, flat tone she's had all night. "But I think there already are cameras out front? Didn't seem to stop them. Him. Whoever."

Cal excuses himself to make a call and steps back inside the cool blue hotel room. First he calls room service and orders a bottle of brandy. He has no idea whether Laina likes brandy but it seems like the appropriate drink for shock. To be on the safe side, he orders some food as well; brandy on an empty stomach might be a bad idea and he has no idea when Laina last ate.

With the order placed, Cal dials the other Cal Murray. What he learns is not reassuring: There was some sophistication to this break-in. There are security cameras already trained on the front entrance, maintained by an independent company the condo board contracts with, but they'd stopped working earlier that same day and a repair crew hadn't yet made it over to check them out. They now suspect the cameras were intentionally disabled. Another disturbing tidbit is that Laina's front door showed no sign of tampering; the intruder might as well have opened it with a key (a theory under consideration). In addition, the intruder had left Laina a gift: an easily obtainable spy camera with a note. Cal's heart races as Cop Cal reports the two words of its message: *Watching You*. Whoever is behind this has proven just how vulnerable Laina is.

By the time Cal disconnects from Cop Cal he's agitated beyond belief. He bursts back out into the cabana. "Whoever busted into your place wasn't some kind of amateur. The security cameras were disabled and you've got to change your locks! I also got a number for you, a guy who'll do an entire surveillance sweep, and you're not going home until all that's done."

Laina looks at him meekly. "Okay," she agrees.

Cal's surprised by her quick acquiescence. But also by his own dominating, protective impulse; his willingness to take command and assert his authority with respect to the question of her safety. *Is this love?*

"Did you know a spycam and a note were left inside your place?" he asks grimly. "The same message, 'Watching You.'"

"Oh my god," she whispers.

"I think we should tell the cops about George Holden."

Pink spots appear on Laina's pale cheeks. "We don't have any proof it was George," she counters.

"You can't protect him if he's behind this, Laina. You shouldn't."

"Let me think about it. Please."

Room service comes and they eat cheeseburgers with bacon and fries with ketchup. They take shuddery shots of brandy and guzzle water. After they've had their fill, they slip down to their skivvies and under the crisp white sheets.

Their bodies entwine in a pose of sheer mutual reassurance, touching at points from head to toe. It's not sexual, Cal realizes. It's more like he's been orbiting adrift and has found his home, each point of contact at foot or knee or shoulder a docking station to bring him in safely.

Happy. Cal's thoughts return to the story he'd told Laina about his mother; it's been forever since he thought about that day.

"Hey," Cal breathes into her ear. "Why'd you ask me about that memory before?"

"Sometimes," Laina murmurs, "when I need to calm myself down, I focus on a really good memory from my past. I try to ground myself there as a reminder that things can and will change. They always do. It's a reminder to myself to hold on for a change for the better."

"I get that." Cal props himself up on one elbow so he can look into Laina's eyes. "But why did you ask for one of my memories?"

Laina tries a wan smile, but there's an infinite heartbreaking sadness on her face. "My stock's run low. I wanted to borrow one of yours."

Cal kisses her on the lips. *This is love.*

Laina snuggles into the crook of his arm like she's a missing puzzle piece. "Tell me a bad memory," she requests. "Tell me something that hurts or something that you're ashamed of."

"Surely you don't need to borrow bad memories as well?" Cal teases. "Don't we all have enough of our own?"

"No doubt," Laina agrees. "I just want to know more about you."

Dazzled by the rush of his own burgeoning feelings, Cal decides to test the boundaries. He tells Laina about Nicole, the girl in Savannah who broke his heart. Not only did she abruptly dump him after ten months of what he thought was pretty serious dating, but she did so in a way that made him realize that while he was falling in love, she was just taking a rebellious side trip from her parents' expectations that she marry a nice *white* Southern boy.

"Is that what you think I'm doing?" Laina queries. "I'm not rebelling against anyone or anything, I promise you. This has taken me by surprise, I admit, but it's not some kind of game for me."

Cal strokes her hair. "Same here," he agrees. "But the really fucked-up thing about Nicole is that once I got, well, a little famous, she tried to win me back. She came over and pled her case, but I'd already taken the job here. Even better, when I saw her, I felt nothing."

"Nothing? Really?"

"I was mostly over the hurt by then. I felt sorry that she'd wasted my time. And a little sorry for her. But nothing *for* her." Cal thinks back on that day, how beautiful Nicole looked but how pathetic and desperate she seemed. The visit had only confirmed for him what he already knew: It was time to get out of Savannah and on to greener pastures. "Your turn," he says to Laina. "Tell me something deep and dark from your past."

Laina hesitates for a moment, tracing circles on Cal's chest with gentle fingers. "When I was eighteen, I was married for five months. I was young, obviously, and, well, vulnerable at that point in my life. He was older, thirty-four, and magnetic. He seemed powerful and that made me feel safe." Laina pauses and Cal gives her time. "Until he started beating me. And I realized the only safe place for me was far, far away from him."

Cal's heart tweaks at the idea of some asshole hitting Laina. He holds her closer. Dots her head with soft kisses.

"But it was a long time ago," Laina adds. "And no one has

ever hurt me quite like that again. But," she adds with a wan smile, "you can see why I'm slow to trust. You've broken my defenses down, Cal Murray."

Cal kisses her. Their bodies press even closer together. But Laina pulls away and holds his face between her two cool palms. "Promise me you'll stop investigating. Please. Let the police do their job and stay out of it. I've just found you and I can't have anything happen to you. Everyone close to me is being targeted!"

Cal knows that if he agrees to this he'll be a liar. Instead, he rains down kisses, working his way from her tender ear-lobe to the nape of her neck.

"I promise nothing will happen to me," he whispers in her ear, aware it's not the promise she asked for, but knowing that it's the only one he's willing to give.

CHAPTER TWENTY-SEVEN

Laina startles awake to the harsh sound of knocking. Reactions flood her system in rapid fire: fear, confusion, panic. *Where am I? Am I safe?*

As she rouses to full consciousness, she realizes she's at the Hotel del Coronado. But where's Cal? She's alone in the rumpled bed. Laina staggers to the door, pulling a sheet around her naked body. "Who is it?" she demands, angry at the crack in her voice that undermines her intended tone of fearless authority.

"It's us! Bringing emergency supplies!"

Laina recognizes the voice and smiles as she opens the hotel room door. Vanessa and Bex burst into the room bearing take-out bags from Breakfast Central (Laina's favorite!) and a heavy tote emblazoned with the logo for the Mysterious Galaxy Bookstore.

"How did you track me down?" Laina asks her friends.

"Cal phoned," Vanessa discloses. "Told me about the break-in last night and that he had to go out. He didn't want you to be alone." Vanessa gives Laina a sly look. "Maybe you want to put on some clothes?"

Laina shrugs into a robe as Bex mixes mimosas. Laina sips at hers, grateful for a little of the hair of the dog and also for the calm efficiency with which her friends set about unpacking cardboard containers loaded with breakfast burritos, along with sides of crispy bacon and biscuits with butter. They've also been to the bookstore, Vanessa announces, presenting the loaded tote bag. Cal thought Laina should stay put at the hotel and Bex thought she might need beach reading.

"Very considerate of the cub reporter," Vanessa observes. "So what exactly is going on with the two of you?"

Laina sips at her drink to avoid Vanessa's sharp eyes. "It's new," she says. "We're figuring it out."

"Give her a break," Bex admonishes Vanessa. "Take your lawyer hat off for one second and believe in love!"

Vanessa gives an undignified snort.

"Tell us about the break-in," Bex entreats. "You must have been terrified."

Laina sketches it out. Coming home after a brutal day. Seeing her door ajar. Her voice breaks and Bex takes her hands in his. Laina soldiers on. Calling the police. Calling Cal. The cops' discovery of the spy camera and its nasty little note. Coming to the hotel. Her friends take it in, sobered and silent.

"What do the police say?" Vanessa wants to know.

"Nothing much yet. The intruder might have had a key."

Bex releases a low whistle. "No wonder Cal wants you to stay here for the time being."

"Do you think he's maybe a little too perfect?" Vanessa challenges. "Didn't all this shit only start going down after he came on the scene?"

"There you go, pissing on romance again," Bex replies huffily.

"Think about it, Laina. When did you meet him? When he ambushed you in the middle of a crisis. Then, despite your proclivity for privacy, he somehow seduced you into an interview. And don't forget he immediately crossed a line by springing an unauthorized question on you! But somehow, he's wormed his way even closer, introducing you to a Hollywood agent, becoming your fucking white knight!"

"You're being ridiculous," Laina protests.

But Vanessa is relentless. "You can't ignore what's happening. One of your clients murdered his brother. Another rammed her car into her lover. A third had some kind of weird sick 'gift' dropped off at her doorstep."

Bex interjects, "Wait! I hadn't heard about that one! How is it I'm behind the times?"

"Vanessa!" Laina interjects. "I spoke to you about that under privilege!"

Vanessa plows on undeterred. "And now you've been warned that you're being watched? Cal's been to your place, right? Before last night? Who's to say he didn't make an impression of your key?" Vanessa pops a buttered biscuit into her mouth and stares at Laina defiantly.

"What possible reason could he have to . . . to . . ." Laina can't even finish her sentence, she's that astounded by Vanessa's theory.

"I did a little research into Cal Murray, cub reporter," Vanessa says grimly.

"You've both been holding out on me! I need another mimosa." Bex refreshes his drink.

"Do you know about the big story he broke in Savannah that propelled him to San Diego?" Without waiting for a reply Vanessa charges on, "He took down a *female doctor*, the head of a medical center, not only exposed fraud and embezzlement but also sex dungeons and a polyamorous lifestyle. Maybe it's a coincidence, but maybe it's not. Maybe he's on some kind of crazy vendetta against women in the medical field. I don't know, you're the shrink, you tell me."

Laina holds her glass out to Bex for a refill. Her head and heart are both pounding furiously. "But I've got nothing to expose!" she exclaims. "You *know* me. There's no fraud or anything like that in my life, and I barely date, much less have a sex dungeon!"

"Well, you do have one secret," Bex observes. "There is Mr. M."

Vanessa sweeps her glinting eyes from Bex to Laina. "Girl-friend, is the identity of Mr. M something that could blow up your life? Because if it is, you need to consult with your attorney right now."

Laina greets Vanessa's gaze head-on. "I swear he's not. He was a stupid mistake, but no."

Vanessa stares Laina down for a beat before continuing. "Okay. But think about what I'm saying. You barely know the cub reporter. Who knows what his agenda is?"

"For what it's worth, I caught a good vibe off the guy," Bex offers and Laina shoots him a grateful glance.

"Let's back up, then," Vanessa continues. "Have you spoken with Harley? Is he open to dissolving the partnership?"

"Yes, I spoke to him, uh, yesterday" is Laina's startled response. *Was that only yesterday?* So much has happened. *Watching You. The sweet and tender vulnerability of last night with Cal.*

"You're relentless," Bex admonishes Vanessa. "Let the woman eat her breakfast."

Laina takes a breath. "It's okay, Bex. It went fine. He's open to it as long as everything is fair."

"What does 'fair' mean?" Bex asks.

"He wants the BETTER LIFE trademark and name, for one thing."

Bex can't hide his astonishment. "And you're okay with that? You've been bitching about the guy forever, how he doesn't pull his weight, how you've carried him on your back while you built the clinic and the brand."

"He's been my friend and partner for a long time, Bex. I want to end things on friendly terms. Particularly now. My practice is in chaos; I don't have it in me to fight."

Laina can feel Vanessa's rapier eyes on her, assessing. To avoid her gaze, Laina busies herself by digging into the tote bag and sifting through the books Bex selected.

"Laina has a point," Vanessa easily agrees. Laina's head jerks up in surprise to see her lawyer lathering another biscuit with butter. Vanessa continues, "Harley and Laina are tied through their reputations even if they part ways. The more amicable we can keep their 'divorce,' the better. But, Laina, do me a favor, just think about the cub reporter without stars in your eyes and the memory of his hands on your—"

"I don't have stars in my eyes," Laina interrupts. "I'm not sixteen." She should have known that Vanessa wouldn't let go of her suspicions about Cal so easily. Vanessa is a shark. It's one of the reasons Laina hired her.

"I'm just saying be careful, okay?"

But even as she reassures her friend, Laina thinks about Cal's rigid determination in pursuing a story. She wonders what Vanessa would make of him snooping inside her walk-in closet. Or how he hangs on to questions like a pitbull who got ahold of a T-bone. She wonders what he's thinking about her situation and worries what he might be doing about it.

In principle, Laina believes in the healing disinfectant of light and sunshine. Secrets are toxic; she knows this all too well. But sometimes full disclosure can be poisonous as well, as she's seen with Clare Hutchinson and Daisy Sullivan. And then there's the question of context. Out-of-context statements can be so easily misconstrued, shaped to fit a narrative. She's seen it happen all too many times in her practice.

She changes the subject and escapes her own unsettling thoughts by proposing they call the desk and arrange for massages in the cabana. "What's the point of being stalked," Laina wryly jokes, "if it doesn't justify a spa day?"

CHAPTER TWENTY-EIGHT

Though he enjoys the thrill of knowing he's on to something big, Cal also can't help the tug of guilt he feels about expressly ignoring Laina's request he stop investigating. He puts in a call to Cop Cal and asks him to see what he can find out about creepy scarf guy, including his whereabouts on the day Franny received her "gift." It would certainly be useful, if not dispositive, if he could place Holden near Franny's condo around the time the package was dropped off. Next up is a visit to the tech firm from which George Holden recently retired. Holden's former firm occupies a renovated industrial building in a gentrifying part of town. Cal chats up a couple of people in the parking lot, hoping to pick up details about the man, but is warily shut down for the most part. The only woman willing to offer an opinion just says that Holden was "odd," and that Cal already knew.

Pulling up his notes from his "astronomy" interview with George, Cal zeroes in on one name: Vincent Corapi, the vice president of Holden's astronomy club, a man George clearly nursed a grievance against. If there's one sure way to get dirt on a person, it's to interview someone else he rubbed the wrong way. A quick internet search turns up three local Vincent Corapis. It's the middle of the workday and Cal suspects he'll have better luck later in the day if he wants to find the right Vincent.

Cal swings by George Holden's place again. It looks shuttered and empty; the RV no longer hulks in the driveway. Nonetheless, Cal parks his car and strides up to the entrance, ringing the bell multiple times and giving the door several sharp raps. Nothing. He turns to leave and sees an elderly woman peering at him from the porch of the dilapidated house next door.

"He's gone. Off on his big road trip, just like that!" the woman croaks. Clouds of white hair, fine as gossamer, ring her shiny pink dome.

"He left today? Was that unexpected?" Cal inquires, again registering that flip of excitement that tells him he might be on to something.

"Yesterday. But good riddance."

"Why do you say that?" Cal probes.

"He was a pervert, that's why," the woman says, drawing herself up to her full height of maybe 5'1" and thrusting her overlarge bosoms in Cal's direction. "Said he had all those telescopes for looking at the stars, but I know he was aiming them into my bedroom."

"Is that so? Why do you think that?"

"I was an actress, you know," the woman informs him. "A dancer. A looker." She pats her nimbus cloud of hair, as if checking it hasn't floated away.

Cal climbs back into his Mercedes. Did Cal, in fact, tip Holden off that he was on to him? Did Holden flee sooner than he'd planned, afraid he was on the verge of getting caught? Was his little "gift" to Laina a parting shot?

If that RV's still local, Cal wants to know. He puts a call

in to Cop Cal and asks for a quiet check on the plates for Holden's RV. His namesake surprises Cal with an unexpected piece of information of his own. "You're sure?" Cal confirms as he processes what this bit of evidence does to his theories about Holden. "All right. Thanks."

Cal next dials Laina, who answers on the first ring. "Holden's taken off," Cal announces.

"What? Since you saw him yesterday?" She sounds startled.

"Yes. The next-door neighbor said he up and left on his road trip."

"What do you think that means?"

"I'm not sure. The guy's one hundred percent a creep. It's possible he was behind it all, got spooked and took off quickly, and yours was the parting gift."

"The thought of him being behind this is completely heartbreaking," Laina says, sadness roughening her voice. "But I guess if he is, then at least the harassment is over."

"Let's hope so," Cal reassures her. "I'm not a hundred percent sure it was George."

"If not George, then who?" Laina sounds alarmed.

"I'm not saying definitively that it's not George," Cal replies. "The guy's definitely weird. But I pulled a favor with that cop friend of mine and Holden alibis out, at least for the package Franny got while I was at her place. He's got fifteen witnesses from an RV enthusiasts club meeting in Chino."

CHAPTER TWENTY-NINE

When Cal returns to the Del Coronado, he finds their hotel room empty, but the sliding doors to the adjacent cabana are wide open, the curtains whipping in the breeze. Laina's not out in the cabana either, but then he spies her walking down along the shoreline, her dark tresses floating behind her. The surf is rough, arcing waves crashing into foam.

Cal kicks off his shoes, rolls up the cuffs of his pants, and heads toward Laina. He calls out to her, but between the rush of the surf and the wind his words are lost. There's an ominous gray ridge of clouds hovering over the shoreline and it occurs to Cal that he might see his first rain since he arrived in SoCal.

When Laina finally turns and sees him, she takes his breath away. A high flush colors her cheeks, from the wind or the exertion of her walk, but it's more than that. She looks lit from within. Almost glowing. She wordlessly reaches her arms toward him and he embraces her, feeling overwhelmed by an emotion he can't quite name, until he recognizes it as *gratitude*. Cal realizes he might be in over his head with how he feels about this woman.

Laina takes Cal's hand and leads him back toward their room. The wind's gotten even more blustery and they have to push against both it and the shifting sand to make their way. They're finally back in their room, Cal shoving the sliding doors closed, when the first streak of lightning cracks the sky. The rain follows moments later.

"There's something I have to tell you," Laina says gravely. She still has that glow and with her wind-disheveled hair she looks like some kind of pixie sprite. "You need to know in order for us to move forward."

Cal very much wants them to move forward. He sits on the edge of the bed and pats the space beside him, inviting Laina to join him, steeling himself for what might come next. Cal thought he'd gotten both smarter and more self-protective since the last time a woman walloped him upside the head, but that doesn't mean it can't happen again.

"I lied when I told you I suspected George Holden."

"Why would you do that?" Cal exclaims.

"Because I was too ashamed to reveal who I suspected was really behind the harassment."

"Laina, you're confusing me. First you thought it was Kelsey, then George. Now you're telling me you don't think it's either one?"

"In order for you to understand, I need to tell you . . . about me and Harley." Laina pauses and looks at Cal with shining, open eyes. But she looks away before continuing. "We were friends first and then colleagues. We were a good team. But then, he started venting to me about Megan, his wife. I listened as a friend would, but tried to stay out of the middle of it the best I could. . . ." Laina trails off.

"But something happened to change that?" Cal prompts her.

"Harley began pursuing me romantically," Laina admits

with a sigh. "He'd pour his heart out to me and tell me no one understood him the way I did. We were together a lot, planning for the new clinic, caught up in dreams about what it might become, and ultimately I succumbed to his pressure to sleep together."

An electric instinct rises up in Cal. A desire to smash that fucker Harley Weida right in his smug face.

"The affair lasted about nine months. We ended it during the height of the pandemic. He was home with his family; I was home alone; it was just too hard. I sobbed for weeks. But then it was like I woke up from some kind of a spell. I couldn't believe I'd compromised myself in that way, professionally or personally."

Uncertain of the right words, Cal takes Laina's hands in his. He's a roiling mass of emotions. Shock at the revelation. Anger toward Harley. Protectiveness toward Laina. Fear about what this disclosure means about Laina's feelings for *him*.

"When we reopened and the plans for the new clinic realigned, I just tried to pretend it had never happened. I focused on the expansion and how through it we would be able to help so many more people," Laina continues.

"And Harley?" Cal can't help but interject. "Did he act like it had never happened?"

"Mostly."

"What does that mean?"

"Every once in a while, there'd be a dig, a kind of veiled threat about exposure and what it could do to both our careers."

"But that's right! To both of you. Why would he threaten to bring you down if he was going to destroy himself too?"

"I think just to fuck with me, honestly. To show he had power over me. The comments usually came with another . . . sexual overture of some kind. So when those calls came in to the clinic about him, I didn't know what to think. I know he's capable of cheating on his wife; I'm living proof. But I don't think he'd *ever* suggest running away with someone, unless she had more money than Megan does. When we finally broke it off, Harley made it quite clear he has no intention of ever leaving her. He likes the lifestyle far too much."

Cal bets he does. He remembers the expensive watch collection Harley has flaunted at their every encounter. *No point in not getting to the point.* "Laina, do you think Harley is the one messing with your patients?"

A spasm of naked hurt twists Laina's features. "I didn't want to believe it. I didn't want to believe he could be so vicious and vindictive. I was even willing to believe poor old George was responsible! Harley is my partner. I trusted him implicitly. But now I know it's true. He could even have made those accusatory calls about *himself*. To make it seem like he was also a victim."

"Beyond possibly trying to leverage you in a split he must have known was coming, how about just a level of batshit crazy? Only someone completely bonkers would pull these kinds of stunts!"

To his surprise, Laina laughs. " 'Batshit' and 'bonkers.' Not exactly diagnoses."

Glad to see her smile, Cal returns it. "You know what I mean."

"I shared everything with him while we were together," Laina admits. "Patient information, even my passwords! I thought we were going to come together personally and professionally, a seamless integration that would make us unstoppable. And of course, he had a key to my house."

The look of wounded vulnerability on Laina's face tugs at Cal's heart. "Could Kelsey have known about your affair?" He has to ask. "Could she have leveraged Harley with that information?"

"Yes. He told me after I confronted him. But she only knew Harley was having an affair. Apparently she secretly recorded his half of a phone call. She didn't know I was on the other end of the line and Harley made a unilateral decision to pump more money her way to keep it quiet. All of this is his doing. At least now you know everything."

Cal digests this information, pulling Laina into an embrace.

"You don't hate me?" Laina asks in a tiny voice.

"Of course not," Cal reassures her. "Harley, maybe. What a manipulative bastard." Cal kisses the top of Laina's head. "The questions, though, are this: What else is he willing to do? Planning to do? And how do we stop him?"

"I have the receipts, Cal. Of our affair. I told him that if he didn't stop, I'll tell Megan everything. Even if it means blowing myself up too. So, we've agreed. We'll dissolve the partnership. He'll get the BETTER LIFE brand and I'll start fresh with my teen clinic."

"And you're asking me to leave it all alone," Cal says flatly.

"Yes. So the two of us can move forward and leave the past behind."

Cal teeters on the edge of two emotions. One is an all too familiar sense of stubborn pushback, recognizable to Cal from interactions with his father. A realization that no matter the worry or care or even love that might lie behind a request, if it felt like an attempt at control, it set Cal's hackles rising. The second is a kind of delirious joy that Laina's as invested as he is in their relationship.

"I'm so glad I told you," she continues. "It's like a weight's been lifted off my shoulders. But please, for my sake . . ." She kisses him lightly on the lips. "And for our sake, please, yes. Just leave it all alone now."

Cal kisses her back, this time deeper. Lust flares between them like a struck match. Thoughts, worries, concerns, and speculations are swept aside as tongues tangle, nipples harden, hands travel, and clothes are shed. The rain outside pounds down as their two bodies merge as one, their cries and murmurs blending with nature's symphony of surf and downpour.

CHAPTER THIRTY

Cal's not as convinced as Laina seems to be that Harley will leave well enough alone; he seems like a master manipulator, the kind who likes to let his victims twist. Having gotten a taste for this particular brand of mischief, will Harley really be so willing to let it go? Or has he simply been able to persuade Laina to protect him just so he can strike again?

Cal's fueled with a determination to find enough leverage on Harley to shut him down permanently. Cal heads to his new apartment for a deep dive down the internet rabbit hole. He ignores the towering jumble of freshly delivered boxes and furniture as he settles down at the kitchen counter with his laptop.

Trolling through Weida's Facebook account reveals lots of pictures furthering the myth of Harley as a devoted family man. Cal goes further and further back in time, watching Harley's life unspool in reverse order: married with two little toddlers; father of one with a pregnant Megan; father of one; newlywed; groom; fiancé; single man. Things had moved fast with Harley and his bride, meeting to marriage in just six months. Cal wonders if Megan got a prenup.

Cal slows as he clicks back through photos of an anniversary party held in the Weidas' backyard back in 2019. Catered, with circulating staff serving both food and drinks. An elegantly dressed crowd of about twenty people or so in addition to the happy couple. He finds Laina in the corner of one shot and notes the grim set of her mouth, the side-eye she seems to be giving Harley, who's holding a glass aloft in a toast to his wife. Cal tries to figure out the point this represented on Laina and Harley's relationship timeline.

What a phony Harley is! With his parade of fancy watches and expensive, understated clothes, his pose as a dedicated husband and doting daddy. Cal rages on Laina's behalf and even on behalf of Megan and the two little girls; all of them deserve better than this fraud, this manipulative asshat who's exploiting them for what they can give him. Laina: professional lift. Megan: old money and status. The adorable blond daughters: the veneer of respectability that makes his true heinous nature seem impossible.

Cal has a rewarding "King of the Mountain" moment as he finally lifts his head from his computer and takes in the spectacular view outside the windows. With his slick new car parked in the garage below and his belongings freshly out of storage and here in the apartment, ready to be unpacked, he not only finally feels like he's home, he feels like he's arrived.

His pleasure is conflicted, as he knows his efforts to dig into everything he can find about Harley Weida are bound to aggravate Laina (if she finds out). But Cal can't help himself. It's in his nature to explore and expose. Knowledge is power, isn't that how the saying goes? And more knowledge is the only way he can truly protect Laina.

Getting up from the computer to stretch his back, Cal decides to give his research a rest and make some progress on his unpacking. He envisions the place all organized and elegant; cooking a gourmet meal to dazzle Laina while she sips wine at the kitchen island and asks about his day.

Pulling himself back from this fantasy (hell, he barely knows how to boil water), he turns his attention to organizing his bedroom, figuring that the simple task of transferring the clothes hanging on racks in wardrobe boxes into the closet will make him feel like he's accomplished a lot in a short amount of time. He's right; after he pulls the two wardrobe boxes out of the room it opens right up. Cal bought a new bed for San Diego, a symbolic gesture largely, but now he's even more pleased. He can break it in with Laina.

Jesus! He sounds like a lovesick puppy. Cal turns his attention back to the puzzle that is Harley Weida. Unpacking once again forgotten, Cal strides to the kitchen. What can he prove? Can he track Weida's movements and show he was responsible for the break-in at Laina's?

Back at his laptop, Cal cross-references the day before with Harley's social media. Harley seems to have documented yet another perfect family evening: playtime and dinner and bath time and books before bed, all meticulously documented, perhaps *overly* documented? Harley certainly made a meal of that particular evening's domestic bliss, more so than on countless other nights. Was he overcompensating? There's no way of knowing the precise time the package was dropped at Laina's since the security cameras were disabled, but it's certainly possible Harley made the trip after his daughters were safely tucked in bed and before Laina made it home.

He needs access to local CCTV. Cal broods, increasingly angry at Harley for the mayhem that has plowed into Laina's life. He's not sure how Harley accomplished everything, but

Laina admitted to sharing passwords and patient information during the course of their affair. A clever man would be
able to manage (and Cal suspects Harley is actually quite
clever under all his bourgeois bluster).

Cal recalls one piece of his father's (often unasked for)
advice that has always stuck with him: The best defense is a
good offense. What Cal needs now is proof of Harley's campaign of harassment. Something to give them leverage over
the guy beyond his affair with Laina, so that Laina's painful
secret can remain under wraps.

Watching

I have a new feed! Something to look forward to. As I flick on my monitors, I don't even check in on my other subjects; I'm too excited to see what my newly placed cameras will reveal.

Three images flicker to life. A modern apartment kitchen with a dining area. The adjacent living area. A bedroom. Labeled moving boxes are piled everywhere; a handful are open, sprouting packing paper and miscellaneous objects: a stack of books, a spill of sweaters, a wall clock. Cal Murray is in the efficiently designed kitchen, unwrapping a blender and setting it on a countertop. He digs back into the same box and pulls out another swathed object. It's a coffeemaker.

Cal pumps his fist in victory. It appears this was his sought-after object. Cal sets about brewing coffee, then digs back into the box and roots around until he unearths yet another swaddled package, which turns out to be a mug.

He has an elegance to his movement, there is no denying that; the confidence in one's body that a trained athlete can hold, even years after their days of sport are behind them. He seems to be singing softly, and as I have no sound on this feed I carefully watch his lips to see if I can make out the lyrics. I can't.

Cal sets about drinking his coffee and booting up a lap-

top that's on the kitchen island. I watch for a while longer, but am almost lulled to sleep by the monotony of Cal reading and sipping, reading and sipping. I get excited when he stands abruptly, but it turns out he's only refilling his coffee cup.

Watching paint dry may have nothing on watching someone else surf the internet. Particularly as his laptop screen is not within my view.

I have other responsibilities to tend to and so log off, counting the hours before I will be able to be back at my post. While I'm disappointed this morning's observations were dull as dirt, I'm gratified that my cameras are in and working. I'm sure Cal Murray will reveal more interesting details the more I watch, and hopefully soon, even though this particular session has been wasted time.

Things are accelerating. I'm someone with no more time left to waste.

CHAPTER THIRTY-ONE

Returning to her apartment is both a relief and a little sur-real. Laina had paid good money to make some changes: new "gotcha" lights on the exterior, a Ring doorbell with a camera and video feed, as well as new locks on the windows and door. She smiles remembering the naked worry on Cal's face as he'd grilled her about the new precautions. *"Did you use the guy my cop friend recommended?"* She hadn't, but she can't deny it's a bit of a thrill to have him acting so pro-tective. The world can be a dark and scary place; it's a com-fort to have someone to cling to, someone to provide shelter from the storm.

And now she's on the way to Cal's new place, a christen-ing of sorts of his new apartment and their new and dazzling intimacy.

Laina picks up a loaf of aromatic fresh bread and a box of kosher salt along with a bottle of wine on her way to din-ner. She'd heard once that bread and salt represented good luck in a new home, and while she can't remember where precisely she picked up this tidbit, it seems like a charming sentiment.

As she drives, Laina takes note of the many changes her

adopted city has seen in the time she's lived here. The sexily rehabilitated part of town in which Cal's new apartment is located is a steel and concrete representation of a kind of human resilience that never ceases to amaze her. People can and do rise from despair and adversity with time and investment, just like neighborhoods. Flexibility, adaptability, and a little bit of courage can truly change destiny.

Laina's feeling courageous herself. Ready to step out and away from Harley. Ready to step into something with Cal. Not that she knows exactly what that something is. But she also feels quite content not to define it just yet. After an admittedly combative start, things have unfolded naturally and comfortably between the two of them. Laina giggles thinking about the footage of her snarling into his cameraman's lens that aired on the eleven o'clock news. A *meet-cute*, as Cal's agent, Ryan, would no doubt describe it.

The same concierge, the impeccably polite Bennet Lau, is on duty and he greets Laina by name as she enters, directing her to the appropriate "no touch" elevator. Laina knows Cal's not quite settled in to his new place yet, but she's curious to see how his taste is reflected in his home. Cal dresses well, which is promising, but how he chooses to construct his environment will reveal even more.

Cal's waiting for her when she steps off the elevator, unburdening her of her packages and sneaking a swift kiss on her lips.

"Bread and salt," she explains. "It's good luck."

"So it is," Cal agrees appreciatively. "A Russian Jewish tradition. Bread so the homeowner never experiences hunger and salt so his life will be full of flavor."

"How did you know that?" Laina's eyebrows dart up in surprise.

"I grew up next door to the Abramoviches. Jacob Abramovich was my best friend for ten years. Anyway, come on in. It's a mess, but it's home."

It is a mess, but one Laina can appreciate. There's a brown cracked leather sofa and matching club chair that look comfortable. An enormous flat-screen TV and an elegant metal coffee table with a glass top. It's all a bit "masculine predictable," but leaned up against a wall are several visually striking framed prints that are kind of exciting, and a vibrant woven rug on the floor provides a lot of warmth.

The wine is opened, the Thai delivery order placed. They take their glasses of wine to the floor-to-ceiling window that hugs the dining area and admire the glittering city expanse.

"To your new place," Laina toasts. "Welcome home."

"Thanks for being the one to christen it with me," Cal replies.

Silence envelops them and Laina thinks it's the comfortable kind until she sneaks a sidelong look at Cal and realizes by the set of his jaw and the crease on his forehead that he's worrying about something. *Funny that I can read him so well already.*

"Okay, spill," she encourages him. "What's on your mind?"

"I want to go after Harley," Cal says. "It's the only thing that makes sense. Expose him for the manipulative bastard he is, in a way that gets him to leave you alone."

"Please don't pursue this," Laina entreats. "Don't you see what it will do to *my* career if Harley is exposed? I can't risk

it. I need to make our split quiet and official. Look forward
and not back."

"And just let him get away with all the crap he's pulled?
Think of how he's hurt your patients!"

"If it allows me to get distance from him successfully,
then yes. You see what kind of man he is. I can't afford to
antagonize him. But I need your expertise, Cal, your help. I
need you to teach me how to keep this all buried."

"That's not what I do."

"I know that, but I can't afford for any of this to become
public. Surely you know how to help?"

Cal reaches for Laina's hand. "I respect your desire to just
move on, but I think you're leaving yourself in a vulnerable
position."

"And how do I know that the temptation of the story
won't be too much for you?" she challenges him, fighting the
telltale flutter in the hollow of her throat. "That my whole
sorry tale won't end up on air?"

"You'll have to trust me."

Laina looks deeply into Cal's eyes. Withdraws her hand
from his grasp. "If you can't leave it alone, I don't know that
I can be with you. I don't even know if I can stay for dinner.
I'm asking you for the last time."

"Slow down. Surely we can talk this out and reach some
kind of compromise?"

Cal's voice has risen and Laina takes a step back and away
from him. She assesses the level of agitation reflected on his
face. Assesses the level of agitation in her own gut. Laina
fights her impulse to escalate this conflict, batting away the
vicious retorts she can feel forming on her tongue.

What do I really want from this man? If I push him away, will he be more or less likely to pursue this agenda? Oh god. Why is trust so fucking hard?

Laina changes tack, rolls her shoulders, and attempts a smile. "Of course we can talk about it."

"So you're staying, then?" Cal asks.

"For now," Laina says. "Can't have you eating all that Thai food by yourself."

CHAPTER THIRTY-TWO

Cal ultimately succumbed, both to Laina's entreaties to leave Harley alone and to the insane chemistry charging between the two of them. They'd broken in the bed just as he had hoped.

Laina had opted not to stay the night and now in the warm light of day, Cal struggles with what had been an implicit promise on his part to leave Harley Weida alone, at least while Laina disentangled herself from him professionally. He notes that in some ways Laina has a kind of charming naïveté, an ability to trust when she ought to be more cautious. Of course, they've both thrown caution to the proverbial winds with respect to each other, haven't they? A little knot of anxiety gathers deep in Cal's belly.

Don't fight the good stuff, he reminds himself. *We all get beaten down, but if we don't learn to open up we don't get to know love.*

That was something Mom used to say. Cal curses himself; he forgot to call her again. Cal checks the time. It's early, before seven. But a plan forms in Cal's mind and he mentally apologizes to Mom while giving her a raincheck.

Forty minutes later, Cal is parked across the street from Weida's decidedly swanky house watching as Megan bundles their two little girls into car seats fastened into her Cadillac SUV. They drive off, leaving Weida's sporty Audi still in the driveway. Cal will leave the fucker alone for Laina's sake but not before he looks him in the eye and hears Harley promise that he will cease and desist. If Cal is going to bury this story for Laina, he needs complete reassurance that Harley's sick campaign of terror is really over.

When Harley emerges, sporting yet another cashmere sweater and yet another expensive watch, Cal is ready to pounce. He's hoping the element of surprise will play in his favor.

"Yo, Harley," he calls out as he nears his quarry. "You got a minute?"

"Not really." Harley grimaces.

"There's no truth to the rumor that caller is spreading, right? You never came on to a patient? Told her you should run away together?"

"Of course not," Harley insists with strained indignation. "It's ridiculous." He waves in the direction of his house. "I have a perfect life, a wife I love, two great little girls. And I also have a practice and a reputation, both of which took me years to build. This is someone's fantasy or an attempt to discredit me."

Cal doesn't comment further on the topic, instead saying, "I understand you and Laina are breaking up your partnership. Why the split?"

Harley shrugs. "A million reasons, not one. But if you had to boil it down, I guess I'd say we just both want different things going forward. It's all amicable, mind you, been coming for a while."

"Is that right? There isn't anything you want to share?

Something that might be relevant to explaining the sordid mess that's plowed through Laina's life in the last few weeks?"

Harley fingers his car keys, clearly itching to get away from Cal. "What has she told you, then?"

Cal's surprised; he didn't think Harley would open up so easily. "Why don't you give me your perspective?"

Harley beckons Cal to follow him a few yards away from where they're standing and points. "Security cameras pick up everything." Harley positions himself so Cal is looking directly into the sun. If it's a power play, Cal's not having it. He slides on a pair of mirrored aviators that protect his eyes and force Harley to confront his own reflection.

"So listen, man, you're right to come to me. It looks like you're fucking lovestruck and you should know what you're getting yourself into."

Cal steels himself for whatever crap Harley is about to spew. A man who's done the things Harley has is no man at all in Cal's estimation. His reporter's nose sniffs the incoming scent of a self-justifying, self-pitying screed. He clenches his fists and wills himself not to hit the guy.

"Did you know Laina and I were lovers long before Megan even came into the picture?"

The mirrored shades are obviously inadequate to hide Cal's surprise at this statement because Harley leers at him. "I guess not. But yes, when we launched the clinic we were together. We split after the first year."

"Why did you split?" Cal's not necessarily buying what Harley is selling, but he might as well listen to the whole sales pitch.

Harley looks at him with that smug, supercilious face,

and Cal wants to hit him even more. "A million reasons, not just one," he says airily, perhaps deliberately parroting his response about the partnership breakup. "But in part because I met Megan and let me just say this, Laina did not let go easy."

"Why didn't you break up the partnership then? Why stick it out?"

"It was the prudent thing to do, professionally. The clinic was just getting a reputation. We had been friends first and I thought we could slide back into that. She assured me we could and it was fine at first. Laina seemed to welcome Megan, even helped throw her bridal shower. But then it became clearer and clearer she was having a hard time letting go of me."

Horrified that a therapist, someone charged with the mental well-being of vulnerable people, would exploit those vulnerabilities for his own ends, Cal interrupts. "I don't know why I should believe a thing you say. You're despicable; the things you've done have had consequences! People have died! How can you sit there and whine about Laina having a hard time 'letting go'! Nothing justifies the shit you've pulled."

Harley gives Cal a sly look. "And just what is it you think I've done?"

Cal is done playing games. "It stops now. Do you understand me? You and Laina are going to go your separate ways and I mean *separate*." He punches an angry fist into his opposite palm.

"Are you threatening me?" Harley's face flushes red and Cal rejoices. He finally got a reaction from the smug fucker.

"If that's what it'll take" is Cal's steely reply. "You got what you wanted. So end it now."

"Are you actually suggesting I pulled all that shit with Laina's patients?"

Cal doesn't dignify Harley's bluster with a response.

"Oooh boy. Have you got it wrong. Not me, buddy," Harley chastises. "Why would I possibly want to do that? Damage to Laina is damage to both of us. I've turned myself inside out to keep our thing quiet. Forked over extra cash to McKendrick, even."

"Stop playing games."

"I'm not."

"So just who is responsible, then?"

"I have no fucking idea. But you can take your threats and shove them."

Cal has had enough. He heads back to his car, slamming his door with satisfying force. He's no shrink, but clearly this guy has no business being one either. He's manipulative, devious, *ugly* in spirit, mind, and heart. Cal's going to have to talk to Laina again, convince her that Harley can't be trusted. Surely she'll see that the exposure of an affair that she'd been seduced into would be less damaging than whatever else Harley might have up his sleeve. Harley should take the full brunt of punishment for his sneaky and sick acts. And isn't Laina the one who keeps talking about the truth being liberating?

Laina had asked him how to bury the story, and Cal has no answer for that. But he does believe that there's power in getting *ahead* of the story. If Harley decides to blow Laina up, she'll inevitably be on the defensive. Cal's father's advice about a good offense being the best defense flashes through his head again, along with this sudden thought: *Maybe I've been too hard on Dad. Just like he's been too hard on me.* The thought's gone as quickly as it comes, but connects up to his next one, which is pity for Harley's two little girls. How can they possibly grow up with him as a father and remain unscathed?

Cal reminds himself to watch his empathy switch. It needs to be kept firmly in the off position in the service of good reporting. He reassures himself that exemptions for children and cancer patients are probably permissible before turning his attention to his next steps.

As he drives, the conversation with Weida keeps prickling at him. He thinks the man is a pathological liar (and makes a note to research the actual definition and characteristics for a better understanding of his adversary). But why would he lie about the timeline of his affair with Laina? Likely an attempt to mess with Cal's feelings for her, get him to not trust her so he would back off. Another sign the deviant is not done with his spiteful games.

Cal marvels at this protective instinct, something novel and delicate within him. Even when he thought he might have been in love before, he's never felt this sense of responsibility for someone else's physical and emotional well-being.

He glances at the clock. Just after eight. Cal bites the bullet and calls home. His mom picks up on the first ring.

CHAPTER THIRTY-THREE

Happy news for a change! The Itos had been thrilled to share they were finally pregnant. Hands clasped and smiles wide, they'd thanked Laina for her support during their infertility journey. Laina couldn't help but beam back at the two of them as a little piece of her brain ticked over the fantasy of a baby with Cal. She'd never thought much about being a mother before, but maybe it's just a question of the right partner.

Laina's making some post-session notes when her office door is flung open without warning. She jumps in her seat. It's Harley, glaring at her like he's Medusa hoping to turn her to stone.

"What was that all about, sending your attack dog after me? At *my house*?"

Laina stiffens. "What? I did no such thing."

"I'll just bet you didn't. He *threatened* me, Laina. We'll dissolve the partnership as quickly as possible. In the meanwhile, while we're still in a shared space, do your best to avoid me and I'll do the same by you."

Harley stalks out, slamming the door behind him. Laina winces. Rubs her temple where a headache is forming like a storm cloud. Cal went to Harley after she specifically asked him not to do so, and after a night of what Laina perceived as trust-inspired fantastic sex.

She tries to rise above the gut punch by reminding herself that people's contradictions are what make them interesting, but it's impossible; all she feels is betrayed.

Cal probably thinks he's protecting her. If he only knew! Laina takes a deep breath.

The white knight attitude is charming in its way, but also old-fashioned and a potential warning sign about future behavior. Trust, that fragile bridge, collapsed again. It's clear Laina will have to find a new tactic to convince Cal that a wide distance is the only thing that should be between him and Harley Weida.

Watching

Projecting the right kind of demeanor can allow one to brazen through almost any situation. In some instances, it's best to be invisible, a technique I'm proud to admit I've perfected over the years. It's enabled me to slide unnoticed and under the radar in a host of situations, allowed me to witness all sorts of naked emotions. This ability is a valuable asset for someone like myself, an observer and collector of human frailties.

In other situations, confidence is needed, and in some instances, arrogance. In order to get into Cal Murray's apartment, I approached Bennet Lau, one of the building's concierges, with precisely the right level of quiet, confident assertion.

Having established my bona fides for access to Cal's apartment with Lau, I don't risk encountering someone else on duty. He greets me now with a friendly smile and sends me right up. This is another thing I've observed: Routine can be my friend; people are easily reassured that routine represents rightness.

I'm frustrated with my camera-feed observations of Cal's apartment. While my recordings revealed that Cal spent much of the day on his computer, making notes while scowl-

ing furiously, the angle of my feed never let me see where those searches were taking him. I need to know what he knows so I can plot my next move. Luckily, my camera did reveal enough of his keyboard that I was able to read his computer password. I also know he's gone out and left the computer behind, so I seized my opportunity. If someone's coming after me, I need to be prepared with every weapon in the arsenal.

I let myself into his apartment and stride to his laptop, wasting no time. I have no idea when Cal will be back and know I need to move quickly. Sliding onto a seat at one of the barstools hugging the kitchen island, I flip open the computer and enter the password: anchorman#1.

I'm in.

The internet search history tells a story, of course it does. Cal has been digging deep, and where he's been going with his research makes my head spin.

Shutting the computer with a decisive click, I calculate my next moves.

CHAPTER THIRTY-FOUR

Cal usually revels in solving puzzles involving corruption, criminality, malfeasance, and wrongdoing; the thirst to do so is the very thing that drove him into investigative journalism. However, the threads of the story line currently in front of him refuse to interlock in any satisfying way. He has to admit to himself that his frustration is colored by his unease about the differing versions of their romantic history presented by Laina and Harley.

Why the different versions? Who is lying and why? It has to be Harley, but why admit to the affair and not the time-line? Is there a gain for Harley in that version of events beyond messing with Cal's head?

While Cal's initial dive into Laina's social media presence back when he first researched her revealed modest disclosure and a highly focused and controlled image, he knows Harley lives way more out loud. Once back at his apartment, he can't resist digging further back in time into Harley's social media, searching for clues as to the truth of the relationship and its timeline.

He feels mildly disloyal to Laina as he does this, but Cal knows he'll feel disloyal to himself if he doesn't.

His search is inconclusive. There are pictures and posts of

the two of them in the pre-Megan days, hiking, at restaurants, in the Silverwood Wildlife Sanctuary, at the San Diego Zoo. But they very well could just be photos of two friends, as there's nothing romantic or sexual in their poses, and no "relationship status updates" that indicated they were ever a "social media official" couple.

After diving down this rabbit hole, Cal decides to further research Laina. Another pang of guilt stabs at his gut, but he reminds himself to not be a fool; this is the reason God invented the internet.

He begins by pulling up the file he'd assembled after their first encounter. All the facts he'd accumulated are there: Berkeley, UCLA, the local girls' empowerment organization she supports, clips about the clinic, articles published on trauma, PTSD, and domestic abuse. It's the perfect profile of the consummate professional successful in her field, the most personal photos being "after" shots of her condo's renovation to her specifications. Cal zooms in on a photo of Laina on her pink velvet pouf inside her newly renovated dressing room. She's posed in front of her accessories pegboard, casually dressed and smiling. She looks adorable, but Cal frowns at the photo, aware that while he can't put his finger on what disturbs him, he's certain that something does.

Cal wants to believe the happy truths about Laina revealed through his research with every fiber of his being. But he reminds himself that no one is perfect; perfection is an illusion that almost always conceals something fetid and oozy, just waiting to seep out.

Digging further back in time, Cal explores younger Laina's online presence, finding a similarly skittish relationship with social media, unusual for a woman of her generation.

Cal frowns and searches a little more, with similarly lean results.

There's no crime in being shy of social media, Cal reminds himself; he himself uses it to check out other people far more than as a tool for his own self-promotion. He has a YouTube channel of his reporting clips, but he, like Laina, tends to keep his personal life more on the down low. He liked it about her when he first delved into who she was, and he likes it about her now.

After almost an hour of sifting through the detritus of the internet, uncertain of why or what he hopes to find, Cal finds Laina in a Berkeley photo spread taken her freshman year. Her hair is way longer, almost down to her waist, but she wears that same serene, shining demeanor that transfixes Cal now. He zooms in on her features but the image is of poor quality and they become grainy and indistinct.

Each of the freshmen in the photograph is captioned with their hometown, showcasing the class's geographic diversity, with Laina's listed as Kent, Washington. Just for the heck of it, Cal searches "Laina Landers, Kent, Washington." Zippo. He digs a little more and discovers Kent has four public high schools. Starting there, Cal tries to see if he can discover which Laina might have attended, but gets stymied when he realizes that while he can email to purchase yearbooks for the graduation year in question, they are not readily available online. He shuts his laptop and rises abruptly. *What the fuck am I doing? What do I think Laina was up to in her high school days that's going to shatter my earth?*

Cal owes Mike a call; they're supposed to meet up to chase down another suspect in the human trafficking ring, but he stands at the center of his apartment gripped by a disturbing inertia. He contemplates the boxes still to be un-packed, the pictures to be hung. He remembers his fantasies of Laina integrated into his life in this apartment, and to his horror, *that* flip churns in his belly.

Cal snaps his fingers as he remembers Laina's confession about her doomed teenage marriage. Is Landers her married name? Maybe she kept it despite the quick divorce? Can a more elaborate picture of the young Laina be revealed by searching her maiden name? Cal does a quick check on the steps necessary to obtain a marriage certificate from Washington State. It's an elaborate process, requiring forms and documentation, and Cal recognizes that he doesn't even know Laina's maiden name, much less if she got married in Washington. She could have run off to Vegas, for all he knows.

Why can't I let this go? He wants to trust Laina, he *does* trust her, he just wants to know her, there's nothing wrong with his digging. Anyway, he'll see Laina later. He resolves to ask her point-blank about Harley's version of events. After all, Cal knows Harley is a monster; maybe Laina can intuit the reason he would lie. In the meanwhile, he'd better get on the stick and start working.

If Cal wants to achieve his anchorman dreams, he needs to break another big story as the next step. Give Ryan an-other sexy set of clips to promote. He can't afford to get distracted. Laina will no doubt clear everything up about why Harley lied, and hopefully Cal put enough fear of god into him that he'll stop his bullshit. He texts Mike that he'll swing by to pick him up within the hour.

All will be well, he reassures himself. *Put your head down and go to work. You'll talk to your girl later and settle your soul.*

CHAPTER THIRTY-FIVE

Laina's invited Cal over to her place under the guise of inspecting her new security system, but she has more than one surprise planned for him. She puts a bottle of white wine on ice and lays out a spread of nibbles: cheese, crackers, olives. She then dresses carefully, inspecting the dresses hung in her orderly walk-in closet cum dressing room and selecting a clingy, deep emerald-green number that she knows complements her hair and eyes.

She puts on a pair of sandals with leather straps that climb up her calves. A necklace is dropped over her head so that a golden heart locket nestles in her cleavage. She sprays a cloud of musky perfume and walks through it.

Staring at her reflection in the heavy-framed full-length mirror on the back wall of her closet, Laina is pleased with what she sees. The green dress is quietly sexy, but the strappy sandals add a killer touch. Cal's explained his theories about women and their shoes, and Laina smiles in anticipation of his reaction.

She's anxious, though, there's no denying that. Laina's hand trembles as she applies a deep crimson lipstick. She has so much to share tonight and so much is at stake. *What if Cal pulls away from me? What if I sabotage myself and fall prey to that all too familiar instinct to push him away? No. These are not possibilities. The evening will unfold exactly as I envisioned it.*

The doorbell rings and Laina checks the new Ring app on her phone and she can see it's Cal outside. *Here we go.*

Cal looks as sharp as ever in a well-cut blazer, dark wash jeans, and an opal-blue button-down shirt. He's brought a bottle of her favorite Sancerre.

"That's so thoughtful, thank you," she says as she ushers him in. "There's a bottle chilling in an ice bucket on the counter, so I'll pop this in the fridge."

When they each have a glass of wine and Laina's taken a large gulp of hers, she shoots a quick glance over at Cal, just in time to see his eyes slide away from hers. Is it her imagination, or is he being unusually quiet? Laina takes another swallow of wine.

"I went to see Harley this morning," Cal says.

"I know," Laina acknowledges. "He told me. He was not happy about it."

"You're angry." Cal says it as a statement of fact.

"I was," Laina concedes. "But I understand you want to protect me. That's flattering in its way."

Cal looks at her with obvious relief in his eyes. "He's dangerous. You're blinded by him in some way that I can't understand. Look at all you've accomplished. I ask you, why would you let Harley screw with that?"

"The answer might not be the neat and tidy little solution you're looking for."

Cal positions himself by the window. His face is largely in shadow and Laina strains to read his expression.

"I'd just like you to be truthful with me," he responds.

"Do you know something that I don't? I nearly slugged Harley! Do you realize the nightmare it could have been for me if I had, and he'd pressed charges?"

"I told you to stay away from him!" Laina twists her hands tighter around the stem of her glass, considering her next words carefully. "Look, Cal, my life's been defined by something that happened when I was a teenager. It's changed the way more than one person has looked at me. I don't talk about it anymore, but I'd like to tell you."

"I'm listening."

Laina stands to flick on another lamp. If she's confessing her sins and their inspirations, it should be under the healing rays of bright light.

And she wants to be able to read Cal's face.

"When I was sixteen, thugs invaded my family home and my mother, father, and brother were murdered. It was a headline grabber at the time, back in Long Island where I grew up. I don't know why I was left to live, unharmed; it haunts me every day. A kind of survivor's guilt, if that makes sense."

Her words swim in the air between them. Laina finds she's holding her breath, fighting that flutter in the hollow of her throat.

"I'm so sorry," Cal says. "But why would that change how anyone feels or thinks about you? It's awful, but you were a *victim*."

"I hate thinking of myself that way! I've fought against it ever since. But I can't deny that the murders and their aftermath affected me."

"How could it not? But I don't understand what this has to do with Harley."

Cal's expression is curious and sympathetic, so Laina feels encouraged to continue. "After the 'incident,' as everyone began to call it, I was sent to live with my aunt and uncle and cousin Danny in Kent, Washington. My aunt Cindy was my mother's sister. They tried, but it was bizarre. I was in a house with a father and a mother and a 'brother,' but none of the people were the *right* people. I felt like an outsider all the time. You get that, I know you do."

Cal nods. And he does get this, she's sure of it; they've talked about the feeling of not quite belonging many times.

Laina sips at her wine. "I was in a dark place. I coped by trying to be perfect, because I never wanted anyone to see how shattered I really felt. I couldn't stand people's pity, so I pretended I was *fine*. Of course, I wasn't. I was always *performing* well, good grades, no obvious behavior problems, I got into Berkeley! But my freshman year, well, I started slipping."

"I saw a picture of you from back then. That article about freshman geographic diversity."

"Doing your homework on me?" Laina says with a little laugh. "Yeah, that was, like, the first week of school. By the end of the quarter, I had married my abuser and was using all kinds of shit to dull the pain. My aunt found me a therapist, who helped me get out of the marriage, off the drugs. She inspired me to spend the rest of my life helping other people change theirs."

"And you've done that! Laina, you're confusing me. I'm sorry all that happened to you, but how does it relate to what's going on now?"

"It started with Clare Hutchinson," Laina says. "When I saw Clare right after the night Peter held her at gunpoint, she told me a partial truth. She admitted to knowing about Peter getting a sex tape but did not confess her partner was Tom, or that she was the one who had sent the video to Peter."

"How does that matter?"

"The point is, the thing that struck me hardest about her in that visit was that Clare was *free*. She was ebullient! After fighting for a marriage in which she felt fundamentally betrayed, she was relieved beyond belief that it was finally over."

"Marriages end every day without sex tapes and hostage situations," Cal replies drily.

"Of course they do. But Clare inspired me."

"To do what exactly?"

Laina walks close to Cal, fully aware of the power of the attraction between them. It's not just physical. She's never felt so seen, accepted, or understood by a man before; it's heady. She knows he'll see things as she does; he has to. "You see, I didn't know about her role in the making or the sending of the video. She portrayed herself as a victim who didn't know she'd been filmed or how her husband got the damn thing, but who found unexpected liberation from the truth coming out. And that got me thinking."

"About?"

"Harley, for one thing."

"Yeah. About Harley," Cal interrupts, his expression now guarded, wary. "He has a very different version of your relationship than the one you shared with me."

Laina takes a deep breath. "I was too embarrassed to tell you the truth, but here it is. He's used me as his *side piece* for years. I thought I was in love with him, and he always kept me just within arm's length. He tortured me before, during, and after his marriage to Megan. And I mean during. He came over and fucked me after their rehearsal dinner."

"That's classy. Why did you allow it to go on?"

Laina can't quite read Cal's expression, but knows that if she can just explain, he'll understand. "Harley had me believing that I couldn't succeed without him. He was my therapist too, until last year. It's taken me a lot of time and work to be strong enough to walk away from him. And when I got the strength, I couldn't help but want to pay him back, just a little bit."

Laina has that glow again; that unusual radiance of purpose she'd had that night on the beach when she'd first confessed her relationship with Harley (and where Cal had felt himself tumbling even harder into love). Tonight, though, her shine is not igniting Cal with its light. He's fighting that telltale uneasy flip deep in his gut, insistent and relentless.

"You made those calls about Harley, didn't you?" he challenges her.

"I did," Laina crows, seemingly delighted that Cal figured it out. "I took a page from Clare Hutchinson and decided to free myself from his control, take the narrative back. Smear his reputation, but keep mine intact."

And this unnatural, beatific glow that Laina radiates? It used to be alluring, now he finds it unnerving.

"What else did you do?" Cal asks in a level voice that miraculously belies his inward turmoil. "Tell me about it, Laina. Please."

Laina takes one of Cal's hands. He fights the urge to flinch as she begins to speak in low, fervent tones. "I've always wondered, just how much pain can people bear? Of course, that question was personal at first; how much could I bear? I felt like I deserved all the pain in the world for surviving while the rest of my family died, and I did everything I could to seek it out."

She's so beautiful, so vulnerable. He wants to hold her. He wants his ugly suspicions disproved. He wants the knot in his stomach to unclench. It won't.

"But I saw how to liberate myself! Inspired by Clare, I made Harley squirm for the very first time in all our years together. From there, it was a natural extension to see how I could use the same philosophy to help my patients. To liberate them from their past narratives, the way I've liberated myself from mine, and Clare did from hers."

Despite the wretched knot at the pit of his stomach, Cal knows he has to continue on with this conversation. The notion of a great love in his life may be dashed against the rocks again, but there's a story here, a big, fat, juicy one.

"Did you have something to do with Daisy Sullivan's photos getting uploaded?"

Laina looks at him, tremulous with what appears to be relief and excitement. She nods her head vigorously. "Daisy was trapped by shame; she needed to be freed!"

"Daisy nearly killed a man! With her children in the car!" Cal's response is quick and tart. "He may never walk again and she's probably going to jail. Her kids will be traumatized for life. You call that freedom?" Cal knows his voice is rising, but he can't help it.

How could she have done such a horrible thing? Worse, how could I have never suspected it?

A frown creases Laina's face. "Well, I never would have

predicted that Daisy would do something like that! She had no history of violence. But I think it's worked out for the best in the end, don't you? Daisy's been proven unfit as a parent, and surely that would have happened eventually. And Brad Sullivan came back, so the kids are reunited with their dad! Clearly a better solution for everyone."

"I don't think Daisy Sullivan looks at it that way. Or Mark Victor." Cal's reply is as sharp as broken glass.

Laina nestles so close to Cal he can smell her shampoo and musky perfume.

"You have to see the bigger picture!" Laina exults. "Take Franny, for example. She needed to knock her father off his pedestal. She knew what he was up to before he was arrested, but she was so determined to protect her image of him that she couldn't accept other kinds of help."

"You left the oil-soaked bill." Cal's voice sounds flat and harsh in his own ears.

"Yes. I tipped the FBI too, about a safe deposit box key Franny had told me about. All for sound reasons, although perhaps not quite with the intended result. On the whole," Laina muses with a speculative half-smile, "my tactics were successful. I think I'll make some modifications, but I believe this kind of therapy will really benefit some of my other patients."

"It can't be legal, what you're doing. It's harassment." Cal takes an involuntary step back and away from Laina but her angelic smile only grows.

"My patients sign a waiver. Anything I deem therapeutic is fair game. Don't you see? It's all perfectly protected. And I'm helping people! Liberation through truth, right?"

It occurs to Cal that the provocative, shadowy doubts

he'd been squelching about Laina are far outstripped by reality. It may not be a clinical term, but she's batshit crazy.

"I knew you'd understand," she continues, eyes and face shining. "We're so aligned, you and I."

"Tell me more," Cal encourages, both sickened and exhilarated by the unfolding details. "I want to understand. You were very clever, weren't you? You turned my attention first to Kelsey McKendrick, and then to George Holden."

"Yes! You were so determined to find the culprit and Kelsey was an easy choice since Harley thought she was behind it from the start. But once you ruled her out, I had to agree. And then, well, George. I felt bad about pointing you in his direction but he was perfect, soon to be off on his road trip, out of town, no longer a threat. If only he didn't have that alibi for the box left at Franny's. I had to do something; I knew you'd keep digging."

"So you scapegoated Harley instead?" Cal asks. He feels as if he's speaking through a fog, needing deep, focused concentration to push even simple words out.

"You wouldn't stop," Laina says simply. "Harley's a bastard. Why not lay the whole mess at his feet?" Laina strokes Cal's jaw. "I knew you'd get it. I've spent most of my life hiding the truth of who I am. People don't always know how to react around tragedy. But we understand each other."

Something shifts in Laina's eyes; Cal realizes that she's suddenly very, very far away from the here and now.

"I want to tell you everything," she whispers. "How I came to. Bound. Gagged. Covered in their blood. I survived, but all the others died."

Cal recognizes he needs to proceed cautiously. He stays silent, fighting his urgent impulse to pull away from her.

"All that blood splattered on the gray tiles," Laina murmurs into his ear. "Splattered on me."

Cal stiffens, but Laina only nestles closer. "You see? I can tell you anything. I can tell you it all. We're so perfect together."

"The appearance of perfection usually masks something completely different, in my experience," Cal chokes out. "Decay. Perversion."

Laina pulls away from him, her eyes suddenly razor focused. Her beatific smile evaporates. "You're supposed to understand," she falters uncertainly.

The hurt in Laina's eyes twists at Cal's heart. Her face is suddenly that of a little girl. Cal's heart is breaking and a rising sense of panic threatens to engulf him. He's been vulnerable with this woman, exposed a truthful side of himself. She's capable of taking intimacies and perverting them; what will she do with his? And now that she's admitting all of this, what does she expect? That he will *condone* her acts? He can't restrain himself any longer.

"How could you squawk at me about protecting poor fragile Franny Goldstein when you had a hand in tormenting her? Even worse, how can you say it worked out for the best for Daisy Sullivan and her poor kids?"

"You are supposed to understand. We're alike, you and I, we've acknowledged it a hundred times," Laina protests.

"Not alike enough for this," he replies as gently as he can. "I'm going to go now," Cal says with the tone one would use to quiet a hysterical toddler, firm but calm. He puts his wineglass down on the coffee table, but when he takes a step toward the door, Laina blocks his way.

"No."

"Laina, you can't keep me here against my will." Cal tries to toss this off lightly, with a casual laugh, but his voice is strained.

"No, but I could scream!" Laina says coquettishly. "I could call 911 and claim you attacked me." A sly look contorts her even features. "Not that I'd do that to you, Cal. Because you're on my side, I know you are. We're the same."

With this threat to call the cops on him, something cracks deep inside Cal. With a rush of horror, he recognizes just how dangerous this woman is.

"I'm actually not so much on your side. Certainly not so much that I came here tonight unprepared."

Laina's eyes narrow. "What do you mean by that?"

Cal's bursting with conflicting emotions: sorrow, revulsion, shame, deep loss, and, yes, *fear*. This woman that he thought he loved now scares the hell out of him. He pulls aside his blazer lapel so Laina can see the lavalier mic affixed inside it. "Do you remember Mike Amis, my cameraman? He's good with sound too. He's outside recording our entire conversation."

Despite his inner turmoil, Cal meets Laina's eyes directly. "You want to scream and call 911? Go right ahead."

Laina remains unfazed by his threat. Her smile only grows wider. "I knew it," she says with delight. "We are bound together. I knew it the first time we talked about the liberating nature of truth."

She presses her body up closer against his, and to his horror, his own body responds. Her hands encircle his neck, her lips are close enough to kiss.

"How long did you suspect? What gave me away?" Laina purrs.

Cal swallows hard. "I couldn't figure out why you and Harley were telling me different versions of your affair. Once I questioned your truthfulness about that, I began to look at everything you'd told me in a new light. Then I saw red ribbon hanging on the pegboard in your dressing room, in a picture you posted on social media. The same ribbon that was on Franny's package."

"What an intrepid little reporter you are," Laina whispers.

Her right palm caresses his neck and drifts lower, to his chest. With a quick yank, she rips the lav mic from Cal's jacket and drops it to the ground. The square heel of her strappy sandal grinds it into the oak floor before Cal can even react.

"Come with me," she beckons, an impish smile on her face. He knows he should run the fuck out of there, but he allows her to take his hand and lead him toward the bedroom.

Is it lust? Pursuit of the story? An all-abiding hope that somehow she is not as crazy as she seems?

Despite his many and conflicted motives, Cal wisely uses his free hand to fish out his cellphone from his blazer pocket and surreptitiously press RECORD on his Voice Memo app before slipping the phone neatly away. A good reporter always has a backup.

Laina ushers him through her bedroom and into her walk-in closet. She pauses dramatically in the center of the feminine and meticulously organized dressing room. With a flourish she swings the tall mirror with the heavy frame away from the wall, gesturing that Cal should come closer.

The mirror's opening reveals a tiny room, outfitted with

spyware equipment and multiple computer monitors. Scanning from screen to screen, Cal gets a jolt when he recognizes the exterior of Franny Goldstein's condo. But when he sees the grainy images of the feeds into his own apartment, he nearly gags.

"You see how aligned we are?" Laina announces triumphantly. "Another woman might be furious you were recording her without her consent, but I understand."

Cal's entire being pulses with *fear*. "Wow. How long have you been spying on me?" Cal asks with feigned admiration, as he scrambles to figure out how to best play this.

"Not spying," Laina replies earnestly. "Learning about you. To help you. To help us."

"Right. Of course. And what have you learned?" Cal asks. Laina stands between him and the door leading out of the closet. He needs to buy time.

"Not nearly enough," Laina answers, moving closer to him with swaying hips and a suggestive smile.

Cal grabs her by the back of the neck and draws her up against him. Kisses her deeply. "If I don't tell Mike I'm okay, he'll be the one calling the police," he tells her. "That's what you get for crushing my equipment!" With a smile and a peck on the lips, he turns her around so he has easy access to the exit. "Why don't you take off that dress while I let Mike go home? I'll be right back. Keep the shoes on."

Laina smiles at him and reaches for her zipper. "Maybe I'll tie some of that red ribbon around my neck. Would you like that?"

"Oh yes."

Cal hurries out of the bedroom and through the rest of the apartment. Once outside, he's careful to prop Laina's front door open. He finds Mike in his parked car, head-phones on and mouth hanging open.

"That's the last time I let you hit on a subject," Mike teases with a wry twist in his voice. "I was about to come in after you."

"Fit me with a new mic," Cal instructs. "Quickly. I switched over to my phone when the first one went down, but I need you to be able to listen in."

"You're kidding me, right, boss? You're going back in there? I'm half amazed you got out of there alive. And what happened to the first lav?"

"Just get me set up," Cal directs. "You have Cop Cal's number just in case. In the meanwhile, this is a story and a half and I'm not losing a front row seat."

Mike fits another lav mic into the lapel of Cal's blazer.

"I won't wear the jacket when I go back in," Cal tells Mike. "I'll drape it over a chair so she can't get to this one."

"I'm not even going to ask," Mike replies. "But, Cal, one word of advice? Don't be an idiot."

"Always a goal." Cal folds his jacket over his arm and strides back to Laina's propped door. "Laina," he calls as he enters. "I'm back."

The open-plan kitchen and living room are empty, just as when he left. Cal enters the bedroom, expecting Laina in her underwear and heels, but finds that room is also empty. "Laina?"

Cal swings open the now closed door to the dressing room. Empty. The mirror/door to Laina's secret lair hangs ajar, all the monitors now blank and dark.

The only other place she can be is the master bathroom, but as Cal approaches it, he fights a sinking sensation, one predicated on the dawning realization that Laina is gone. He marches back through the unit, throwing open closet doors, but his suspicion is confirmed.

Shit. Cal walks back into the bedroom and stares into Laina's now darkened spy center. He sinks down onto the bed and runs his hands through his hair. *Now what?*

His hands drop to the bedspread. Stroking the silken texture, Cal's consumed by memories of how openly he shared his body, heart, and mind with Laina, and tortured by the realization that he knew her not at all.

His cellphone vibrates and his heart gives an involuntary little lurch. *What does it mean that I still want it to be her?*

It's Mike, and Cal hits the DECLINE button. He needs a minute.

With the adrenaline thrill of the story gone, Cal's fully feeling his loss. Another woman he completely misread. How can instincts that serve him so well professionally be so disastrous personally?

His phone vibrates again. Mike again. Cal declines the call for the second time. Finally, with a heavy sigh, he hoists himself off Laina's bed, crosses out of the bedroom and into the center of the apartment. He pauses for a last look around, desperate for clues that might explain Laina. Clues that might explain himself. Finding none, he pulls open the front door.

Lights blast into his eyes. Cal recoils.

"On your knees!" a commanding voice barks. "Hands over your head!"

Cal reels backward. He may be partially blinded, but he can see the glint of light on badges and drawn guns.

She fucking called the cops on me.

Cal's heart is pounding so hard he thinks it might explode. He silently offers up an apology to his mama for everything he's done wrong.

He's been prepared for this moment his whole life, but how could he ever be ready?

"That's right!" The commanding voice continues as Cal sinks to his knees, arms raised above his head. "Don't give us a reason to fuck you up."

Someone laughs in the darkness. It's an ugly sound, full of menace. Cal feels his insides turn liquid. A flashlight flares directly into his eyes. He instinctively drops one hand to shield his eyes.

"He's reaching!" someone shouts.

"No! I'm not!" Cal thinks he's shouted this, but at the same time wonders if he even said it aloud. He wonders if this is how he is going to die.

Indistinct yelling penetrates the miasma of fear paralyzing him. Voices he recognizes. Mike. Cop Cal.

In the nick of fucking time.

CHAPTER THIRTY-SIX

"What you don't understand about Laina is how genuinely kind she is," Bex says earnestly into the camera. "I was never her patient, just her friend, but she completely supported me before and during my decision to transition. And this is something no one knows: She paid for a lot of my surgery and other treatment. I never would have been able to do it so quickly without her."

Seated at one of the station's editing bays, Cal rewinds the footage and freezes on Bex's handsome, confident face, wondering what it is about the clip that's making him uneasy. Cal realizes it's that he tends to think of Laina in the past tense, while Bex always refers to her in the present. As well as insisting that Laina could in no way have participated in the acts of which she's accused because of his personal experience of her open heart and generosity.

Is it possible that Laina was genuinely kind as well as intrusive and hurtful? Perhaps.

Cal broke the story of the "crazy therapist" to spectacular ratings. He's now preparing a magazine-style multipart exclusive as a follow-up. Cal's piece has shaped up to be about the very question that had so tormented Laina, an irony not lost on Cal: How much pain can people bear before they break? And in particular, what pain did Laina have to bear and how did it break her? He and Mike have been filming, and Cal's been working with his producer to shape the segments into a compelling arc. Ryan is salivating, crassly commenting that "You're in the middle of the story, baby. This is on trend. I bet I can get you a deal at Netflix."

The revelations have been startling. Cal wasn't the only person Laina was spying on. Several of her clients also had been so blessed, including Franny Goldstein, a young schoolteacher named Michelle Marshall, and a newlywed named Carmen Hidalgo, who Cal has since learned had accused Laina of siccing the cops on her husband for domestic abuse. With Cal's full recognition of this additional inherent irony, Cop Cal confided that all of Laina's tapes of Carmen and her husband revealed nothing but harmony between the couple, although Carmen has proven herself to be a self-injuring klutz.

Cal knows a lot more now than he did that night in Laina's condo; like the good reporter he is, he's pieced the scattered shards of the story together.

Laina Landers was born Alaina Beckett. Her story about the home invasion that killed the rest of her family is true. Her father, a businessman with some shady associates, was reputed to have brought the disaster on himself by double-dealing a Colombian drug cartel.

This revelation breaks Cal's heart. How might Laina have been different if violence hadn't convulsed through her young life?

I could have loved this woman, maybe I do love her, despite how very damaged she is.

He tracks Alaina Beckett to Washington, where she be-

came Laina Landers, dropping the *A* of her first name and
legally taking on the surname of her aunt and uncle. Cal remembers how he'd thought her name sounded made-up
when he first heard it, like a comic book supervillain, and a
pang of sadness reverberates through his body. Another
irony.

He finds ample evidence of the truth of Laina's account
of her first marriage, tracking down the marriage and annul-
ment records as well as the police reports documenting the
abuse.

Laina's story aligns from there too. She graduates Berkeley, goes to UCLA, ends up in San Diego. Meets Harley
Weida, launches their clinic. But he still has a million questions and Cal knows he may never get all the answers, especially since it seems as if Laina has vanished into thin air.

Cal's reporting on the "aftermath," as he thinks of it,
and has interviews completed not only with Bex but with
Laina's former patient Carmen Hidalgo, as well as Kelsey
McKendrick (who'd also spoken largely in Laina's defense).
Vanessa Calabres declined to be interviewed, as Cal expected
she would, as did Harley Weida. A cloud of scandal de-
scended on Weida as word leaked out about the anonymous
phone calls left on the BETTER LIFE voicemail (Cal suspects Abi gossiped), finally waking Megan Weida up to the
fact that her husband was a serial cheater. Cal's last attempt
to get Harley to sit for an interview revealed that Harley had
moved out of the Weida home.

As best as Cal can puzzle it, and largely based on Bex's
timeline of gossip about "Mr. Mysterious," he's come to believe more in Laina's ultimate version of the affair than Harley's recitation. When Cal revealed to Bex in the course of

conversation that Mr. Mysterious was, in fact, Harley, a light dawned over Bex's face as he exclaimed, *So much makes sense now!* Cal still can't quite reconcile the strong, successful, independent woman he thought he knew with a Laina consigned to trembling weakly in the shadows under the control of a manipulating deceiver, but his recently acquired knowledge has forced him to sadly reconsider.

Confusing contradictions abound. Michelle Marshall, in a move that surprised Cal, not only agreed to expose her private affairs on camera but also sang Laina's praises. She might have left Michelle the revolting "gift" of a jarred fetus, but Michelle defended the move as one that ultimately helped her resolve her trauma.

It's precisely all these conflicting views of Dr. Laina Landers that are making Cal's piece so dynamic, while slicing his heart to shreds.

The person Cal most wishes to interview is Laina, for the story, sure, but also to come to an understanding of the woman and her motives, and to reconcile how and why he fell so deeply under her spell. He's deathly afraid of ever seeing her again for the very same reasons. Cal perpetually presses on the remembered wound of Laina telling him that the answers to his questions were not going to be neat and tidy. She was dead right, nothing is neat. Nothing is tidy.

Cal arrives home after a day cutting at the studio and greets the concierge on duty. (Bennet Lau has been fired for allowing Laina access to Cal's apartment, which she was apparently easily able to wrangle by claiming she wanted to arrange surprises for "my fiancé.") He checks his mail and finds a surprise among the bills and circulars: a series of three postcards from some of the United States' great public parks: Carlsbad Caverns in New Mexico, Zion National Park in Utah, and Big Bend National Park in Texas. Each of the numbered postcards is addressed to Cal and filled with cramped, tiny handwriting. They are from Laina's creepy scarf-stealing patient, George Holden.

Dear Mr. Murray,
You came to interview me about astronomy but recent events have led me to believe that you may actually have been interested in information about my former therapist, Dr. Laina Landers. I have nothing but the best things to say about Dr. Landers. I've seen the stories about her, but she helped me more than I can say. Regards, George Holden

Dear Mr. Murray,
Regarding Dr. Landers's theories of "liberation through truth," I'm writing to say I fully agree with her methodology. I must confess that after my daughter died, I became obsessed with the granddaughter of my next-door neighbor. She was so young and vital, and once I discovered I could spy on her with my telescope, I couldn't help but do it all the time. But once I confessed this to Dr. Landers, I felt freed of my obsession. Regards, George Holden

Dear Mr. Murray,
I've also heard about the room Dr. Landers set up to secretly record her patients. I sincerely hope

that my spying was not the inspiration for that on the doctor's part, although I suspect it might be so. As I often confided in the doctor, one does learn so much watching someone who is unawares. Regards, George Holden

Cal has the impulse to crumple these crazy postcards up and pretend he's never seen them but resists, his mind already spinning about how he can work them into his cut. He remembers the old lady who lived next to George, utterly certain he was spying on her, and marvels at people's capacity for self-deception, his own included.

Watching

People litter pieces of themselves everywhere, all the time, without so much as a glance backward.

Social media is splashed with happy, shiny portraits (the posters of which want the world to believe is their truth, even though we've all brushed against the darker side of a life lived online). Google aggregates every search we make and uses that data to tailor personal results, perpetuating confirmation bias. Alexa will order things based on our conversations. Even a computer-run home refrigerator can be hacked to access an entire household's data. Doorbells have cameras. Spyware can be ordered online. Nanny cams spy inside our bedrooms. CCTV grids hover over every city. Data breaches exposing our most personal details are commonplace. Even so-called secure hidden platforms can be accessed, screenshot, and stored before they are wiped. We all spy on one another all the time, leaving digital fingerprints as unique as our actual finger pads. We are all complicit in this. We've accepted it. We give it all away.

Dwell on all of this a moment; what you're serving up without a thought will stagger you.

And the intimate things people have confided to me in the course of my years as a therapist? That they've no doubt also shared with their inner circle at a minimum, the members of which have no doubt passed along details to their inner circles at a minimum? We all talk, and all stories get twisted in the telling.

So it was inevitable I needed to see more, that I thirsted to see the few truly private moments people held back, what they would reveal as the skins of all façades peeled away. I spied on George Holden first, after his confession about watching his young neighbor. I thought it would help me understand him, and it did. He's happier than he's ever been, I know that in my bones. Michelle Marshall is another success story. I understand she and her boyfriend recently got engaged.

I can admit the results I had with Daisy Sullivan were not what I anticipated, but she needed to be freed from her shame, that much is undeniable. I might have hastened an inevitable breakdown, but she was well on the way, and now at least Brad is back to care for his children. So much depends on perspective.

The patient I miss most is Franny; I would have liked to be able to treat her these last lingering weeks of her life. If only Cal hadn't been so convinced that the secret to the harassment lay with the Goldsteins. I had to use that, of course, to throw suspicion away from myself; what other choice did I have?

I wonder if Franny's finally knocked her father off his shiny pedestal. With her death sadly inevitable, I dearly hope she can take this important step as she reconciles the life she's lived (particularly as I suspect that the oil-soaked bill and the anonymous tip I made to the FBI about Satchel's safe deposit box key may have hastened her decline).

I do carry remorse for some of the things I've done, of course.

Consciousness of guilt. Regret. Self-recrimination. Penitence. How often have I walked those steps alongside a patient? Too many to count. But over the years, I've watched countless souls twist themselves through endless mental gymnastics that just drained their time, energy, and spirit without providing real relief or resolution. Long ago, I learned to squarely acknowledge any pinch of regret and then pack it up and stow it away where it can never find the light again. I believe in looking forward, not back.

Despite my determination to only focus on the future, I can't help but play a game of "if only" when I think about Cal Murray. I've divined that he's doing a follow-up story on me, which is, of course, flattering, but I still nurse the sore wound of his rejection. I thought he truly saw and accepted me for who I am. It's particularly bitter, because I abhorred and avoided press before I met him, but somehow he got past my defenses. Being the only survivor of a family slaughter put me under intense media scrutiny when I was a teenage girl, and let's just say, it wasn't pretty; I should have known better.

But my strength of purpose in my mission has only intensified. I helped so many people! Countless patients. I helped Clare Hutchinson—I saved her life, for god's sake! And I helped her with her children after their father murdered his brother. I know I could have helped Carmen Hidalgo (if only she could have brought herself to face the truth of her situation). As Cal once pointed out to me, I'm not a hundred percent responsible for my patients. I can only fulfill my oath to serve them in the best way I know how.

Most important, I know I can still help so many more.

My ability to become invisible has served me yet again. The media, including Cal, report that I've "disappeared," which is ridiculous. I was prepared, that's all. Cash is still king, and my go bag was ready with plenty of it. Being conscious of what we unwittingly share has made me a student of privacy; I know how to protect mine. I'm resettled now, near the ocean, of course, and am enjoying my new start, even looking forward to the icy chill of winter, so different from the balmy SoCal living to which I'm accustomed.

It didn't take me long to establish myself here, with a new identity, including conforming professional credentials. I knew the need to reinvent myself again might arise, so I was ready. And this relocation has come at such a pivotal time in my research and theories! I'm genuinely excited by the possibilities that lie before me.

But more on that later.

I have a patient waiting.

ACKNOWLEDGMENTS

I conceived and wrote this book during the worst of Southern California's Covid lockdown, wondering, as I was writing, "How much grief and pain can any of us carry before we break?" The answer, of course, is different for everyone, but I explored my own limits as I explored those of my characters.

As was the case for many people, my priorties shifted during the pandemic. I am truly grateful for the clarity I've gained about who and what is important in my life, so the gratitude expressed in these acknowledgments is particularly heartfelt.

In the process of conceiving, writing, and editing *Privacy* I was helped by many people. My editor, Anne Speyer, and I had an excellent collaboration in which she consistently encouraged me to do better and go further. My publishing whisperer, Janet Cooke, read every draft and was ever constant in her support. Darryl Taja and I had many conversations about race in America and his friendship and openness allowed me new perspective. I'm grateful to my twin, Felicia Henderson, for the belly laughs and for always being frank about many messy subjects, including race. Kudos to Kingsley Smith for letting me grill him about the TV news business and for answering all my random oddball text questions so quickly. I'm grateful to the therapists I spoke with who informed my creation of Laina (not that she is any of them!), including Robin Sax, Bonnie Greenberg, Shandiz Zandi, and Analia Rey. Shout-outs need to go to Gracie Corapi for reading early drafts and providing consistently smart feedback, not only about prose but about marketing as well, and to my other trusted early readers: Michelle Raimo, Sean Smith, and Hannah Phenicie, who always see the best in me but aren't afraid to deliver some tough love. Thanks must also go to Laina Cohn who lent me her gate house and her first name for inspiration. I also want to acknowledge Linda Mills, a fantastic cheerleader, friend, and boss, as well as my entire team at NYU LA and my colleagues at NYU Global; I'm proud to be a part of the NYU community. And to the rest of my beloved family and friends, you know who you are and how much you mean to me, especially my kids, Rafi and Xander, and my husband, Gary.

I am also very grateful for the support I've been shown from the entire team at Penguin Random House over the course of five novels. I feel blessed by this faith and thank Kara Welsh, Kim Hovey, Jennifer Hershey, Jesse Shuman, Allison Schuster, Melissa Sanford Folds, Loren Noveck, Scott Biel (for the beautiful cover design), and Dana Blanchette (for the equally beautiful interior design). I'd also like to acknowledge the heroes of the BBD sales team. I know how hard they all work to support authors, including this one, and I'm deeply grateful.

Additional thanks to my agents, Jeff Kleinman and Claudia Cross at Folio Literary, for all their support at every stage of the process.

And to my readers, thank you! If you like my work, please share the love. Post reviews, tell your friends, and write to me! I write back.

NINA SADOWSKY is an author, filmmaker, and educator. Her previous novels are *Just Fall, The Burial Society, The Empty Bed*, and *Convince Me*. She has written numerous screenplays and produced such films as *The Wedding Planner*. She currently serves as site director for NYU Los Angeles, a "semester abroad" program for advanced students considering careers in the entertainment and media industries. Sadowsky also has several television projects in development.

ninasadowsky.com
Facebook.com/ninasadowskythrillers
Twitter: @sadowsky_nina
Instagram: @ninasadowsky